Also by Matthew Cody

Powerless
The Dead Gentleman

super

matthew cody

Alfred A. Knopf  New York

THIS IS A BORZOI BOOK PUBLISHED BY ALFRED A. KNOPF

Visit us on the Web! randomhouse.com/kids

Educators and librarians, for a variety of teaching tools, visit us at RHTeachersLibrarians.com

Library of Congress Cataloging-in-Publication Data
Cody, Matthew.
Super / Matthew Cody — 1st ed.
p. cm.
Summary: In this sequel to POWERLESS, the superpowered kids of Noble's Green are once again threatened by an unknown force that may be trying to steal their powers.
ISBN 978-0-375-86894-8 (trade) — ISBN 978-0-375-96894-5 (lib. bdg.) — ISBN 978-0-375-89979-9 (ebook)
[1. Supernatural—Fiction. 2. Superheroes—Fiction. 3. Supervillains—Fiction. 4. Pennsylvania—Fiction.] I. Title.
PZ7.C654Su 2012
[Fic]—dc23
2012008220

The text of this book is set in 12-point HoeflerNew.

Printed in the United States of America
September 2012
10 9 8 7 6 5 4 3 2 1

First Edition

For Jack and Stan,
who filled my childhood
with dreams of flying.
And for Alisha and Willem,
always.

Acknowledgments

My wife, Alisha, and my son, Willem, get a special place in the dedication, but they've put up with enough to earn an extra thank-you here as well. An extra-big thanks also to my editor, Michele Burke. *Super* was the first book that we could really roll up our sleeves and work on together, from start to finish, and the experience was a joy. Thanks to my friend and agent, Kate Schafer Testerman, who continues to guide me through the wilds of publishing, and tells me to take a breath every now and then. She's right, it helps.

And lastly to all the great teachers, parents, librarians, and young readers I've met over the last few years who've asked for a sequel to *Powerless*—I told you it was coming!

Prologue

The night terrors had started a year ago. The doctors said he'd grow out of it, that it was hormonal and normal and nothing to be alarmed about. This is what they told his parents. The doctors never really talked to Michael.

Night terrors. The name alone was enough to cause nightmares. But these weren't nightmares. Nightmares were bad, but Michael had never had a nightmare that left him sweaty and shivering at the same time. He'd never had a nightmare that made him scream so loud that his parents had to call 911. Nightmares were for children. They were the stuff of spooky closets and monsters under the bed. Michael's dreams were haunted by something far, far worse.

The problem was, he couldn't remember what. He'd awake in a panic and for a few seconds he would know—he could see it so clearly, it might as well have still been in the room with him. But try as he might, he couldn't hold on to it. It vanished. The fear was the only thing that stayed behind. He could feel it in his sweat-soaked sheets, he tasted it in his mouth, which had gone dry from the screaming. But he couldn't give it a name.

In the sleepless, dead hours of the night, he was thankful that his mom and dad had stopped barging into his room every time it happened. The terrors were bad enough without Michael having to feel guilty about waking the entire house. Of course, they were probably awake anyway—no one could sleep through that kind of screaming—but the doctors had advised them to stop drawing attention to the problem. The doctors couldn't make the terrors go away, but they could lessen the embarrassment a little, at least.

Tonight, as on so many nights, Michael found himself sitting upright in bed trying to quiet the sound of his own wildly thumping heart. This time he'd awoken pressed up against the headboard as if he could climb it to safety. It was always something like that. Sometimes he woke up on the floor, sometimes he'd made it as far as the bedroom door, but he always seemed to be trying to get away from the outside. Away from the windows. The source of his fear lay beyond the walls of his house.

The doctors made a point of correcting him when he said things like that. They reminded him that the source of his terror was his own subconscious, an unfortunate combination of teenage anxiety and a flood of hormones. The doors and windows were just objects that his subconscious had fixated on. If only the doctors would explain that to his subconscious.

It didn't happen every night, but when it did, Michael would sit awake in the dark, alone, until dawn. He actually felt safer with the lights off. Flip on a light in a dark room at night, and the window becomes a two-way mirror. You can't see out, but anyone, or anything, can see in.

And it was an especially clear night tonight. The moon hung, a half circle, above the branches of the oak outside his bedroom. It was an old tree, old enough to reach up three stories to his window. When he was younger, he used to fantasize about leaping out and climbing the tree to freedom. He'd loved the oak, the open sky beyond, even the dark peak of Mount Noble looming in the distance. For him as a kid, the window had been a part of his recurring dream of flight, and in that nighttime fantasy, he leapt from the tree and kept going straight up into the sky. Even today he could almost feel the tickle of the leaves against his legs as he skimmed the treetops. But the window held no such fascination now. He stared at the branches and shivered. He always stood off to one side, out of sight. It wouldn't do to stand in full view of the yard beyond. Not at night. Not ever at night.

His room was stifling, and the humid air clung to his skin like a wet sweater. Despite Pennsylvania's midsummer swelter, Michael always slept with the window shut. His parents had agreed to run the air conditioner for him, but it was a weak old contraption that never managed to cool the upstairs rooms. He longed to throw open the window and let the mountain breeze in. He wanted to smell something other than his own sour sweat.

What was he afraid of? What did he think was out there?

Asking that question was like chasing a name on the tip of his tongue. But he was closing in on it. Just a little farther . . .

His hands pressed flat against the windowpane without his say-so. It felt good, this sort of numb distance that he was suddenly experiencing. So much better than the cord of fear that had twisted in his gut for so long.

With just a little effort, he clicked the locks open. First one, then the other. A wind blew through the oak's branches outside, their tips brushing the window. It had the unnerving effect of sounding like someone tapping on the pane. The fear started to creep back into his stomach. Breathing deep, Michael leaned his forehead against the cool glass and watched as his breath fogged it up. What was he afraid of? He wasn't asleep anymore. The terror, whatever it was, couldn't hurt him now.

The wooden tracks squealed a bit in protest as Michael slid the window open. Mountain air and the musty-dirt smell of cut grass and green leaves washed over him at once. The air tasted so very good, and the night breeze cooled his feverish skin. Smiling, he leaned out the window and tested the nearest tree limb, tracing lines in the bark. The branch was sturdy and surprisingly smooth in places where it felt like it'd actually been rubbed flat, almost polished with use. Here a handhold, there a foothold. For the first time, Michael really examined the windowsill. Even in the dim moonlight he could see the scuff marks where the painted wood had been rubbed thin. Someone had climbed out of this window and into this tree before. And they'd done it many times.

But who?

Carefully, Michael put one foot on the windowsill, in the exact spot where the paint was nearly worn bare. His long arms braced against either side for support and balance as he pulled himself up into the open window. It was a dizzying height, a full three-story drop to the yard below, but Michael felt surprisingly sure. He wasn't scared of heights per se, but he also wasn't normally adventurous enough to go tree climbing in the dark. And yet his hands knew where to hold on. His other foot had already found a place on the branch where he could pivot away from the window, secure in the knowledge that this was the right one. No, not knowledge. Michael still had no memory of ever actually climbing this tree, but it was like his *body* knew how. His muscles remembered what his mind had forgotten.

But how do you remember something you've never done?

Hand over hand he climbed while his feet found other branches that he just knew would support his weight. There were plenty of weak limbs this near the top, but he easily avoided those. Only minutes ago he'd been lying in his bed

5

paralyzed with fear, and now here he was doing daredevil feats in the dark. Although he was sure-footed here up top, the way down was still something of a mystery to him. The leaves were thicker just below; the branches there felt foreign. He had no sense of the path down. So little moonlight made it through the leaves that the space below him was nearly pitch-black. It would be hard to see where he was stepping down there.

That was an adventure for another day. Perhaps tomorrow, when there was sunlight to see by. For now he'd content himself with sitting at the top of his tree and watching the clouds drift in front of the moon. It was as peaceful as he'd felt in months, just listening to the creaking of branches bending with the breeze, the crickets chirping somewhere nearby. In the daytime such sounds were always interrupted by the gunning of a car engine or the buzz of a neighbor's lawn mower. It was only at this hour of the night in Noble's Green that the human sounds disappeared and you could really listen to the subtle sounds of nature, of the mountain itself.

Which was why the sudden rustle beneath him was so alarming. It was not the sound of windblown leaves. This sounded more like something *moving* among the branches, moving with a purpose. But it sounded too large to be a squirrel or bird, and yet it didn't have the weight of a human being stumbling through the foliage. This was a sneakier sound. Almost like slithering. Like fabric being pulled through the leaves. Up the leaves. Climbing the tree.

The fear came back and wrapped him up like an iron chain, so tight that he couldn't breathe. Something was coming up the tree for him. Michael tried to make out a shape in the darkness below, but nothing moved, at least nothing that he could see. And the sound was getting louder, getting closer. His open window was still several feet away, the drop to the yard much more than that.

He'd just started to inch his way back when he caught a glimpse of something. It was confusing at first, because he thought he was just spying his own shadow against the thick floor of leaves below, but that was impossible. The moon wasn't nearly bright enough in the sky to cast shadows at night, especially in the depths of this tree. He was looking at an outline, a form of someone roughly his size and all in black. But the dimensions were all wrong: it stretched and crept along the branches toward him. A form with shape but no mass.

The shadow looked at Michael and opened its mouth.

Michael pushed off with all his strength, leaping for the window. Branches slapped him in the face, cutting and scraping against bare skin, but his hands found the window's ledge. His bare feet tore against the wood, getting bloodied and picking up splinters as he scrambled to find purchase. Up over the windowsill he hauled himself, too terrified to look over his shoulder, and dropped himself onto his bedroom floor.

In an instant he was back on his feet and slamming the window shut. As he flipped the latches locked, he saw something still moving in the tree, the dark shape crawling among the dark branches where he'd been sitting. He threw the curtains closed and sprinted down the hall to his parents' bedroom.

They were waiting for him. They'd heard the crash as he'd come through the window. They wore exhausted, worried expressions as he fell into their arms, crying uncontrollably. But their worry turned to something worse as they spotted his cut and bleeding hands, his torn feet. They sat him down and cleaned his cuts and asked him what had happened this time, how he'd gotten hurt again, but Michael couldn't answer. He didn't know.

Something had happened. He'd seen something terribly *wrong* and yet terribly familiar, but he couldn't tell his parents what it was. He'd known just minutes before, but it was gone now.

The night terror had stolen it away.

Chapter One
The New Kid

"We need a name," said Eric. "Like a secret society name or something. A league name."

"A league?" asked Daniel. "You mean like major league baseball?"

"Ha. You know what I mean. We need to call ourselves something. I can't say *The Supers of Noble's Green* with a straight face."

"But *The League of Justice* would be different? You want that on a T-shirt?"

"I don't want anything on a T-shirt," said Eric, rolling his eyes.

"How about *The League of Junior Superheroes and Their*

Friend Who Really Just Wants to Go Swimming? That would strike fear into the hearts of evildoers everywhere."

"Okay, okay! Forget I brought it up."

The two friends were quiet for a moment, listening to the sounds of summer. The buzz of cicadas rose and fell. Tangle Creek burbled below them. A train whistle blew somewhere in the distance.

"Did you pick a superhero name?" asked Daniel. "Because I think *Compulsive Naming Guy* hasn't been taken yet."

Eric groaned, covering his face with his hands.

"Kid List Maker?"

"You know, Superman was lucky that all he had to worry about was kryptonite. He didn't have you."

"The Brainstormer? Wait, that almost sounds cool. Scratch that."

Eric reached his hands out as if to strangle Daniel.

"Do you yield before my superior wit?" asked Daniel. "Can we please go swimming now? I'm melting up here in the sun."

"Fine. Just let me make sure the coast is clear."

And with that Eric stepped off their perch on the trellis of the Tangle Creek Bridge, hidden from view beneath the bridge's roadway but still a full thirty feet above the greenish water below. But he didn't fall. Eric never fell. He flew.

Tangle Creek Bridge was notorious. The approaching road, a lonely, poorly maintained stretch of Route 16, veered sharply into a hairpin curve just before narrowing onto the one-lane bridge. While this helped to slow down oncoming traffic, it also meant that drivers had little time to gauge the conditions before they crossed. In the winter if the bridge was icy, or anytime someone was driving carelessly during a rainstorm, the old bridge was a deathtrap.

But for this, the summer before their eighth-grade year, the little-used bridge had served as Daniel and his friends' secret swimming hole. The water directly underneath was deep enough to dive into and clear of the jagged rocks and sandbars that were so common along much of the rest of the creek. There was an easy-to-climb trellis that led to a spot halfway up, where you could do a pretty excellent cannon-ball; or if you were really brave, you could keep climbing to the platform just beneath the very top for a straight cliff-style dive.

Or, if you were Eric, you could fly.

Daniel had spent much of the summer watching Mollie and Eric approach the bridge from the north, keeping low and barely skimming the water as they flew, just enough to kick up a spray that would cool you off on a hot summer afternoon. Or if they were looking for a real soak, they'd fly a loop up and over the bridge, then free-fall into the deep green water.

Though Daniel wasn't a flier, of course, he did like to hold on to Eric's arms and tag along as they skimmed the creek—that was better than any water ride in any amuse-ment park in the country. He'd tried it once with Mollie, but she'd dragged him so low that he'd gone face-first into the creek. Daniel had hit so hard that he nearly lost his trunks, and when he'd come up for air, Mollie had been doubled over snorting and laughing herself blue.

Today, Daniel was feeling in more of a high-dive mood. Low impact, high altitude. And he liked climbing up to enjoy the other great thing about Tangle Creek Bridge—the scenery. The old bridge itself looked like something off a postcard. The bleached-wood trestles and low stone wall that made it so treacherous also made it a local landmark. Tangle Creek was framed on either bank by green forest, and the water ran clean—it was free of the soapy suds or oily sheen that polluted so many of the lakes and rivers closer to the more industrial parts of Pennsylvania. Noble's Green might feel like the small town that time forgot, but sometimes that had its advantages.

Daniel sat on his bridge perch, in no hurry, and enjoyed the breeze. Wildflowers were blooming along the bank, and they'd sweetened the already sweet air.

A machine-gun-like succession of small sneezes broke the idyllic moment.

"Hi, Rohan," Daniel said as he glanced down to see his small friend climbing up the last few feet of the trellis while struggling to hold a handkerchief to his nose.

"Wild . . . wild geraniums," Rohan said. "Very bad on the allergies."

Daniel offered him a hand up, thankful that Rohan pocketed the snotty handkerchief before accepting.

"You diving?" asked Daniel.

"Me?" answered Rohan. "I'm not the high-diving type,

thank you. You may enjoy hitching a ride with Eric, but it just gives me motion sickness. I'll go down a ways and try a cannonball. Hey, where is Eric, anyway?"

"Making sure the coast is clear."

Rohan squinted at Daniel—it was odd to see Rohan without his ever-present inch-thick glasses, but he'd left them on the bank with their shoes and towels. But Daniel knew that while *he* might be a blur to Rohan, the rest of the world—the trees on the far bank and even the distant peak of Mount Noble—was uniquely visible to his friend. Rohan could make out the gathering raindrops of the highest cloud. Even beyond.

Daniel thought about what Rohan had said about hitching a ride with Eric. His friend was only half right. Daniel did love that feeling of pretend flying, the freedom, the taste of the cold air. But every time Eric took him along, it was a bitter pill. Flying was glorious, and as Eric liked to say, there was nothing else like it. But it was also a stinging reminder of just how ordinary Daniel was. He wasn't a flier—he was a passenger, a guest. At best, he was just along for the ride.

As if on cue, there was a sudden rush of wind, a swirl of movement in the air, and Eric was back. He stayed floating just a few feet away from Daniel's perch but still high above the water below.

Eric didn't wear a cape, and though he might not have a code name (yet), he was still the unseen superhero of Noble's Green. Only a handful of other kids knew it, but he was the reason the town bragged about being the safest place on earth and could mean it. Lowest accident rate in the country, practically zero crime. An abnormally high number of UFO sightings, most of which were oddly kid-shaped, but that was all.

Mostly thanks to Eric.

"What are you two jabbering about?" Eric asked.

"I just got here," answered Rohan. "We haven't even started our jabbering."

"So what do you have planned for us today?" asked Daniel. "I'm gonna try a high dive, Rohan's doing a cannonball, but you're doing something awesome, right?"

Eric shrugged, but Daniel knew it was false modesty. The Supers of Noble's Green were the best-kept secret, probably in the world, but Eric loved the chance to show off for his friends. And why not? The Supers were a special group of kids, each with a unique power. Mollie flew at super-speed, little Rose could turn invisible, Rohan could hear a baby cough in the next town. But Eric was different—a flier who was also super-fast, super-strong, and super-tough—he could do almost anything. He was a superhero even to the Supers.

It was hard for Daniel to believe that he once hadn't trusted Eric. Impossible to believe these days, after all they'd been through.

Eric started rising, slowly, into the air. Then, with his arms down at his sides, he rocketed upward and disappeared into the sky like a missile.

"What do you think?" asked Rohan. "Corkscrew cannonball?"

"Nah," said Daniel. "He did two of those last time. I think he'll pull out an oldie-but-goodie. Maybe a thunder dive."

"Meh. Thunder dive is very last summer. Too old-fashioned."

"Says the boy who wears ties to school."

"Watch it. Ties are cool."

They sat there for a few moments searching the heavens, squinting against the bright afternoon sun. Of course Rohan spotted him first.

"Uh-oh," said Rohan.

"What? What do you see?"

"He's coming down and . . . Oh, no!"

"What?"

"Belly flop!"

Then Daniel saw him—arms and legs out like a parachutist in free fall.

"Aw, man!" said Daniel as he held on tight and closed his eyes.

There was a brief echo of laughter as Eric plummeted past them, followed by a monumental splash. It was the kind of splash that you feel in your toes, a cracking explosion that ended in a thirty-foot-tall plume of water that soaked everything in sight: the bridge, the bank, and—just as Eric had planned—Daniel and Rohan.

The two square inches of skin where Daniel's butt met the seat were the only area of his body that did not get soaked by the cannonball tsunami. Every other spot was drenched. Rohan whined about water getting up his nose as Eric came floating up for air. That kind of fall would have flattened anyone else, but Eric just smiled.

"So, judges," he said. "What's my score?"

"I'll give you a ten for style," said Daniel. "But your form was a little off. Five point five."

"You get zero point zero from me," said Rohan. "I'm going to be tasting creek water for a week."

Eric put his hands on his head in mock outrage. "What? Well, I'll just have to try harder next time!"

"No!" said Daniel. "No next time! Not necessary!"

But it was too late. Eric was already peeling off into the sky above in preparation for his second super-soaking belly flop of the day.

"Way to go," said Daniel, elbowing Rohan in the ribs. "Better hold on to something— What is it?"

Rohan had that faraway look on his face that meant he was sensing something that no one else could. It could be a small distraction, like a particularly delicious smell from several miles away, a baking pie in the next town over. Or it could mean trouble.

"Rohan?"

"There's a car coming," his friend answered. "Too fast."

Daniel understood immediately. He looked up to see Eric plummeting once more out of the sky, oblivious to the approaching car. Daniel tried to wave him off, was shouting at him to slow down, but Eric didn't hear. He connected with the water just when Daniel heard the motor above their heads as the car neared the bridge.

When the second splash passed, Daniel opened his eyes to see Eric ricocheting back up out of the creek, laughing as he flew up toward them. But as Eric landed on the trellis, the laughter stopped. He heard what Daniel was already hearing—the screeching of tires and the scraping of metal from the bridge above.

Daniel grabbed Eric by the shoulder and shouted in his ear. "Car! It's going to—"

His words were lost in a jaw-rattling crash, and then the world went strangely silent for a moment as a sleek black Porsche came flying over their heads, falling.

Then not.

Eric was there. Hidden from whoever was inside, he had a grip on the underside of the car and had stopped its fall. It was a surreal moment as the car floated high above Tangle Creek, held up by Eric, just a few feet away from where Daniel and Rohan were sitting.

The driver's side window was open, and a pale-faced teenager leaned his head out. He still couldn't see Eric beneath him, but he looked straight at Daniel—a bewildered, questioning look on his face.

"Uh," answered Daniel. What else was there to say?

Then the car shook. It quivered for half a second, and Daniel noticed something shocking—Eric was straining. Veins bulged in his neck and his arms were shaking under

17

the Porsche's weight. Then he fell, and the car fell with him. They hit the water together, Eric disappearing beneath it. The car bobbed on the surface for a moment, then followed. The driver abandoned the sinking vehicle just before it was swallowed up by the creek.

But no sign of Eric.

Daniel wasn't a great diver, but he managed to hit the water safely. Under the surface it was chaos as the sinking Porsche churned up the dark creek silt, and as the escaping air from the car bubbled and roared all around him like a whirlpool. Daniel was only an average swimmer, but his arms cut through the water with a strength that surprised him. Fueled by concern for his friend, Daniel managed to swim through the muddy water until he spotted a shape down there other than the sinking car. Eric wasn't moving, and when Daniel got close enough, he saw that his friend's leg was trapped beneath the vehicle. The farther the car sank into the soft bottom, the more stuck Eric would become.

Surprisingly, the car rolled easily off Eric's leg when Daniel gave it a shove. It hadn't had time to settle into the mud and silt, and Daniel pulled Eric out of the muck and kicked for the surface. They came out of the water near the shore, and Daniel grabbed a fistful of reeds with one hand as he pulled Eric's limp body behind him with the other. Someone was there to grab him and help him onto the bank. Daniel saw a face, the pale one in the car window. A boy a few years older than Daniel.

"Here, let me," said the boy, and he began to do CPR on

Eric. It didn't take long before Eric coughed up a lungful of green water and replaced it with a groaning breath of air. He was alive.

"You . . . you saved his life," said Daniel, but the boy shook his head.

"No, you saved him. You pulled him out of there."

"Eric?" said Daniel. "You okay?"

Eric nodded and rolled over onto his stomach. He vomited up a little more creek water and moaned.

"He'll be all right," said the boy. "He just needs a minute."

"Really," said Daniel. "Thank you."

"Theo," the boy said, holding out his hand. "Theo Plunkett."

Daniel started to return the handshake but froze when he heard the last name. *Plunkett?*

"You all right there?" asked Theo. "Still shook up?"

"Uh, yeah. Sorry. I'm Daniel . . . Corrigan." Daniel had trouble getting out his own name. It stuck there in his throat.

Plunkett?

Theo looked back at the water. Daniel turned and saw a rather stunned-looking Rohan watching them from the far bank. The Porsche was gone. Lost on the bottom of Tangle Creek.

"Man, my dad's gonna kill me," said Theo, staring at the bubbles rising to the surface. "That's the second one this year."

19

Chapter Two
Mollie Lee

On August 13, at 2:53 p.m., summer ended early for the Supers of Noble's Green. A new Plunkett was in town.

That evening, an emergency meeting was called at the tree fort to discuss the disturbing development. Nearly everyone was in attendance, and invitations were even sent to super-bullies Clay and Bud (who didn't show, of course). Eric, Mollie, Rohan, Louisa, and Rose sat together in the dark, and by flashlight and candlelight they debated what should be done.

Meanwhile, Daniel was at home babysitting his little brother.

When Daniel's parents announced that they were reviving an ancient tradition known as the weekly date night,

Daniel had at first been thrilled. This meant that once a week he'd have his evenings free while his parents went to dinner and a movie, and that in turn meant more time to sneak away to the tree fort. What he hadn't taken into account was the unthinkable possibility that his mom and dad wouldn't be taking his little brother, Georgie, with them. Apparently, date night was just another excuse to invoke the slave labor clause of parenting, which read: *The older child shall, from time to time, be drafted into all manner of unpaid, onerous tasks. Such as, but not limited to, scooping the cat's litter, mowing the lawn, and guarding a three-year-old.*

It confirmed what Daniel had long suspected: parents had second children just to make sure they got their money's worth out of the first.

Bath time with Georgie was the worst, by far. Getting him to eat dinner was a pain, but Daniel refused to get caught in the same trap as his parents. If Georgie refused to eat his vegetables, Daniel didn't push it. He just scooped the broccoli off the plate and went straight to dessert. He'd figured out long ago that successfully babysitting a three-year-old required a careful combination of threats plus bribery, and handing Georgie an ice cream sandwich was more potent than a brown paper bag full of cash.

But after dinner came bath. Ever since Georgie had learned how to get out of the tub on his own, he'd adopted a new game, the rules of which were aggravatingly simple — Daniel turned his back for two seconds and Georgie would leap out of the bath and run, dripping, down the hall at full speed shouting, "I'm a stinker!" all the way to the living room. Daniel would then spend the next ten minutes cleaning wet, soapy footprints off the floor and wet, soapy baby-butt prints off the sofa.

He'd just finished mopping up the last of tonight's collateral bath damage and gotten Georgie into bed when Daniel heard a familiar tap-tapping at his attic bedroom window. Mollie had insisted they create a secret code—a special rhythm to the tapping that would identify it as her. When Daniel had sarcastically asked just how many other people in Noble's Green could fly up the three stories to his window, Mollie had answered him with a punch to the arm. And so the secret code was born.

The tune Mollie had chosen was the Darth Vader theme from *Star Wars*. Mollie added her own lyrics. They went, "Daaaaaniel is a butt-head, dum-da-dum, dum-da-dum."

"It's unlocked, Mollie," Daniel said, interrupting her before she could make up a second verse.

Mollie floated into the room like a gently blown leaf, settling with a plop on the edge of his bed. She'd really mastered the graceful entrance. So different from her first trip through that window, over half a year ago, when she'd crashed into his room, exhausted and terrified. Of course, that had been the time of the Shroud, when fear had been a constant among the special children of Noble's Green.

"Your room's a total mess," said Mollie, eying the stacks of books and unfinished-model pieces littering his desk and bedside table. Daniel and Rohan had recently gotten into World

War II era battleships and were trying to create a complete model of the Pacific fleet. But as summer arrived, the two spent more and more time outdoors and less and less time on their plastic armada. Now every patch of space that wasn't already taken up with detective books and comics was being used for bits of the U.S.S. *Independence* and H.M.S. *Nelson*.

Mollie idly kicked at the flight deck of the U.S.S. *Intrepid* and made a face.

"It's a work in progress," said Daniel. "So tell me what you saw. Did you get over to Plunkett's house?"

Mollie nodded. "We did a flyby, but we couldn't get too close without being seen. Nothing to report, really. At least nothing freaky. There are moving vans parked out front and a big black limo. No other cars."

"Well, their Porsche is going to be in the shop for a while, I suspect. Once they drag it out of Tangle Creek."

Daniel thought about this for a few minutes, chewing the inside of his cheek and tapping his fingers on the Sherlock Holmes–style pipe that sat on his desk. His mom had found it at an antiques store and picked it up for Daniel as a surprise. He liked to hold it, to imagine that it helped him focus in the way that his hero Holmes focused. But he didn't like to put it in his mouth, because the tip still tasted like bitter tobacco.

"I gotta say I'm surprised that Plunkett had any family at all," said Mollie.

"He was an orphan. Theo must be a great-great-grand-cousin or something. I didn't have much time to interrogate him before the fire department showed up."

Herman Plunkett had officially disappeared over half a year ago. Though a missing-persons investigation was ongoing, the Noble's Green sheriff's department hadn't mentioned foul play. Nor had anyone connected the dots between Plunkett's disappearance and the mysterious collapse at the Old Quarry around the same time. No one suspected that Herman Plunkett, aka the Shroud, lay buried under that mountain of rock and rubble.

"Well," said Mollie, "hopefully they'll pocket the silverware and Plunkett family portraits and be on their way. Eric's totally freaked out—he wants to keep an eye on them around the clock, like a stakeout or something."

"Yeah, we have great luck with those," Daniel said.

"But Rohan said that we're all overreacting. He said there's no reason to suspect that Herman's family has anything to do with the Shroud."

"He's right about that," said Daniel. "It's not like I'm worried about a family of Shrouds moving into Plunkett's old house, but I am worried."

"What about?"

"You said that they were probably just here to pick up the family heirlooms and stuff, the valuable things. That's what scares me."

Mollie was up on her feet, pacing the room. She was always full of nervous energy. Daniel worried at first that she would tromp all over his model pieces until he noticed that her feet weren't actually touching the floor. She was hovering about four inches above the mess. She was literally walking on air.

"So you think that there's something in the Plunkett house that's dangerous?" she asked. "Some secret about . . . well, about us?"

Daniel looked at the girl floating in his bedroom. He thought about Eric, flying high over the Plunkett house, spying from the safety of the night sky. There were certainly a lot of secrets in this town to discover.

Daniel shook his head. "I hope not. And I think most of Plunkett's secrets got buried with him in that Shroud-Cave beneath the quarry. He was such a paranoid old kook that I doubt he kept anything in his home. I'm just being overcautious."

Daniel wanted to reassure Mollie, but he couldn't shake a certain memory. Plunkett had once shown him a hidden safe in his study where he kept a file on the Supers, complete with pictures and names. Daniel felt a sharp pang of guilt as he remembered how Plunkett had doctored one of those photos to fool Daniel into believing that his friend Eric was actually the Shroud. For a time it had worked, and Daniel had convinced the rest of the Supers too. He'd been manipulated by Herman into casting doubt on his friend. It was something Daniel would never forgive himself for. And he'd never suspect his friend again.

Daniel had destroyed those photos, but who was to say that Plunkett hadn't made copies? And what if they were still in that house, in that hidden safe? What would someone think when they saw those pictures of the children of Noble's Green, soaring through the air or lifting cars over their heads? And worse, what would they *do*?

"Rohan's probably right that there's nothing to worry about," said Daniel. "But I just want to make extra sure that Plunkett didn't leave anything behind. We should've done this a long time ago."

"What do you want us to do, then? Break in? I don't trust that place. Plunkett probably rigged his home up with alarms and booby traps and who knows what!"

"Maybe. Which makes the new Plunketts a kind of happy accident, in a way."

"How so? Spill it, Sherlock," said Mollie. She was getting impatient with Daniel, but she was always getting impatient with someone. When you were talking with Mollie, it was hard to keep on her schedule. The rest of the world moved in slow motion compared to the fastest girl alive.

"No need to worry about security systems if you're invited in," said Daniel, twirling his pipe for emphasis.

Mollie stopped moving just long enough to snort. "So you're going to just bike over there and ask for the house tour?"

Daniel smiled. The problem with his superpowered friends was that they had so much power, they often overlooked the simplest solutions. Most of life's difficulties didn't require super-strength or super-speed to fix. Most of the time you just needed your brain and a few guts.

"I'll go over tomorrow to check on Theo. It's the neighborly thing to do."

"Theo Plunkett just totaled his dad's Porsche! I'm sure he's in the mood to make new friends."

"Can't hurt to try."

Mollie rolled her eyes, but she didn't argue any further. She didn't have any better ideas, and the fact that someone was snooping around inside Plunkett's mansion—another Plunkett no less—had them all on edge.

With that settled, Daniel sat back in his chair and tapped on his pipe thoughtfully. There was something else that had been bothering him.

"How's Eric?" he asked.

Mollie shrugged. "He's embarrassed. It's not like him to mess up like that. The car was way heavier than he'd expected."

Daniel nodded, but he wasn't sure he agreed. Eric was strong, and getting stronger every day. And even if the car was too much, that didn't explain why he'd nearly drowned. Eric was the most powerful person Daniel had ever met, but today he hadn't even had the strength to swim.

Daniel was worried about his friend, and he planned to talk to Eric about what had happened at the bridge as soon as he got the chance. But for the time being he had other things to focus on. If Herman had left those photos behind where they could be found, they would all be in danger.

The Shroud was dead and gone, but would he ever stop making them afraid?

Daniel would start his investigation tomorrow. Theo Plunkett was about to make a new friend, whether he liked it or not.

Chapter Three
The Plunkett Family Name

That night Daniel dreamed of the Old Quarry, and of the Shroud. He was fighting his old enemy again, but this time he was fighting alone. As the black-cloaked Shroud overwhelmed him, Daniel reached for the glowing meteor stone pendant around Herman's neck. That shard of Witch Fire meteorite was the source of the villain's strength, and Daniel had torn it from the Shroud's neck once before, rendering him powerless. But this time, as he grasped the hunk of burning black rock, his own hand caught fire. Green flames licked along his fingers as Daniel cried out in pain. The Shroud was speaking to him, telling him how Daniel could make the pain go away by giving in to the stone's power, but he refused to listen. Eventually his hand burned down to nothing, and all Daniel could do was clutch the stump that had once been his hand. All the while Plunkett's voice whispered his name.

In the morning when Daniel awoke, he made himself a little rule—no more Shroud talk before bed. His day was mostly filled with chores—mowing the lawn and watching Georgie while his mom tended her flower garden—but as soon as he could slip away, Daniel pedaled his bike along a route he hadn't taken in months; one that he'd hoped to never take again.

The Plunkett estate was hidden away at the end of a private drive just off Cedar Lane. The towering mansion had been empty since Herman's disappearance, a lonely place of gathering dust and wild, overgrown gardens. But Herman's house had felt deserted for years. The old millionaire had lived a hermitlike existence, playing the part of the infirm, doddering eccentric to the hilt. With the exception of a visiting nurse and a few gardeners, no one came to or went from that house, even when Herman was still alive. Or at least that was the charade, the carefully crafted play, that Herman had put on for years. In truth the villain had had the run of Noble's Green as the Shroud, flitting in and out of the shadows, stealing the powers and memories of generations of the town's gifted children. Over many years he'd used his influence, his money, and his frightening abilities to control the town in unseen ways, to dominate and terrorize the children while keeping the adults ignorant of their town's strange goings-on. In the end, he died a bitter and paranoid old man. Herman trapped himself in his own lie, like a bottled spider.

Which was why it seemed all the more surreal as Daniel walked his bike up the main drive and saw the change that had come over the Plunkett house. The front yard was buzzing with an army of gardeners trimming the shrubs and pulling weeds. Men on ladders were applying a new coat of paint to the peeling facade, and the heavy curtains were drawn back and every last window was thrown wide open. Someone was airing out the place—like they were expunging what was left of old Herman. Daniel remembered the distinctive smell that had permeated the house, a mixture of musty paper and mediciny ointments. It was the kind of smell that left dust in your nose.

Now it smelled of cut grass and fresh paint.

Two enormous moving vans were parked next to the long garage. Seeing the vans there, Daniel was instantly transported back to his first day in Noble's Green. He'd met Mollie on that day, and that chance meeting had sparked the greatest adventure of his life. It had introduced him to a world he'd never dreamed possible.

A year later and here he was, confronted with a new mystery. There was a puzzle here, a problem that needed working out. And though their current situation wasn't nearly as dire as their long battle with the Shroud, it was still serious. Who was Theo Plunkett? What danger might he and his family, even inadvertently, pose to his friends?

Somewhere deep down, Daniel had missed this feeling. He had to admit it—despite last night's bad dreams, it felt good to be on the case again.

And so he found himself walking briskly, lightly even, as he approached the front door. He even hummed a little song he made up on the spot. It was mostly tuneless, but upbeat. His own detective-movie soundtrack.

He was ringing the doorbell—and just hitting his theme song's crescendo, the soaring flourish that signaled to the audience that here was the hero—when he caught his reflection in the glass door. The hand he was holding up to the doorbell wasn't there. There was nothing except a charred stump.

When Daniel blinked everything was back to normal. Five skinny fingers. Five chewed-on nails. It had all been in his mind, a flashback to last night's nightmare, but the image left a chilled pit in his stomach despite the hot summer's day. Daniel would've sat down on the step except someone was coming to the door. So he took a few deep breaths—in through the nose and out through the mouth—and concentrated on not throwing up.

The door inched open just a crack, and a shriveled face peeked out. Beady eyes blinked at him from behind thick plastic glasses. A familiar, liver-spotted bald head poked forward, its mouth turned up in a thin-lipped snarl.

As if the dream flashback hadn't been enough, Daniel was now staring into the face of Herman Plunkett, returned from the dead. But this Herman carried a bit more poundage. Where the old one was stick thin, this one was more . . . pear-shaped. But the generous double chin couldn't hide the family resemblance. It wasn't Herman, but it was unmistakably a Plunkett.

"Eh?" said the old man. "What do you want?"

"Granddad?" called a boy's voice from inside the house. "What are you doing up?"

The old man threw Daniel a sour look and then shouted back over his shoulder. "The door wouldn't stop buzzing. Someone has to answer it!"

Theo Plunkett appeared behind the old man and gently put a hand on his arm. "I told you to ring your bell if you needed anything. I could've gotten it."

"You can't hear the doorbell with that music contraption in your ears, so how are you going to hear my bell?"

"Hey, Daniel," said Theo with a wry smile. "Give me a minute, will you?"

Daniel nodded and waited as Theo and his grandfather disappeared inside. Apparently the Plunkett family genetics didn't stop with looks—a sour disposition was obviously a dominant gene. He could still hear the old man chastising poor Theo, even with the door closed.

After a few minutes Theo returned. Fortunately, this time he was alone.

"Sorry about that," he said. "Granddad's seriously lacking in social skills."

"No problem," answered Daniel. "Your granddad just . . . surprised me. I didn't think Herman had any family."

"Granddad's actually Herman's brother, Oliver Plunkett. They got separated when they were toddlers. Grew up in different parts of the country, didn't even know the other existed. By the time they found each other, Herman didn't want much to do with our side of the family. Granddad said they had been apart so long that they had nothing in common except a knack for making money. But if you ask me, they were two peas in a pod. Both cranky and stubborn. That's why they couldn't stand each other—they were too alike."

Theo cocked his head and looked down at Daniel. "Did you know Herman well? I only met him once, but he didn't exactly seem like the type to make friends with little kids."

Daniel decided to let the "little kids" remark go. Theo wasn't *that* much older than he was. A couple of years, tops.

"I knew him," said Daniel. "But I wouldn't say we were friends. Seeing your granddad there was like seeing a ghost."

So Herman had a brother, and that brother had had a family. The story made sense, and Daniel could picture Herman's reaction to finding out he had a sibling—he'd manage to see him as a threat to the carefully constructed fiction that he'd been working on all those years. The delusion that he was somehow doing good, that he was a protector and not a predator. Herman had needed to stay friendless and alone, lest anyone get close enough to make him face the truth about his life.

For some reason, out of everyone, he'd chosen Daniel to confide in. He'd had the deranged thought that Daniel would believe the lie too. That he'd support him in it and even take up his legacy.

About that, just like everything else, Herman had been wrong.

But he'd also been almost superhumanly devious, so Daniel wasn't prepared to let his guard down just yet. Theo and his granddad were still strangers. And they were still Plunketts, after all.

"Really, I just came by to see how you were doing," Daniel said. "That was some accident yesterday."

"I'm fine. Just ruined a pair of shoes. And a car, of course. How's your friend?"

"Eric's okay, thanks to you."

Theo shook his head. "No way. Like I said before, you did the rescuing. He owes you, not me."

"Yeah, well, I think he wants to thank you anyway. In person. Would it be all right if I brought him by sometime?"

"Sure. Technically I'm under house arrest, but I'll get out of that soon enough."

"Grounded, huh?"

"No, I mean I'm under *house arrest*—as in I was arrested. See, technically, I just turned fifteen, so technically I can't drive. I kind of borrowed one of Dad's cars. He's down at the police station trying to get it to go away. He's good at that sort of thing." Theo shrugged and put his hands in his pockets like he was trying to act embarrassed, but he wouldn't drop his cocky sneer.

"Still," he said, "I guess I'm lucky to be alive. Weird to

survive something like that without a scratch, huh?" He held on to Daniel's gaze for a long time—uncomfortably long. Daniel thought about that moment yesterday when they'd looked at each other as Theo's car was miraculously suspended midfall and, just for a few seconds, floated in the air.

"Yeah," said Daniel. "It was a heck of a scare. Funny at times like that how things seem to go in slow motion, right? Like a movie."

"Sure," answered Theo, not breaking his stare. "Slow motion."

He looked like he might say something more, but he was interrupted by a car coming up the long driveway. The limousine that Mollie had described was pulling up in front of the house.

"All hail the conquering hero," said Theo. "Dad's home."

The stretch limo parked and a large, thick-necked chauffeur got out and greeted Theo with a tip of his cap. Then he swung around to the rear of the car and opened the door, stepping back to make room for . . . a dog. A giant golden retriever bounded out of the car. It had some kind of slobbered-on stuffed animal in its mouth, and it was coming straight for Daniel.

Tail wagging, it reared up on its back paws and playfully pounded Daniel on the chest, nearly knocking him onto his backside. A long string of saliva dangled precariously in front of Daniel's face as the dog presented his chewed-upon trophy for inspection.

"Better give in," called a man's voice. "Barney won't give up until you give Mr. Pickles a throw."

"What's . . . ," said Daniel as he struggled to keep his balance against the big dog's weight. "What's a Mr. Pickles?"

"Mr. Pickles is what's left of my son's favorite stuffed rabbit-bear. Looked a little like a rabbit when we first got it, a little like a teddy, but not very much like either. He's more of a headless mop these days, thanks to Barney."

A middle-aged man, double-chinned and balding and dressed in a pair of outrageous Bermuda shorts, had exited the limo and was strolling up the drive, a big grin on his jowly face. Daniel could see the Plunkett in him, only the thin sneer had been replaced with the good-natured smile and extra pounds of someone who enjoyed life—perhaps a little too much. Daniel liked him instantly.

"He's right," said Theo. "Barney won't take no for an answer."

Daniel put his hand out and tried not to visibly flinch as Barney dropped the soggy mass of fur and stuffing that was Mr. Pickles into his open palm. Then the dog plopped down again on all fours and lowered his head to the ground, while sticking his butt up in the air in a classic puppy pose.

Daniel gave Mr. Pickles a throw, a long line of slobber trailing behind it, with Barney in hot pursuit.

Daniel searched for something to wipe his hand on.

"Sorry about that," said Theo.

"Aw, it's just love!" said Theo's dad. "Barney's more dog than even he knows."

"That's okay," said Daniel, resorting to his pant leg to dry his Barney-ized hand. "He's nice."

Theo's dad stuck out his hand, careless of the dog spittle on Daniel's. "I'm Theodore Plunkett. I see you've met Junior."

His grip was firm. A businessman's handshake.

"Daniel Corrigan. I was there at the . . . accident. I was just coming by to check up on him."

"You mean the scene of the crime?" Mr. Plunkett was eying Daniel's bike, parked just a few feet away. "I approve of your choice of transportation, son! Eco-friendly and cost-effective and, most importantly, legal! Junior, here, could learn a thing or two from you, I suspect."

Theo shook his head but didn't say anything. Daniel couldn't help but wonder if this seemingly good-natured ribbing was for real. If Daniel had taken the family car out and wrecked it—underage, no less—his dad would have grounded him for life. He'd look like Grandpa Plunkett by the time he reached parole.

"Well, Mr. Plunkett, that bridge *is* dangerous. My gram used to say that it was a deathtrap."

"Well, I'm just glad no one was seriously hurt," said Mr. Plunkett. "Cars can be replaced easily enough. But kids are expensive."

Daniel smiled at Mr. Plunkett's . . . joke?

"Why don't you come back tomorrow, Daniel?" said Mr. Plunkett. "Junior and I have to have a father-to-criminal talk, but I'm sure Theo'd like a tour of the town. A bike tour!"

Daniel looked at Theo. After the earlier "little kids" comment he wasn't sure how Theo would react, but he was happy to see Theo grinning.

"I'd be up for it. You free?"

"Sure," said Daniel. "Be happy to."

"Good!" said Mr. Plunkett, clapping his hands. "That's settled then! Now, Daniel, say goodbye to Barney."

The big retriever had finished mauling Mr. Pickles and had trotted back over to where the humans were talking. He wagged his tail appreciatively as Daniel patted his head and said his goodbyes.

Chapter Four
Clay the Terrible

Daniel was halfway home when he realized he had never even stepped inside Theo's front door. He'd been stonewalled, but whether it had been an accident or on purpose was hard to know for sure. He hadn't gotten so much as a peek inside Herman Plunkett's old home, but the trip hadn't been a total waste of time. He'd made some kind of connection with Theo, and maybe he could use that connection to get inside the mansion at a later date. At the very least, he might have made a new friend.

A friend with a taste for stealing his father's cars, apparently. This was an aspect of Theo's life that Daniel doubted he'd ever understand.

Daniel had just pulled into his subdivision when he saw Rohan standing on the sidewalk, waiting for him and pointing at something overhead. It was still late summer, but the sun had started dipping lower earlier in the evening. The days were getting shorter. Against the backdrop of a burnt-orange sky, Eric appeared. He whipped up a few prematurely fallen leaves as he landed—a glimpse of the change of seasons to come.

"Hey, you talk to the new kid?" asked Eric. Eric loved to make an entrance, but he never *acted* like he was making an entrance. Daniel wondered at what point flying kids had begun to seem everyday. When precisely did such things stop being absolutely mind-blowing? He honestly couldn't remember.

"Earth to Daniel," said Rohan. "Did little Plunkett put you into some kind of trance? Eric, I think our friend's been zombified."

"Huh?" asked Daniel. "Oh, you mean Theo? He actually seemed okay."

"Did you get inside?" asked Rohan. "Did you do any sleuthing?"

"I couldn't get past the front door. But I did meet some of the family. Turns out, Theo's grandfather is Herman's brother. He looks just like a plus-sized Herman. It's creepy."

"Well, I'm glad you were able to meet the folks," said Eric. "But that doesn't help us figure out what Theo's game plan is."

"Actually, I think it does," said Daniel. "They were nor-

40

mal people, Eric. Theo's obviously super-spoiled and way too full of himself, but I don't think he has any kind of game plan other than driving his dad crazy."

Eric let out an unconvinced laugh and mumbled something under his breath.

"Eric apparently doesn't take well to other kids saving his life," said Rohan. "He holds a grudge for the strangest things."

"For the record, Daniel did the saving," said Eric. "And I don't have anything against the kid."

"But . . . ," said Rohan.

"But Daniel went over there for a reason. C'mon, you two are as freaked out about a new Plunkett in town as I am."

Daniel didn't answer. He just shrugged as he hugged the street's shoulder, walking his bike toward home. They had reached a portion of the road where the sidewalk ended, and you had to keep one eye on oncoming traffic at all times. Unless you were Eric, of course. Daniel felt sorry for the tractor-trailer that was unlucky enough to come barreling into him.

"Look, it's weird, all right? And I want to make sure that everything over there in Plunkett's home is nice and safe, but I just don't want to judge Theo on the stuff his crazy old granduncle did, okay?"

"Unfortunately, we don't have much evidence one way or the other," said Rohan. "Stealing his dad's car for a joyride is a strike against him, but he did act pretty heroically when he saved Eric—or helped save Eric, anyway. The two kind of cancel each other out in my book."

Eric shrugged at this. Daniel couldn't understand why it bothered Eric so much that Theo had saved him, but it obviously did.

"So," continued Rohan, "all we have to go on is Theo's name. He's a Plunkett. Let's hope he's just a quirky kind of Plunkett and not on the psychopath side of the family tree. But until we know for sure, we need to be cautious."

Daniel nodded. He himself had told Mollie that they needed to be careful, and he supposed it was natural for them all to be suspicious of that family—Daniel included. But Theo was the new kid in a strange town, and only Daniel knew how that felt. And how important it would be for Theo to make real friends.

But something else was on Daniel's mind, something that had been worrying him almost as much as Theo Plunkett.

"So . . . ," Daniel began. "Speaking of the creek, how are you feeling, Eric?"

Eric shook his head and smiled. "I was wondering when you were going to get to that. I was hoping to keep your detective brain distracted enough with Plunkett family conspiracies. . . ."

"I'm not using my detective brain on this one. We're friends, that's all."

"You and Rohan are like two old ladies," he said.

"I've been asking him the same question," said Rohan. "It looked to me like Eric didn't just lose his grip on that car. Looked like he depowered or something."

"I'm fine!" said Eric. "That car was heavy, and I guess I must've blacked out for a sec. I just overdid it splashing you two with those cannonballs. No big deal."

"We've all seen you handle worse than that car," said Daniel.

"Yeah, well, I'd like to see you two try to lift it!"

Daniel had never seen Eric this defensive before, which in itself was in some ways the most alarming thing of all. Or perhaps Eric was just tired of the questions, and maybe Daniel was looking for problems where there weren't any. The easiest explanation would be that Eric had just been overly tired. Why couldn't Daniel simply accept that and move on?

Because as Daniel had learned, in Noble's Green the easiest explanation was almost never the right one.

He let the issue die for now, and the three friends walked a while farther without saying much of anything. Soon they came to the lonely intersection that marked Daniel's street, Elm Lane. Rohan's family lived on the corner, so he waved goodbye and headed indoors for the evening. Eric's own neighborhood of Briarwood was several miles away, but that wouldn't mean much to Eric. He could be home in minutes. But it was still a little surprising when Eric made the turn with Daniel onto Elm.

"You're not headed home?" asked Daniel.

"Huh? Oh, in a while. I just thought you might want company."

Considering that for the last ten minutes his "company" had been silent and grumpy, Daniel guessed there was something else going on here.

"Eric, is there a reason you're not going home right away?"

Eric stopped walking, shoved his hands into his pockets, and stared at the sky.

"Bob's back," he said.

"Bob? Oh, your mom's boyfriend?"

"Yeah. Only now he brought all his stuff. Mom says he's making a commitment, but I think he finally got kicked out of his apartment. Staying with us is rent-free."

"Oh, I see."

Daniel had learned months ago that Eric's home life was anything but perfect. His mom worked double shifts at the diner to pay the mortgage on their tiny Briarwood house, and when she wasn't around, her on-again, off-again boyfriend treated Eric like dirt. The guy was rude at the best of times, but when he drank, he became downright scary.

Which in turn scared Daniel. Bob had no idea what Eric really was, or what he was capable of. Daniel worried about the day that Bob pushed Eric too far.

"I thought your mom had dumped him last time for good," Daniel said.

"It's never for good. My dad was lousy too, but she kept

on taking him back until he finally disappeared. In the end he found a family he liked better, I guess, which was fine with me. My mom and I don't need anyone else. We definitely don't need Bob.

"Anyway, Mom's back to pulling long hours, and Bob popped open his first beer of the day around noon. It'll be at least seven or eight before he's safely passed out on the sofa."

"Well, you could eat dinner at our house. My dad's cooking tonight, so I can't promise it'll be good. I can pretty much guarantee the opposite, actually. But I can promise there'll be no Bobs at the dinner table."

Eric smiled. "Thanks. That sounds awesome. Even the dad-cooked meal."

The two of them started up Elm, past the flickering early-evening streetlights. But they hadn't gotten very far before Eric put out a hand, stopping Daniel in his tracks.

"Smell that?" Eric asked, wrinkling his nose.

"Hmm? What?"

"Something awful."

Daniel looked around, sniffing. "Dinner?"

"No, it's . . ."

Then Daniel caught wind of it. A smell unlike any other in Noble's Green. A smell that was so super-terrible, so nauseatingly horrific, that it could only belong to one person.

Bud.

The fat bully stepped out of the woods just a few yards ahead. He was out of breath and struggling with something in his ham-sized fists. Whatever it was, it was heavy even for the big kid. He was so preoccupied with hefting the large whatever-it-was that he didn't see Eric and Daniel standing in the road.

"Evening, Bud," said Eric.

Eric's voice so startled Bud that he dropped what he was carrying. He yelped in pain as a large rock landed on his foot.

"Ow! Ow! Ow!" cried Bud as he hopped around on the other foot. At the same time, the smell—that distinctive Bud odor—grew instantly stronger. A hard-boiled egg soaked in milk and left in a hot car.

Daniel covered his face with his sleeve and tried not to barf. Of all the superpowers in Noble's Green, Bud's super-stink had to be the worst. In more ways than one.

"Sorry, Bud," said Daniel. "We didn't mean to surprise you."

"Aww, man!" said Bud, struggling to keep his balance and massage his foot at the same time. "Why you gotta sneak up on people?"

"We were just walking along the street," answered Eric. "You're the one who came skulking out of the woods. What do you got there, anyway?"

Bud suddenly seemed to remember his dropped parcel, and he took an obvious step forward to put his body between it and Eric and Daniel.

"This? Nothin'."

"What Bud meant to say," came a voice from behind them, "is that it's none of your business, Boy Scout."

From the opposite side of the street stepped Clay

Cudgens, Bud's wicked, and far more dangerous, partner. Where Bud was a giant slab of flab, Clay was lean and mean. And powerful. Clay was at least as strong as Eric and just as hard to hurt. He reminded Daniel of a feral dog. He'd bitten the hand of everyone who'd reached out to him, including Daniel.

"Well, this looks familiar," said Eric. "You gonna brag and threaten us until I have to finally kick your butt? Again?"

Clay couldn't fly, and what's more, he was terrified of heights. That was Eric's only advantage, but so far it had always been enough. So far. At that moment Daniel could feel the tension between the two boys strain to the breaking point. It was taut between them.

"That wasn't helpful," whispered Daniel.

"Just skipping ahead to the fun part," Eric whispered back.

"Look, Clay," said Daniel. "We were just on our way home when Bud came stumbling out of those woods. We're curious what he's up to, is all."

"And I said it wasn't none of your business. You got trouble with your ears as well as your head?"

Daniel shook his head. "I'm trying to *avoid* trouble here, Clay. But you make it really hard."

"Sure." Clay smiled. "You want to avoid trouble because you've got flyboy there to back you up. You'd be wetting yourself if you came around the corner alone and found me waiting for you."

Actually, that last part was absolutely true. Daniel had

already had a bad run-in with Clay, one that had ended with Daniel falling off a mountain. If it hadn't been for Eric's timely rescue, Daniel would've been a puddle of goo at the foot of Mount Noble. While Clay had ultimately helped the Supers in their final battle with the Shroud, that truce had been temporary, and these days Clay seemed even more determined to make their lives miserable. Clay was right: Daniel was scared of him. And with good reason.

"If Daniel came around the corner and found you," said Eric, "you'd smile and ask how he was doing. Then you'd go peacefully on your way. Otherwise I'd hear about it. Then you'd hear about it." He pointed one finger up at the sky. "You and me, we'd have a nice long talk. Up there."

Clay glanced worriedly skyward. His mouth twitched in anger, but there was fear in his eyes.

"Fine. You go your way, we'll go ours. We weren't hurting nobody anyhow. C'mon, Bud."

Bud began waddling past them, his cloud of stink trailing behind.

"Bud!" said Clay.

"Huh? Oh! Right!" Bud turned around and bent over the fallen hunk of rock he'd smashed his foot with.

"Oof! Gimme a hand, Clay, won't you?"

Clay snarled in annoyance and walked over to his partner, all the while keeping his eyes on Eric and Daniel.

"Pick it up, lard-butt!"

"It's heavy!" complained Bud, his face turning red from the effort.

"Hold on, let me get a look at it first," said Clay, bending low. Daniel noticed that while Clay was looking, he wasn't touching.

"That's just a rock," he said at last.

"But it's a funny shape! Kinda. Man, I hauled it all the way here, just like you asked."

"You're an idiot."

Something was bothering Daniel. Something was wrong with this situation. Something about the rock, and the direction Bud had come from. He'd hauled it all the way from where?

Eric was apparently curious too. He'd already approached the two boys. "You guys having trouble with your pet rock?"

"It's kinda heavy," answered Clay. "But I bet you could pick it up, no problem."

Something in Clay's voice, something in the suddenly too-friendly smile.

"Eric," said Daniel, "be careful."

"What? What's there to be afraid of? We're all friends, right, Clay? You don't mind if I hold your pet rock for a minute."

He lifted the bowling-ball-sized stone like it was nothing. "Huh. Can't say I see what's so special. What is this, limestone?"

Limestone. The Old Quarry. All at once, everything clicked together in Daniel's mind. He knew, without a doubt, where Bud had been and, worse, what he'd been looking for.

"Eric!" Daniel said, moving toward his friend. Clay had taken a step back, but he was looking intently at Eric, like a hyena waiting for its next meal. "Drop it!"

"Huh?" said Eric. "What's wrong?" He gave Daniel a confused smile, but he did as he was told. He let the rock fall with a thud to the ground.

"It's limestone," answered Daniel, glancing over at Clay. "From the Old Quarry. But they weren't looking for limestone. They were looking for Plunkett's stone."

Eric's smile disappeared. He understood now. Placing a hand on Daniel's chest, he gently pushed him away from himself and Clay, but as he did so, he never took his eyes off the bully. Daniel's heart was pounding in his ears. He knew what his friend was thinking, knew that the memory of that final fight with Herman Plunkett was still fresh in Eric's mind. In the Old Quarry, the Supers had stood united against the Shroud and his black meteorite, a shard of the Witch Fire Comet itself, an alien stone that had stolen the powers of generations of superpowered children and had very nearly defeated them all. In the end, with Clay's help, they had won. Plunkett was dead, buried under tons of limestone rubble. His body was still there. And so was the Witch Fire meteorite.

They'd been allies for that one night, but now there was going to be trouble. Bud took the hint and stepped back too. Far away from Eric's quiet rage.

"What?" said Clay. "Bud's starting a rock collection, that's all— Hey!"

Eric had grabbed Clay by the shirt collar, yanking him close.

"It's not enough to be a bully? You want to be a super-villain now, is that it?"

"Get your hands off me!"

One hand holding Clay by the collar, Eric leapt up to the sky . . . and fell. His feet didn't get more than a few feet off the ground before something in him gave out and he collapsed back to earth.

"What the . . . ?" Clay shrugged Eric off and stumbled backward, his face twisted in confusion. Eric wobbled to his feet, barely able to stand. Daniel recognized that dazed look on his friend's face—he'd seen it before back at the bridge.

"Hey, what's the matter with him?" asked Bud.

No one answered. No one said anything. But a mean smile crept across Clay's face, making his already ugly face even uglier. It was never a good thing when Clay Cudgens smiled.

"Hey, Eric," said Clay. "You okay, man? You need a hand?"

Before Daniel could shout a warning, Clay gave Eric a hard shove, knocking him backward.

Eric was lifted up and off the ground by the force of Clay's little push, and he landed with a loud smack that knocked the wind out of him. He lay there clutching his stomach and gasping for breath.

"Well, well," said Clay. "Here's an interesting twist!"

"Whoa," said Bud, and the air took on the tang of spoiled meat.

Clay stalked toward Eric's helpless form, cracking his knuckles as he walked.

"Man, payback hurts, don't it?"

Eric struggled to stand up, but he just couldn't get his breath. Daniel was at his side, but even with help Eric could only make it to one knee. If he didn't get better fast, they were both in serious trouble.

"Maybe I'll just give you to Bud," said Clay. "I bet even lard-butt over there could whup you now."

"Hey!" said Bud.

"But just to make sure, I think I'll soften you up first. This'll be fun."

Not that long ago, Daniel had watched Mollie Lee stand her ground against Clay. She'd been protecting Daniel at the time, and though she was super-fast, she was no match for Clay's strength. If the two of them got into a fight, Daniel doubted that Clay would even feel it. But she hadn't backed down; she'd stood up for a boy she barely even knew.

Daniel tried to hold on to that memory of Mollie, her face full of stubborn bravery. He kept it foremost in his mind as he put himself between Clay and Eric.

"Leave him alone, Clay."

Clay's smile grew wider and, if possible, uglier.

"I'm surprised at you, New Kid. I'd have thought you'd be halfway home by now. You're gonna need a place to change your shorts."

Clay laughed as he stepped over to the edge of the line of trees and wrapped his arms around a sturdy maple. Its trunk was too thick around for Clay's arms, but he dug his fingers into the bark and pulled. And pulled. The veins in his neck bulged and his arms began to shake, but after a few seconds there was a deep-sounding crack. A snap of splitting roots and the whole thing lurched out of the ground, taking a giant chunk of earth with it.

He lifted the tree above his head and grinned like a maniac.

"I should flatten the both of you!"

"Clay, man," said Bud, "what are you doing? You'll cream Daniel with that thing!"

"Then he'd better move!"

Clay assumed Daniel would run away, of course. Just as he assumed that Eric could take the hit. After all, he'd seen him take much worse. But only Daniel knew how very weak his friend was right now. That thing would kill him.

"Clay!" shouted Daniel. "Wait! Don't!"

"Catch!" said Clay.

In a cloud of leaves and dirt, Clay tossed the tree. It was a lazy throw, but it still spun toward Daniel, a thousand pounds of deadly wood. Daniel barely had time to react. He needed to run, he needed to . . .

The leaves settled and the dust was making his eyes water, but Daniel was surprised to discover that he was still alive.

Clay was still standing over the hole left by his uprooted tree. He was frozen still and he was staring, openmouthed, at Daniel. At the tree overhead.

Daniel looked up to see the giant maple tree suspended above. He quickly glanced over his shoulder to see if Eric was behind him, but his friend was still on the ground. In fact, Eric's face held the same shocked expression as Clay's.

Daniel was holding the tree. Alone. Over his head. All by himself. A thousand pounds of solid wood and dirt.

No one said anything for a long time, until at last Bud broke the silence.

"Whoa," he said.

Chapter Five
First Flight

The first time Daniel had flown, when Eric had taken him on that ride over the forests of Mount Noble, the cold wind had stung Daniel's face and the tingle of vertigo had made his stomach do flip-flops the whole way. It had been thrilling but also terrifying. He'd held on to Eric with white-knuckled fingers, his arms around his friend like a bear trap. The whole flight had been a back-and-forth battle between the joy of flying and the fear of falling. After all, he hadn't really been flying—Eric had been the one in control. Daniel had just been along for the ride.

This time was different. Daniel didn't feel the cold; or rather, he didn't feel it in the way he'd ever felt it before. He was aware of the wind blowing, and he felt the sensation of it, just not the pain. He knew it was cold, but the cold could never hurt him. And as for holding on to Eric, well, that would have been hard since Eric was little more than a spot on the ground below him. And getting smaller by the second.

Daniel was flying. Really flying. He wasn't sure *how*—this wasn't like walking or running, where you have the solid impact of earth-meets-foot to remind you what you're doing. He just felt certain that he could, that the power was there. He could move mountains. Or fly over them.

At last Daniel was super.

After the fight with Clay, Daniel was as shocked as anyone else, even more so, to find himself wielding an enormous tree like it was a baton. If this had been a comic book, Daniel knew, he'd have had something heroic to say, a well-delivered superhero quip aimed at the villain he'd just thwarted. Instead, he went with the obvious:

"Eric! I'm holding a tree!" he said.

"I know!" answered Eric. "But how?"

"I don't know! What do I do with it now?"

"Put it down!"

"Where?"

"Anywhere except on me!"

Bud was already long gone, and Clay was retreating as well. Daniel caught a glimpse of the boy's face before he got out of sight, though. Clay's already puglike features were contorted with hate—hate for the Supers and hate for Daniel. It would have concerned him, and it probably should have, except that Daniel's brain didn't have room for Clay Cudgens anymore. Things were different now.

Daniel dropped the tree with a loud thud that tickled the bottoms of his feet. It would take five grown men to just budge the thing, normally. Yet to Daniel it had felt no heavier than a folding chair. He stared at his hands. They didn't look any different, but if he concentrated, he could feel something, a buzz, the vibration of energy in his muscles just waiting to be released. It started near his heart and ran through his veins, from his fingers to his toes.

"Eric, what's going on?" he asked.

His friend shook his head. "I don't know. How do you feel?"

"Not that different, really. Just sorta tingly, I guess. My heart's going crazy, though."

"Try something else," Eric said. "Pick up Bud's rock."

Daniel looked over at the bowling-ball-sized piece of limestone. He reached out his hands to scoop it up.

"Uh-uh," said Eric. "Try one-handed."

Daniel placed his fingers around the rock. Bud was a big kid, and he'd barely been able to carry it with both hands. Daniel hefted it easily, balancing it in his palm like a basketball.

"Man," said Eric. "Can you do more?"

Daniel placed his other hand on the rock and squeezed.

It took some effort, but after a few seconds of trying, he shattered the rock between his palms. Eric had to duck to escape the flying shrapnel.

"More powerful than a locomotive," said Eric. He pointed up at the sky. "Able to leap tall buildings?"

"No way," said Daniel. Then, "You think?"

"One way to find out."

Daniel looked up at the sky. Stars were just starting to wink at them through the blue-pink firmament of twilight. He took a deep breath, letting the air fill his lungs, then felt that vibration turn into something more, like a current of electricity. His calves were twitchy, eager to jump. His arms were already stretched high above his head, almost involuntarily reaching skyward. His body was telling him to go *up*.

And he did. He flew. One leap and he kept going, shouting as he soared through the heavens higher and higher, all the while willing the ground to stay away. He was a creature of the air now. Nothing else mattered, not even the sound of Eric calling his name. Beneath the howling wind and his own laughter, he was only barely aware of Eric's warning, calling to him like an echo.

"Wait! You're going too fast," Eric shouted. "Don't go too high!"

Daniel didn't understand. How could he be too high? This was glorious. This was flight! This was everything that Eric and Mollie had experienced but Daniel had only ever imagined. This was freedom.

This was every kid's dream.

The world was receding. Even the roar of the wind was becoming little more than a faraway humming in his ears, like a lullaby. His eyes were closed. Why were his eyes closed?

The ground hit him like a wrecking ball to the face. Or rather, Daniel hit the ground. When the earth beneath him finally stopped spinning, Daniel opened his eyes to see that he'd plowed into a bank of fir trees. Pine needles were drifting down around him like a shower of snowflakes. After a few minutes Eric came running toward him. Daniel's head throbbed with a dull ache that kept rhythm with his heart pounding in his temples.

"What . . . what happened?" Daniel asked.

"You . . . flew too high, too fast," said Eric. "You get that high, you start to run out of oxygen. Man, you scared me. I didn't know if you were tough enough to survive a fall like that."

Daniel stared at him, not comprehending.

"Daniel, you flew."

Daniel looked around him at the snapped pine branches, the gout of dirt that had been torn up as he'd skidded to a halt. He remembered the wind. For some reason the air smelled differently up there. It was hard to talk past the knot in his throat. The words just weren't there, so he nodded instead.

"Wow, Daniel," said Eric. "You really flew. And that tree . . . how'd you do that?"

Daniel cleared his throat, suddenly self-conscious.

"I don't know . . . puberty?"

"Man, come on!" said Eric. "This is serious!"

"I know! I know! But I don't know what to say. I have no idea what's happening to me!"

"Do you feel like you could do it again?"

Daniel shifted his weight beneath him and thought about the wind. He felt that same tingle in his hands and feet, just a bit weaker now. He concentrated on it as his feet began to lift off the ground. Then he suddenly felt dizzy. His stomach flipped over on itself and he had to sit back down.

"Whoa, whoa, take it easy," said Eric, putting a firm hand on Daniel's shoulder. "You just about killed yourself last time, you know."

Daniel took a deep breath and looked up at the stars. How far had he gotten? Must've been pretty far to start losing oxygen. He'd heard of climbers running out of air on the top of Mount Everest, and that was nearly 30,000 feet. Eric was right—Daniel hadn't even realized what he'd been doing, or how fast or how far he'd been flying. It was as if the wind had just pulled him along, and he hadn't had a care in the world. Not a fear.

"You were fly-drunk," said Eric.

"What?"

"That's what Michael used to call it. You get up there with nothing but the wind and you kind of lose yourself. It's easy to do, but it's dangerous. Michael used to joke that friends don't let friends fly drunk." Michael was one of the Shroud's last victims. He'd had his powers, and his memory, stolen from him on his thirteenth birthday, but before that he'd been the greatest flier Noble's Green had ever known.

"Eric, has anything like this happened before? I mean, someone getting powers who wasn't born here?"

Eric thought for a minute. "No, not that I can remember. But we don't get a lot of new kids here anyway, so maybe it was just a matter of time."

"I can't believe this," said Daniel.

Eric smiled. "So, I guess . . . welcome to the club, Super."

Daniel shook his head. He certainly didn't feel that super now. The nausea was passing, but he still felt weak and tired, like he'd run a marathon in hundred-degree heat. All he wanted to do was sleep.

"I feel terrible. I don't think I could fly now if you pushed me out of a plane."

"Well, maybe it's a slow process—you getting your powers. Maybe because you weren't raised here, you just haven't stored up enough . . . superpower or whatever. You've got a small gas tank."

Daniel shrugged. It didn't sound right to him, but he was willing to go with any explanation for the time being. He was so tired, it hurt to think, but through the haze, one thing did occur to him. A worrying thought.

"Eric," said Daniel, "why didn't you come after me?"

"What do you mean?" asked Eric. Daniel noticed that his friend wasn't looking at him. Eric always looked you in the eyes when he talked to you.

"When I flew off, you didn't follow me. If you were so worried about me, why didn't you follow me? Eric, look at me."

Eric looked at Daniel, and what Daniel saw in his friend's eyes was something he'd never seen there before: fear.

"You didn't fly after me because you couldn't," said Daniel. "Right?"

"I tried, but . . . it just . . . disappeared."

Daniel shook his head. Eric's power disappeared. At the same time that Daniel's appeared.

"Like back at the creek?"

Eric nodded.

"Eric . . ."

"No! Don't say it, Daniel. Don't even think it."

"Come on!" said Daniel. "*Your* flight and *your* strength go missing just as I become super-strong and start to fly!"

"No. You're not like him. You are not the Shroud!"

"Look, I'm not saying I am, but—"

"Just forget it, Daniel. Get the idea that your powers and my problem are somehow connected out of your head. You're becoming a Super because you *deserve* to be, Daniel. You are not becoming Herman Plunkett. And whatever's going on with me, we'll fix it. I'm already feeling better. I've probably just got the super-flu or something stupid like that."

Reluctantly, Daniel nodded. He didn't believe him, but he was too tired to argue anymore and too exhausted to think clearly. But he remembered that night not so long ago when he'd woken up in a cave in the Old Quarry, to discover Eric unconscious and the Shroud whispering offers in the dark. Offers of power. He'd said no to them all. He'd said no then.

"Another thing," said Eric. "Though I can't wait to see Mollie's face when you fly past her window, let's not tell the others just yet, okay? You and me can figure this out together, but I don't want to worry them."

"Okay. But if it gets worse . . ."

"If it gets worse, then we'll talk."

Eric helped Daniel dust himself off as best he could. But Daniel's hair was still in a tangle, and he looked like he'd been belly-crawling through the forest.

"I think we'll walk the rest of the way, what do you say?" Eric said.

Daniel nodded, and the two friends headed for the lights of Elm Lane and the Corrigan home.

"That dinner offer still stand?" Eric asked.

"Of course," said Daniel. "We need to celebrate with some really terrible food."

Eric chuckled, and then the two walked in silence past the now-glowing streetlights. But all the way home, Daniel imagined that he could hear whispers in the dark.

Chapter Six
Superheroing 101

That night the dream returned. After dinner, and a groggy goodbye to Eric, Daniel barely made it back to his room, where he fell asleep without even taking off his clothes. He was back in the Old Quarry, fighting the Shroud. As before, he wrestled with Herman Plunkett, struggling to tear the meteorite pendant from the old man's throat. Again, as his fingers closed around it, they burned away like butter against a hot stove. The details were all the same, like a recording of a dream rather than the actual thing. The same up to the end, when suddenly the Shroud disguise melted away, revealing the weak old man beneath. Herman was pleading with Daniel, begging him for something—mercy? But Daniel didn't listen. He stood over his fallen enemy and held up his ruined right hand. The flesh was gone, but in its place was a hand made all of green fire.

Daniel woke up clutching his hand tightly to his chest. He quickly counted the fingers to make sure they were all there. He lay there for a few moments, staring at the ceiling while he worked out the phantom pains from his hand, and he noticed something odd. Normally he woke up looking at the sunlit window, but this time he was staring up at the bookshelf, which was clear on the other side of the room. As he rubbed the sleep from his sticky eyes, the rest of the room came into focus.

He was on the floor. He'd been sleeping on the hard wooden floor at the base of the bookshelf, but he had absolutely no memory of how he'd gotten there. The ache in his fingers was gone, only to be replaced by a very real crick in his neck and a stabbing pain in his lower back—at some point he'd apparently rolled atop a piece of H.M.S. *Nelson*.

The bed was wrinkled, but the covers were undisturbed, and nothing else in the room seemed to be out of place. So without a better explanation, Daniel must've been sleep-walking. He'd never done that before, but then, recently he'd been doing a lot of things he'd never done before.

He could fly, for one thing. Or at least, he had flown. He'd had the power yesterday. He'd soared as high as any Super dared go.

But where had the power come from? Was Eric right when he said that Daniel was finally a Super, or was there another, darker explanation? In his dream he'd stood over Herman, his hand made of emerald flame. *Witch Fire* . . .

Daniel sat up and tried to rub some warmth back into his bare arms. The mornings were getting cooler, and autumn would come early this year. But there was a chill in Daniel's bones that had nothing to do with the changing seasons. He stood in front of the bookshelf and flexed his fingers as he looked down once more at his bare hand. He didn't wear a watch and he owned only one ring, a ring he'd never worn.

Reaching up to the topmost shelf, Daniel retrieved a very special book. It was a hardcover, a very old edition of *The Final Problem,* with a black-ink-and-gold-embossed illustration on the front showing Sherlock Holmes battling his arch-nemesis, Moriarty, over the Reichenbach Falls. The book was unusually light for its size because Daniel himself had hollowed out the inside pages to make room for a small ring of polished black rock. He flipped the book open to the hollowed-out middle and looked at the ring. The ugly circle of black rock looked like it had been carved out of coal, but Daniel knew better. It had been a gift from Herman Plunkett himself, who'd told Daniel that he'd crafted it from the very same meteorite that gave Plunkett his power-stealing Shroud abilities. The old villain had intended it for Daniel to use as his protégé.

Daniel had never worn it, but he hadn't destroyed it either. He hadn't tossed it into the deepest bottom of Tangle Creek or buried it far off in the remote woods. But worse than that, he hadn't told anyone about it. He'd kept it here on his bookshelf, a secret. He'd convinced himself that this was the safest place for it, that he was keeping it out of the wrong hands. But safe from whom? His friends?

There had been several times over the last few months when he'd come close to telling the Supers about the ring, but each time he'd chickened out at the last minute. He'd had it for so long now, and to tell them would be admitting that he'd kept something from them, something that could turn into a threat to all of them. The longer he went without telling, the guiltier he felt. The guiltier he felt, the harder it was to tell his friends the truth. He was stuck.

He set the book down on his desk and stared at the ring inside. When it caught the sunlight from a certain angle, it took on a kind of greenish, oily sheen. Daniel remembered the emerald fire that had burned from the Shroud's pendant; he remembered the green flame that had consumed his hand in his dream the night before.

His subconscious was not subtle. And his subconscious was probably right. The ring was dangerous, and he should just destroy it now. He should take a hammer to it until it was just so much dust. But what if Eric was right and Daniel was a Super now too? Herman Plunkett had said that Daniel's own grandmother had lost both her powers and her memories by merely touching a piece of that meteor stone. The slightest touch and she'd been changed forever. Made less.

And last night Daniel had flown.

Now the ring held a different kind of fear for him. It was like a venomous snake in a basket, and to get rid of it you might have to risk being bit.

Daniel's hand fell away. He closed the book's cover, leaving the black ring in its hiding place, untouched. And there it would stay, for the time being at least.

Daniel stood and stretched. Other than the stiff neck and aching back, he didn't feel any different today than any other day. He certainly didn't feel more powerful. But then last night he'd been aware of the power only when he'd actually been using it—he hadn't felt super-strong until he'd found himself holding a thousand pounds of tree above his head. He hadn't known he could fly until he actually flew. What should he do now? Should he test himself again, try lifting something heavy? But what could he lift . . . ?

"Hey, Georgie!" Daniel called. Daniel's room was in the attic at the top of the house, but his little brother slept downstairs, in what was once the nursery but now had to be carefully referred to as the "big-boy room." Normally, if Daniel so much as whispered in the direction of his door, Georgie would come running.

But today there was no answer. As Daniel went down the attic steps, he caught voices drifting up from the kitchen downstairs. Everyone must already be at breakfast—they'd let him sleep in. Perfect. Daniel didn't want his nosy little brother around to see what he was about to attempt.

Inside Georgie's room was a piece of Corrigan family history in the form of a cherrywood dresser. It was squat and thick, barely coming up to Daniel's chest, and it had been used as a diaper-changing table by Daniel's gram. She'd used it to change Daniel's mother when she'd been just a baby. Gram had kept it here in this house for years, always intending to pass it on as a keepsake, but there was one problem—it was too heavy. It was a monster of craftsmanship, but it was also so solid, no one dared move it from its spot. In fact, Georgie's room had become Georgie's room simply because that changing table was already in there, and it wasn't going anywhere. From now on, it came with the house. People came to the changing table; the changing table did not come to them.

Listening at the top of the stairwell, he could hear the clink of plates being cleared, which signaled his family was finishing up breakfast. It was now or never.

"All right," he said, sizing up the dresser. "It's just you and me!"

Daniel wrapped his arms around the dresser's edge. His skinny limbs certainly didn't look any more muscly, but then, to look at Eric you'd never know that he could lift a car over his head and not break a sweat. At least, not usually.

Daniel gave the dresser a tug. Then a shove. He grunted. He pushed and he pulled, and for a moment he thought he felt something give, but it was just his knees popping. After a short time of useless struggle, he gave up.

Had yesterday been just a fluke? By some weird quirk of Noble's Green super-physics, had he been given powers just to see them fade away again? Daniel looked out Georgie's window. His little brother's bedroom overlooked the front yard. It didn't have the same breathtaking view of Mount Noble that Daniel's attic room had, but above the trees he could still get a look at the clear morning sky.

He peered up at the blue sliver in Georgie's window and remembered what it was like to be up there, alone with the wind. He needed to know. He needed to see if he could still . . .

"Fly! Fly! Georgie fly!"

Georgie came into the room wearing nothing but his pajama shirt, a hat made from a brown paper bag, and a bath-towel cape. Daniel's little brother disdained pants.

"Charge!" shouted Georgie with his arms outstretched as he ran straight at Daniel. Daniel caught his little brother and, in one fluid motion, spun him around. Georgie exploded in giggles.

"Fly! Georgie fly!"

Daniel twirled his brother in three complete circles before letting him collapse at his feet.

"More! More, Daniel, more!" Georgie was so dizzy, he couldn't even wobble himself up to sitting, but he still wanted to go again.

"Not now, Georgie. My arms are tired."

"Mooooore!" Georgie pumped his legs in the air, kicking at something that wasn't there, but Daniel wasn't in the mood.

"Georgie, I can't, okay? I'm not strong enough!"

"Everything all right in here?" Daniel's mother appeared

in the doorway holding a bagel and a glass of orange juice. She frowned when she saw Georgie doing bicycle kicks on the floor. "Uh-oh. Is Georgie counting down?"

Counting down was Corrigan family code for when their youngest was near toddler-meltdown. It was a signal to drop everything and secure any and all loose objects. Georgie's tantrums were forces of nature.

Daniel looked askance at his brother, but Georgie just blew him a raspberry in return and giggled.

"No," said Daniel. "False alarm."

"Well, I'm glad to see you're finally awake," said his mother. "Georgie needs to get dressed, and you need to grab a bite to eat. I told Eric that you could take a bagel and juice with you."

"Eric?"

No sooner had Daniel said his name than his friend stepped into view. He was smiling at them behind a mouthful of bagel and cream cheese.

"Sorry about the surprise visit," Eric said, "but I wanted to get an early start."

"A start on what?" asked Daniel.

"Superheroing 101!"

"You boys and your games," said Daniel's mother as she began stripping Georgie out of his bath-towel cape and paper-bag hat. "Just be home for lunch."

"Superheroing 101?" asked Daniel as the two of them climbed the steps to his room, out of earshot of his mother.

71

Eric smiled as he shrugged. "I flew over here this morning. Powers are back to full. How are you feeling?"

Daniel thought about the changing table. Solid. The unmovable object.

"Nothing. Looks like I'm back to my ordinary, measly self."

"Well, let's put it to the test. I wanna figure out what's going on." Eric pointed to Daniel's feet. "Put on a pair of clean socks and grab your shoes. Class is in session!"

The morning chill gave way as the sun appeared above the trees. It was going to be a warm day after all, maybe one of the last of the season. The sky was all clear blue, but the air down on the ground was hazy and still sticky with western Pennsylvania humidity, even this early in the morning. They hiked out into the neighboring woods until they reached a small clearing. The weeds were waist high in places, and Daniel's jeans kept getting snagged on sticker bushes. But it was private.

"Okay," said Eric. "First things first. Fly. But this time, go slow!"

"I can't go at all!" said Daniel. "I told you, I don't have any powers!"

"Did you have any powers yesterday morning?"

"No."

"But you did by the end of the day. So we need to test it, to be sure. It's called the scientific method. You see, I know that because I go to a fine public school—"

Daniel held up a hand and cut Eric off. "Okay, enough. I'll try. Just shut up."

Eric grinned like a fool, but he did, in fact, shut up.

Daniel concentrated. He felt nothing except a slowly building urge to sneeze. He gave a little hop. Nothing.

"See?" he said. "I'm a dead battery."

"Give it a real try," said Eric. "Arms up!"

"C'mon!"

"Arms *up*!"

With a sigh, Daniel lifted his arms and stretched his fingers skyward. Eric watched him expectantly.

"Up, up, and away!" said Daniel.

Nothing.

"Okay, then," said Eric. "So the flight's gone. What about the strength?"

"I tried it out already. Couldn't even scoot a piece of bedroom furniture. Is that scientific enough for you?"

Eric rubbed his chin. Then he lifted up off the ground, just a few feet, and hovered there. Daniel couldn't help but feel a little stab of jealousy, like something nipping at his insides.

"Your powers seem to have disappeared," Eric said. "And mine are back. When the Shroud stole powers, they never returned. Ever."

"Maybe mine's just temporary. Like I'm a Shroud . . . lite?"

Eric shook his head. "I don't buy it. If you're a power thief, why aren't you stealing my powers right now?"

"Doesn't prove anything," said Daniel. "The Shroud's powers worked on touch."

"Good point. Let's try it out."

Before Daniel could even protest, Eric reached out and grabbed him by the hand. Skin-on-skin contact.

"Don't worry," Eric said. "If I fizzle out again, I think I can handle a fall of eight inches."

Daniel took a breath and waited. And again nothing happened.

"Really try," said Eric, still holding Daniel's hand. "Try to will my power away from me. Picture yourself flying!"

Daniel did as he was told. He visualized himself floating there, free of earth, free of gravity itself.

Still nothing. And for once Daniel was glad.

"Huh," said Eric. "Well, I'd say my hypothesis still stands. Whatever you are, you are not a Shroud."

"We don't know that for sure. This is hardly a definitive test."

"Eh, it's good enough for me. So what else do we know so far?"

Daniel began listing the facts on his fingers. He was good at this part. This was about evidence—detective work.

"The first time you experienced any kind of power loss was at the bridge, right?"

"Right," said Eric. "And you didn't do anything super back there, did you?"

Daniel had been thinking about this. "I did push that car off you."

"In the water," said Eric. "That car was still full of air and might not have settled yet. That's a maybe at best."

"Okay, we'll put that into the insufficient-data category."

"Now you're sounding like Rohan."

"Speaking of, he might have some ideas about all this."

"No!" said Eric suddenly. Daniel was so startled by his friend's outburst that he actually took a step back. Eric noticed and immediately regained his composure.

"Sorry, I just— Until we know more, I'd like to keep this between us, okay? Rohan's a worrier and Mollie . . . Just between us."

Daniel nodded. The truth was that Eric was a hero to them all, and Daniel couldn't imagine telling them that Eric was losing his powers and that Daniel might be the cause of it. Better to keep it a secret for now.

"Between us," agreed Daniel. "So the second time you experienced a power loss was last night?"

"Yeah," said Eric. "I felt fine right up until I squared off with Clay."

"At which point *my* powers kicked in," said Daniel. "Any other times you're not telling me about?"

"Nope. Where's that leave us?"

Daniel looked at his fingers. Two times now Eric's power had failed him. And he'd been present on both occasions.

"Inconclusive," said Daniel. "And our attempt to repeat it just now was a failure. . . ."

"So we wait and see."

Daniel nodded, but he was frustrated. Daniel wanted to

be *doing* something—he was a detective, and that meant that he looked for answers. He didn't just wait around. But what else could he do?

"We'll stay in touch," said Eric. "If I have another of my episodes, I'll let you know. If you start flying around the treetops, you let me know."

The two friends shook hands and said goodbye, and Daniel picked his way through the trees as Eric flew off into the distance. The morning so far had left Daniel with equal parts relief and frustration. His thoughts were a tangle, and he was at the same time disappointed and guilty at feeling disappointed.

The morning didn't get any better when he returned home to find a smirking Theo Plunkett waiting for him. Eating Daniel's lunch.

Chapter Seven
Theo and the Bridge

"Terrific sandwich, Mrs. Corrigan," Theo was saying, crumbs spilling out of his mouth as he talked. "Pastrami's so thin, it reminds me of Manhattan's best."

"It was two for one on lunch meat at the local grocer," said Daniel's mom. "But thank you anyway."

Theo Plunkett was sitting at Daniel's kitchen table contentedly munching Daniel's lunch. It was so surreal that for just a second, Daniel feared he might be back in his dream.

"Theo, what are you doing here?"

Theo shrugged. "You said you'd take me on a tour of Noble's Green today. You forget? Your mom was nice enough to let me wait here for you. She makes a terrific pastrami on rye."

Daniel had forgotten. After yesterday evening's events he'd forgotten about Theo Plunkett altogether. He seemed like such a minor concern now, a nuisance. And now the kid wanted a tour?

"Oh, yeah, right. And your dad's okay with it?"

Theo snorted. "Heck, yeah. You made quite an impression on him yesterday. Thinks that it'll be good for me to spend some time with a fine, upstanding citizen such as yourself."

Theo must've caught the look Daniel's mother was giving him, because he hastily dropped the smug smile and looked sheepish.

"I mean, I'd really like to make some friends around here too," he said. "It's hard being the new kid, you know?"

"So," said Daniel's mother. "Theo here tells me he's the boy from the accident the other day? The one with the *car*?"

The way Daniel's mom stretched out the word *car*, she might as well have been saying *life sentence without parole*. Of course she'd heard the story of the creek accident (the edited one, anyway—no need to mention the flying boy), and she hadn't had much good to say about someone who made first impressions by stealing his father's car and driving it off a bridge.

"Uh, yes," said Daniel.

"But we're going on a *walking* tour today," added Theo. "I've sworn off, uh . . . other people's cars."

78

Daniel's mother was unamused.

"I told Theo's dad I'd show him around," offered Daniel.

"Promised, actually," added Theo.

"Right," said Daniel. "I guess I promised."

His mother eventually relented, but Daniel could tell that she was still wary. So was Daniel, for that matter.

Daniel's mother shoved a pastrami sandwich and a banana into his hands and told him to be home before dinner.

Once they were outside, Theo gave him a good-natured slap on the back. Daniel grunted as he wolfed down the food. Theo was obviously misreading Daniel's sour mood. It had little to do with Theo per se. Daniel just didn't want to see anyone right now. He wanted to be up there in the sky.

"Hey," said Theo. "Sorry about all this, but my dad was driving me crazy and I just had to get out of the house. He was on the phone with the mechanic and shouting about the cost of all the repairs to the Porsche. Like we don't have the money or something. I think he was just trying to guilt-trip me."

"So," said Daniel, offering what he hoped was a slightly friendlier tone, "is your dad going to take it out of your allowance or what?"

Theo laughed. "Allowance? Good one, Daniel! That's something I like about you, man—you've got a crazy sense of humor."

Daniel smiled, but he hadn't meant the question as a joke. He wondered just how rich Theo's family really was.

"Should we get going?" Theo asked.

"Sure. We could go up to the Mount Noble Observatory. You can get a great view of the valley. There's a bus that leaves from Main Street, and I don't think your dad would object to us using public transportation."

Theo held up a hand and shook his head. "Actually," he said, "I had someplace else in mind."

The Tangle Creek Bridge had a new temporary guardrail installed where Theo's car had broken through—a short concrete wall capped by two orange plastic barrels. The whole thing looked out of place alongside the rustic old bridge. It felt wrong, but not nearly as wrong as Daniel felt standing there with Theo. They were suspects returning to the scene of the crime.

Theo stood at the edge of the rail, hands in his pockets, looking down at the creek below. The sun hadn't reached this side of the bridge yet, and the greenish water looked black in the shade. Daniel stood a foot or so behind him. He was painfully aware of how casual he was trying to appear, and how badly he was doing it. This was the last place he wanted to be.

"You know," Theo said, "you wouldn't think that a person could survive a fall like that unhurt. Guess I'm lucky the car landed so . . . softly."

"Yeah," answered Daniel. "My gram would've called it a miracle."

"Would've?" asked Theo.

"She passed away last year."

Theo pulled his eyes away from the dark water. "Sorry. I've never lost anyone. Not anyone close anyway. I barely knew Uncle Herman."

"Gram was great. She had a wicked sense of humor— you'd have liked her."

"Bet I would have. We would've argued about one thing, though."

"What's that?" asked Daniel.

"I don't believe in miracles," answered Theo, slinging his legs over the guardrail. "I wanna get a better look."

Daniel scrambled to keep up with the older boy. Theo's long arms and legs made it an easy thing for him to swing over the side and climb down the scaffolding supports. Daniel was used to climbing up from the creek, and he found doing it in reverse both tricky and a bit scary. He wondered what would happen if he fell. Would it be the long drop to the water below, or would he fly?

"Watch yourself," Theo said as Daniel's foot slipped on the scaffolding. "Here, take my hand."

Daniel did as he was told and proceeded cautiously until he found himself safely perched near the diving point, in the same place he'd been when he'd watched Theo's car careen over the edge.

"So this is your gang's hidden swimming hole, huh?" As Theo talked, he leaned as far as could out over the creek— one hand on the scaffolding and the other stretched out in midair, like he was trying to touch the distant shore.

"Well, yeah."

"But I guess it's not so hidden anymore. With all those fire trucks that showed up after my accident, I guess the secret's blown, huh?" Theo looked over his shoulder at him, and as the two boys made eye contact, Daniel had a worrying realization.

Watching Theo dangle over that deep creek brought Daniel back to that afternoon a few days ago, when he'd watched the car plummet off the bridge only to be caught midfall by Eric. One moment in free fall, the next perfectly still, floating in space. It had lasted only a second, but it had been long enough for Daniel to lock eyes with Theo Plunkett and to recognize something in the boy's face. Theo had known in that moment that something impossible was happening to him. He couldn't see Eric, and in his state of shock he probably hadn't been able to process much, but Theo had understood that he should have been falling and he wasn't. He knew that much, at least. And that much was dangerous.

Daniel cursed himself for not thinking of it sooner. Of course Theo wanted to spend time with him, of course he'd brought him here, to where it had all happened. Daniel had been so caught up in his own extraordinary experiences of the past two days that he hadn't seen what was really going on.

He wasn't investigating Theo Plunkett. Theo Plunkett was investigating him.

"How's your friend Eric?" asked Theo. "He back up and swimming?"

"Sure," said Daniel, trying to sound unconcerned. "He's fine. I think I told you that yesterday—"

"I'd like to see him," interrupted Theo. "And that other kid, the Indian one."

"Rohan."

"Right. I've got a few questions about that day, you know? Keep playing it over and over again in my head. And there are parts I just can't figure out."

Theo was watching for a reaction, Daniel could tell. But Daniel had matched wits with another Plunkett a lot more wily than this spoiled rich kid. If he could handle Herman, he could handle anyone.

"What are you confused about?" asked Daniel. "I was here—I saw the whole thing."

"Well, that wave, for one thing," said Theo. "Where did that water come from? Certainly none of you could have made that splash from the creek thirty feet down."

"There was a spot shower. We get those sometimes up here; they blow in off the mountain, but I wouldn't call it a wave."

Theo didn't answer right away. But he smiled unconvincingly.

"That must be it. Still, I'd like to meet your friends. It's hard being new and all, you know?"

"Sure. Of course. They'd love to meet you too."

"Great," said Theo. "That's settled then. Tell you what— my dad's going out of town in a couple of days, and though he won't want me leaving the house, I can probably have people over. Why don't you all come over to our place? We'll order pizza. You do have pizza delivery in this town, right?"

"Of course we do."

"Awesome!" And with that Theo began pulling his shirt up over his head.

"What are you doing?"

"It looks like it's going to be another hot day. Don't know how many more of those we'll have, so I'm not going to waste it!"

Theo dove, with perfect form, into Tangle Creek, leaving Daniel by himself at the top. He hadn't invited him in, but then Theo seemed the sort who was used to doing things alone.

Which was just fine with Daniel. The last thing he wanted to do was jump. He'd had enough of this creek to last him for good.

Daniel had told Eric that Theo wasn't a problem. He now knew that he'd been very, very wrong.

Chapter Eight
The Tree Fort of Justice

The next day, while Theo sat in his palatial mansion and endured whatever passed for punishment in his family, a new meeting of the Supers was called. Approaching the tree fort by bike was slow going for Daniel, as he had to pedal along an old, rarely used road that eventually wound around the mountain's north face to the Old Quarry. But long before completing that treacherous route, Daniel veered off on a secret footpath into the thick forest. He was walking his bike along the trail, as he had many times before, when he heard a girl's voice giggling in his ear. It was a clear, sunny day, and despite the thick foliage there was plenty of light here in the woods. He looked around him, and despite the laughter, Daniel was alone.

No one was there, or at least no one he could see.

"Hi, Rose," he said.

The giggling stopped and the woods were quiet except for birdsong and a few chirping crickets. Silently, Daniel began counting to himself. He made it to seven before the giggles exploded again into a snorting laugh.

"Oh, how did you know?" asked the girl's voice.

"There's only one invisible girl with that laugh, Rose," Daniel said. Actually, there was only one invisible girl, period. From the sound of it, she was somewhere to his left. Squinting, he could just make out tiny footprints stirring the underbrush, as if someone was rocking back and forth on her feet.

"Aww, I wanted to surprise you!" said the unseen Rose.

"You did surprise me," answered Daniel. "You did much better this time. You were quiet for almost seven seconds. That's a new record!"

She giggled again, but this time it was a proud laugh. Though he couldn't see it, he had the feeling the invisible girl was blushing.

"Where's your sister, Rose?"

"Louisa's up the trail a ways. I wandered off again."

"She's going to be worried about you. Come on."

If little Rose was the smallest Super, then her older sister, Louisa, was the most . . . reluctant. Whereas the other Supers reveled in their abilities, Louisa's intangibility only served to make her self-conscious. The two sisters' powers were linked in a way—Rose couldn't be seen unless she wanted to be, and Louisa couldn't be touched. But whereas Rose spent most of her time with the Supers totally invisible, Louisa almost never activated her power. Mollie had told Daniel once that she thought Louisa was afraid she'd somehow get stuck that way, unable to touch or feel anything ever again.

Daniel knew it was simpler than that—Louisa just wanted to be normal. Louisa and he were alike in a way: they both pretended to be something they weren't.

"Hey, Rose, can you do me a favor?"

"What?"

"Can you turn visible now? Now that you've surprised me and all, it would be nice to see who I'm talking to."

"Oh, sure."

Rose popped into existence next to him, standing in the shade of a small evergreen. Nearly six years old, the youngest Super had her sister's long black hair and nut-brown eyes.

"Rose! Rose!"

Louisa came out of the woods a little ways ahead of them on the trail. She was obviously relieved to see her missing sister, but not panicked. By now they were all used to Rose disappearing, literally.

"There you are!" Louisa said.

"I surprised Daniel!" said Rose, giving her sister a huge grin. "I went seven seconds without laughing!"

"Good for you," said Louisa. "Hi, Daniel."

Whenever Louisa said hi to Daniel, she smiled in a way that made Mollie roll her eyes and Daniel feel sort of queasy. Louisa was pretty, and she treated him a lot better than Mollie did (she had never once punched him in the arm, for starters). But Daniel wasn't ready for crushes. Fighting super-villains was simple. Crushes were complicated.

"Hey, Louisa," he said. "Am I the last one here?"

"Yeah, but don't worry. The fliers only just arrived, and it takes them, what, like two minutes from town?"

Daniel chuckled in agreement, but the picture of Eric and Mollie soaring above the trees soured his mood. Now that he knew what flight really felt like, his jealousy was worse than ever. He didn't like it, and he certainly wasn't proud of how he felt, but it was there. A bitter lemon stuck in his throat.

The three of them walked the rest of the way up the trail, and when they finally got to the tree fort, the rest of the Supers were there waiting for them. Tucked away in the woods on the south face of Mount Noble, the Supers' tree fort was a cross between a hidden base and a makeshift museum. No one really knew how old the fort was. The inside was filled with comics, drawings, and other mementos left by previous generations of superpowered children, and the outside had been added to and repaired so many times over the years that there was probably little of the original structure intact. The newest addition had been a lookout crow's nest up top, which gave the whole thing a ramshackle, pirate-ship appearance. It was as if Captain Hook's *Jolly*

Roger had been wrecked upon the branches of two great trees.

Eric and Mollie were perched in the crow's nest, waving as Daniel approached, and he spotted Rohan in the topmost window, his face in a book. Rohan wasn't a flier, but he would have been the first to arrive, regardless. He was just like that. His powers meant that he was easily distracted, but though he might not know where he was at any given time, he always got there early.

Once inside, before any official business could be sorted out, each Super had to sit through Rose's story of how she had surprised Daniel. She told it to everyone, individually, and each time a new detail appeared. By the time she got to Mollie, Rose had Daniel screaming like a girl and running away. While everyone else rolled their eyes at Rose's little embellishments, Mollie simply nodded, and said, "Yep. Sounds like Daniel."

The Supers ran their meetings informally, and really only Rohan and Eric still insisted they be called meetings at all. Not too long ago, they had opened each meeting with a reading of the Rules—a set of commandments supposedly handed down from the first superhero, Johnny Noble. But Daniel had discovered that the Rules had actually been planted by the Shroud as a way of controlling the Supers. He'd used fear and a false history to keep the kids in line.

Since that discovery, the Rules had been abandoned, and now each meeting began with a simple *hello*.

"Hi, everyone," said Daniel. "Thanks for coming."

Daniel cleared his throat as he talked. The Supers were spread out before him, sitting on old beanbags, crates, or rugs on the floor. Even speaking in front a group of friends gave him a small case of the jitters. Louisa and Rose were up front, and Louisa's staring wasn't making it any easier on Daniel's nerves. So he chose to focus on Eric in the back, who gave him a supportive thumbs-up. The two hadn't talked about Daniel's powers problem since yesterday, and Daniel wasn't planning on bringing it up here either. He'd called them together for another reason altogether.

"So, uh," began Daniel, "I guess you already know that we've got a new kid in Noble's Green and that he's a Plunkett."

"Plunketts are bad," said Rose. "They're scary."

"Shh," said Louisa. "Let him finish."

"That's okay, Louisa. Yeah, Rose, Herman Plunkett was scary. But this isn't Herman. It's his grandnephew, Theo."

Mollie stuck her tongue out at this and started to say something, but Eric caught the move out of the corner of his eye and kicked the crate she was sitting on. Mollie, faster than lightning, must've thumped him, because one minute Eric was grinning and the next he was rubbing his nose, which was already turning an angry red. Eric liked to keep the meetings orderly, but this earned him more than the occasional punch from Mollie.

"We don't have any reason to believe that Theo is as dangerous as his uncle was," said Daniel, pausing for effect. "But he is dangerous."

That got their attention.

"But you were defending him yesterday!" said Eric.

"That was yesterday morning. He stopped by for a visit later that afternoon, and I now think that he could pose a serious problem. He's onto us. I think it's only a matter of time before he finds out about the Supers."

The room was quiet while he told them about their trip back to the Tangle Creek Bridge. As he talked, he knew they were all thinking the same thing, because they all shared the same fear—if their secret got out, there was no telling what might happen. Men in black cars coming to take them away, scientists who would want to study them like lab rats. Daniel had to be careful not to create a panic. He knew he needed to be a bit dramatic, if for no other reason than to get them to be serious for ten seconds, but he also didn't want this to get out of hand. Theo was a Plunkett, but he wasn't the Shroud.

Luckily, Rohan followed up with a logical question. "You said he's asking questions about the accident, but do you think he has any more info?"

Daniel shook his head. "Not yet. All he knows is something strange happened. He knows his car should've plummeted into the creek, not floated gently down."

"Well, duh," said Mollie.

"I'd hoped the shock would've confused things," said Rohan. "It was only a few seconds before he fell."

There was an awkward pause as everyone processed the unspoken part of what Rohan was saying—that Theo fell because Eric dropped him.

"Anyway," said Daniel, moving on, "Theo knows something's up, and he wants to talk to us. Specifically, he wants to talk to Eric and Rohan. He's invited us over to his place for . . . pizza."

"Doesn't exactly sound like the plan of a criminal mastermind," said Rohan. "A pizza party?"

"I think he's dangerous; I didn't say he was evil," said Daniel. "He's stumbled onto a mystery, and I think he's determined to solve it."

"Just like you were," said Rohan, smiling.

"Yeah," answered Daniel. "And you all took a big chance by telling me the truth."

"So, what do you think we should do?" asked Rohan. "You know him better than any of us—do you think we should tell him?"

"He did save Eric's life," said Louisa. "I mean, with Daniel's help he did. I can't imagine Herman Plunkett doing something like that."

Mollie threw up her hands. "I can't even believe we're talking about this! No, we are *not* going to tell him anything! Daniel was different. We can't compare the two of them."

"Well, Daniel is special, that's true," said Louisa.

"I was going to say that Daniel is *totally* unthreatening. He was a skinny new kid who was getting picked on by Clay and Bud. He needed our help."

"Gee, thanks, Mollie," said Daniel.

"You know what I mean," said Mollie. "Theo Plunkett has powers we don't have."

"Like what exactly?" asked Rohan.

"He's rich," answered Daniel, before Mollie could say it. "Mollie's right. I hate to say it, but she's right. I was just a kid, but I still could've caused trouble. But Theo's family . . . if they found out about you guys, who knows what could happen?"

"Are you worried about black helicopters, stuff like that?" asked Rohan.

"I'm trying not to sound that paranoid, Rohan. But though I don't want to judge Theo by his family, we can't ignore it either."

"So what do you suggest we do?" asked Eric.

Daniel scratched his head. Once again here he was acting like the leader of this bunch. And once again he was feeling not quite up to the task, but he hoped it didn't show. They were looking to him for ideas. "I think we should take him up on his offer. We share a pizza, we hang out, and we convince him that you all are as ordinary as can be. We bore him to death so that he stops snooping around."

"That won't be hard for Rohan," said Mollie.

"Quiet, you," said Rohan. "But what if that doesn't work, Daniel? What if he's as persistent as you were?"

Daniel shrugged. "He can't do anything on a hunch. He'd need proof."

"Which is all the more reason to go over there," added Mollie. "If Herman left anything incriminating lying around in that big old house of his, this could be our best chance to get it."

"Right," said Daniel. "Herman had a hidden safe in his study—he showed it to me once. I don't know the combination, but if someone had the power to get inside that safe without having to open it . . . What do you think, Louisa? You can make yourself intangible, but if there is anything in the safe, you could phase that out too, right?"

All eyes turned to her. Of all of them, she was the last person to volunteer for a bit of espionage, but she was also the only one with the power to get into that safe, unnoticed.

"Yeah, my powers work on touch," she said. "I guess so."

"Great!" said Daniel. "So Rohan, Eric, and I will say yes to the pizza party, and we'll bring Louisa along too."

"I wanna go!" whined Rose.

"Sorry, Rose. This is a big-kid thing."

"It's always a big-kid thing," said Rose, folding her arms in front of her chest. She'd pout for a while, but she'd get over it.

"Louisa and I will need to slip away, so we can find the safe while Eric and Rohan convince Theo that we're a bunch of perfectly normal kids."

"What's that?" asked Rohan. "Sorry, I got distracted by a colony of black ants under the fort. Sounds like the queen is getting ready to lay more eggs!"

Mollie slapped her forehead. "We are doomed."

"It'll be fine," said Eric. "I promise."

Daniel nodded and let out a breath that he'd been holding for the last ten minutes. They had a plan now, at least.

It was decided that they should take Theo up on his offer sooner rather than later, and Louisa, Daniel, Rohan, and Eric agreed to try to meet there tomorrow. High-stakes espionage was a lot tougher when you needed your parents' permission.

Once the meeting was adjourned, the Supers drifted away in groups. Eric followed Daniel, but he didn't say anything about the powers, as Mollie always seemed to be within earshot. It would have to wait until another time.

The plan was set. The game was afoot.

Chapter Nine
Safety in Numbers

It wasn't so much the lying to Theo that made Daniel uneasy (he'd actually gotten quite good at that part); it was the feeling that they might be walking into the lion's den. True, it was his own plan, but each time he'd dealt with Theo, or Herman for that matter, he'd been alone. There was something comforting in having friends around him, but it also meant that there were that many more people he had to watch out for. Whenever he'd visited old Herman at his home, it had played out like a cleverly calculated chess match: Plunkett had used that very analogy to describe their competitive relationship. And after the bridge, Daniel felt pretty sure Theo had inherited more than a little of his granduncle's wiles. Theo would be watching Daniel and his friends for the slightest mistake, and Daniel would be watching too.

Not surprisingly, when Daniel called Theo to invite himself and his friends over, Theo had been all niceness. Theo's parents were leaving that morning on business, and the grounds staff had the day off, so other than his granddad, they'd have the place to themselves. Daniel remembered how alone Herman had been in that cavernous old house. All he'd had was a nurse and a few gardeners for occasional company. Herman and Oliver Plunkett had chosen very different lives, each scorning the other's. It seemed to Daniel that Oliver had gotten the better deal. He at least had a family, something other than money to leave behind. He at least had people around him.

Daniel, Eric, Rohan, and Louisa agreed to meet outside the Plunketts' house the next day. Daniel spent another night haunted by nightmares, and he woke up just in time to wolf down a quick breakfast before Mollie Lee appeared on his front porch. He was already in a testy mood. Perhaps it was only nerves about the mission, but it might also have been something else: Though he hadn't wanted to admit it to himself, each morning he woke up hoping to be . . . Super. But he wasn't. Each day began and ended with him staying the same. Ordinary. It was looking more and more like that one incident was nothing more than a fluke. So when he saw Mollie Lee scowling at him from the other side of the screen door, he really wasn't in the mood.

"What?" he asked. He didn't even bother to say hello.

If Mollie was put off by this, it didn't show past her already put-off veneer.

"First, you're a jerk for putting together your plan without including me," she said.

"Huh?" Daniel blinked at her in confusion.

"Everyone is going over to Theo Plunkett's house except for me and Rose. You benched me with the six-year-old."

"But— What?"

Mollie continued talking. As usual, she seemed interested in only one side of the conversation. Hers.

"And second," she said. "I'm going with you today whether you want me to or not. You can't stop me."

Daniel rubbed his temples, trying to process exactly what it was she was going on about. Mollie was mad because she hadn't been asked along to Theo's? Because Daniel hadn't invited her to meet someone she clearly had no interest in meeting, on a mission she openly scoffed at?

"Uh, fine," he said. "You're right. So let's go."

That stopped her. Mollie had dug her heels in, ready for a fight. She wasn't used to getting her way without one, and most of the time she even seemed to enjoy it. But Daniel wasn't going to give her one today. She was right when she said he couldn't stop her from coming along if she wanted to, so why try?

"I said let's go." Daniel pushed past her. "I don't want to be late. We're not all super-speeders, you know."

For maybe the first time ever, Daniel was a step ahead of

Mollie Lee. He was already across the lawn and to the sidewalk when she finally shook the stunned look from her face and caught up.

"Well, good," she said, marching along next to him. "I'm glad that's settled."

"So am I," answered Daniel, still determined not to take the bait.

Mollie wrinkled her forehead in frustration, burying her eyebrows beneath her dark bangs. She kept up her angry pout all the way to the Plunkett house, while Daniel stayed smugly silent. Eric waved at them from the entrance to Theo Plunkett's drive. Louisa and Rohan were standing nearby.

"Rohan heard you two coming," called Eric. "He said, 'Here comes Daniel, and Mollie's with him. And she sounds angry.'"

"How could I *sound* angry?" asked Mollie. "We haven't said a word to each other the whole way!"

"You're breathing angry," said Rohan, not looking at anyone in particular but seemingly fascinated with his own shoe. "It's very distinctive."

"You're really annoying," said Mollie.

Rohan shrugged.

"Since we're all here," said Eric, "should we head on in? No sense in waiting around."

"Sure," said Daniel. "But let's just review the plan first."

"There's a plan?" asked Eric.

Daniel ignored him. "Once inside, we'll hang out for a while, until I get up to go to the bathroom. After a few minutes, Louisa, you tell Theo you have to go too. I'm sure a house that big has plenty of bathrooms."

"I'm not good at lying," said Louisa. "Just so everyone knows."

"It's a tiny lie," Daniel reassured her. "Just tell him you have to pee."

"I get all blushy," said Louisa.

"You'll do fine," said Daniel. "Just excuse yourself and instead of finding the bathroom, we'll find Herman's study. The safe is in there."

"What are you hoping to find?" asked Eric.

"I'm hoping nothing," answered Daniel. "But Herman kept tabs on everything in this town, including all of us. We've got to make sure there's nothing in there that could be dangerous for any of you."

"Just us?" asked Louisa. "Aren't you just a little bit worried about yourself?"

Daniel avoided looking at Louisa as he answered her. "I don't have powers. I'm not in any danger."

See? he wanted to say. *Lying is easy—it's the easiest thing in the world. Look how good I've gotten at it.*

He felt Eric watching him but ignored him. It was time to focus on the job at hand.

"While Louisa and I check out Herman's safe, you three need to keep Theo occupied so he doesn't get suspicious."

"Easy," said Eric. "We'll just compliment his driving."

"Be careful," said Daniel. "He's cleverer than you think." Daniel knew they shouldn't underestimate Theo Plunkett.

He'd underestimated Herman, and they'd all nearly paid for it with their lives.

"What's the signal when you're all clear?" asked Rohan. "Should we come up with a birdcall or something? How will we know you're done in the study?"

"Um, you'll know when we're done because we'll be done and we'll come back," answered Daniel.

Mollie snorted as she started making birdcalls under her breath, and now it was Rohan's turn to shoot her a look. "Of course. I just meant, you know, in case you two get into trouble."

"We'll be fine if we're careful," said Daniel. "While I don't want Theo Plunkett learning the truth about the Supers, we won't be in any real danger in there. We're not dealing with the Shroud this time."

The group went quiet at the mention of their old enemy. Even Mollie looked thoughtful. Daniel realized that they'd all been cracking jokes at each other just to keep their minds off him. Except for Daniel, none of them had ever set foot in Herman's house. Daniel had talked to Herman Plunkett face to face, and he knew him to be a deranged and dangerous old man, but still just a man. The rest of them had only ever dealt with the Shroud—the shadow in the dark, the thing that haunted their dreams, the legend. Most of them hadn't even seen his real face. No one wanted to show it, but they were scared.

"Seriously," said Daniel, giving what he hoped was a reassuring smile. "We'll be fine. I promise."

Chapter Ten
New Friends and Old Enemies

Theo was delighted to see them. He answered the door wearing his usual smile and exuding the seemingly good humor that Daniel had come to expect. What Daniel didn't expect was the way Mollie and Louisa treated Theo. From the moment he opened the door the two girls . . . changed. With Louisa it was a subtle shift—she developed this new habit of flipping her hair whenever she laughed, which was often and at every joke Theo made, at every story he told about his trip to such-and-such island or so-and-so European city. With Mollie it was a more obvious and therefore more startling transformation. Mollie didn't deck anyone, not a single punch, and she smiled. She smiled a lot and almost exclusively at Theo. This was an altogether unrecognizable Mollie Lee.

Daniel should have seen it coming. Theo was good-looking enough, but it was more than that. Theo had what Daniel termed the *Girl Wink*. Pizza was offered to everyone, but Mollie got hers along with a wink. Tour of the house? Everyone was invited, but Louisa was invited with a wink. Daniel didn't think Theo was consciously flirting—after all, the girls were each at least two years younger than he was. But for Theo it just kind of came naturally. He had two modes that Daniel had witnessed so far—snide and charming—and today he was switched to full-on charm.

Eric noticed it too, but whereas Daniel was bemused, muddled, and bewildered by it all, Eric seemed to be experiencing something else. He was quiet. He rolled his eyes at every girlish giggle. When Theo wasn't looking, he mimed that he was shoving his finger down his throat and vomiting. Eric was jealous.

As thrown as he was by this sudden upending of his once-stable, predictable circle of friends, Daniel forced himself to put who-was-flirting-with-who out of his brain and focus on their mission: to get inside Herman's hidden safe. Theo gave them a brief house tour, but touring Herman's old home was awfully depressing. Even with the windows thrown open, the house couldn't shake the feeling of claustrophobia. What little warm sunlight managed to find its way inside was gobbled up by the water-stained carpeting and peeling wood paneling. The Shroud's gloomy mansion was where cheer went to die.

As the tour passed the closed door to Herman's study, Daniel caught Louisa's attention and gave her what he thought was a conspiratorial look. She just blinked her eyes back at him shyly and smiled, causing Daniel to go an instant burnt red. Now she was back to flirting with him! Things were going terribly.

Fortunately, the billiard room was at least bearable, and once they'd settled in, Mollie's competitive instincts overrode the spell cast by Theo's looks and charm. After getting soundly thrashed three games in a row playing pool, Theo dropped the wink. Meanwhile, Rohan and Eric were having a contest to see who could hold the most pizza in his mouth.

It seemed as good a time as any to do a little spy-work.

No one seemed to even notice when he announced he was going to the bathroom, and for a moment Daniel worried that his friends had forgotten the plan. But on the way out he caught Rohan crossing his fingers for luck, which Daniel assumed was meant for him and not the pizza-eating contest. Herman's study was up the stairs from the basement game room and just down the hall, past the grandfather's room. As he tiptoed quietly past the old man's door, Daniel could hear him snoring away. He must be napping. Daniel couldn't picture the old man's evil twin, Herman, napping in the middle of the day. The Shroud had probably been too busy plotting, pulling at his webs, to ever sleep.

The study door was unlocked, so Daniel didn't wait for Louisa. Inside, it looked just as Daniel remembered. The air in there was stale and smelled of musty paper. Of all the windows in the house, these had stayed shut, the curtains drawn. Stacks of books were balanced upon more stacks of books. The well-worn reading chair sat empty against a wall covered in framed sketches, ink-and-brush illustrations of Herman Plunkett's comic-book heroes and villains. Among the drawings was a picture of a man in a black domino mask: Herman's most memorable creation, Johnny Noble. Of course, Johnny had been both Herman's real-life nemesis and his greatest work of fiction. The stone pendant that gave the Shroud his power-stealing abilities had come from the same meteor that had made Jonathan Noble into a superhuman. Although the historical Jonathan Noble had disappeared in a dreamlike blur of childhood hero-worship and town folklore, Daniel knew that the real Johnny was the one person Plunkett feared. The old man had taunted his enemy in the pages of *Fantastic Futures, Starring Johnny Noble,* replaying their rivalry in four-color, nine-panel grids. He recast their roles as those of superhero and supervillain.

The most twisted part of it all was that, in the real world, Herman truly thought himself the hero. He had deluded himself into thinking he was saving the world from a generation of reckless and dangerous super-kids. It was only in the pages of his own art that the truth came out and his villainy was exposed.

Being alone in that old study brought back too many

disturbing memories, and Daniel was glad when Louisa stuck her head in the doorway.

"Mollie's telling stories about the Old Quarry," she said.

But when she saw the alarmed look on Daniel's face, she quickly added, "Not *those* kinds of stories. Old ghost stories and stuff. I think she's just showing off for Theo."

"I guess he is sort of good-looking. Or whatever."

Louisa smiled. "He is, but it kind of wears thin after a while. To get out of there I used the bathroom excuse, but I don't think he believed me. I warned you, I just hate lying."

"Sure he believed you," answered Daniel. "He has no reason not to. After all, why would you sneak off just minutes after I left? Why would we want to be alone together . . . ?"

Louisa raised her eyebrows at him.

"Oh," said Daniel. "You think he thinks that we . . . I mean you and me . . ."

Louisa didn't say anything. He wished she would say something.

Daniel cleared his throat, but even that sounded awkward to his ears. This was not part of his plan. Detective work and ungainly romance did not work well together.

"Let's get to it, then," he said at last. "The safe, I mean! Before, ah, before anyone comes looking for you."

Daniel walked over to the cabinet on the far wall and swung it open, revealing a small mounted safe. If Daniel had been half the detective he dreamed of being, he would have memorized the combination when he'd watched

Herman open it all those months ago. But Daniel was bad at numbers.

Luckily, he had the best safecracker in the world—one who didn't even have to open the door.

"Well, there it is," he said. "What do you think?"

Louisa studied the safe's dimensions. It was maybe two feet wide. "Well, I could poke my head in there and look, but I wouldn't be able to see anything," she said. "Could be tricky, but I suppose I could just reach in and pull out whatever's in there."

Louisa could extend her intangibility power to other people or objects that she touched. It would be simple for her to reach inside, but Daniel understood her hesitation: without being able to see in first, she'd have no idea what she was actually grabbing. Daniel imagined Louisa's hand reaching toward a viper, coiled in the dark and waiting to strike.

But that, of course, was ridiculous. They had more cause to worry about tripping some kind of silent alarm. They would have a hard time explaining that to the police.

"If you don't want to try it, I'll understand," said Daniel. "We could always try to sneak in when Theo's not home and let Eric just pull the door off."

Louisa shook her head. "No. I can do this. If Eric opens that safe, it's going to be *obvious* Eric opened that safe. He's not exactly subtle."

She looked at Daniel and smiled. "I want to help you guys out. I'm part of the team, even if I sometimes don't act like it. I just don't get the same . . . thrill out of all this that you do."

"I don't get a thrill out it," Daniel answered. "But it's important."

"Of course it is. It's important and you are trying to help us all. Your heart's always in the right place. But don't fool yourself that you don't love it, Daniel. You love the mystery, the adventure. Admit it. So does Eric. The detective and the superhero; you guys are the world's finest partners."

Daniel opened his mouth to protest but stopped himself. She was right. Daniel didn't enjoy the danger his friends were in, but he craved the excitement of a new mystery to solve. He hadn't realized just how bored he had been, especially these last few months of worry-free summer. And especially now, he felt like he needed this focus, he needed something to occupy his thoughts other than the memory of flying. This, at least, kept his mind off it.

"Stand back," said Louisa, "and let me at that safe!"

Daniel positioned himself in the door to act as lookout while Louisa placed her thin brown fingers on the safe's door. There was no outward sign that she was activating her power, no flash of light or whoosh of sound. Her hand just slipped inside. As easily as one might dip their hand in a tub of water, Louisa had reached in through the solid steel door until it was nearly up to her elbow.

"Now's the tricky part," she said. "I have to let my hand go solid again so I can feel around, but still keep the rest of my arm intangible. This always freaks me out a bit, to be honest."

A gruesome thought occurred to Daniel: he wondered what would happen if she allowed her whole arm to become solid again while it was still inside the safe. Best not to think about that, he decided.

Daniel didn't think it was a good idea to talk to Louisa while she was concentrating. After a minute of silence she let out a frustrated sigh. "Hmm, there doesn't seem to be anything in there. It's empty. . . . Wait, I found something."

Louisa's arm came out of the safe holding a piece of paper. It was a single sheet, folded over once.

"Is that all?" Daniel asked, trying to keep the disappointment out of his voice. "No folders or cases or anything—"

"Daniel," Louisa said, staring at the paper, "it's for you."

"What do you mean?"

Louisa held it out, and written on the front in big cursive script was his name—Daniel Corrigan.

"Looks like someone was expecting you," said Louisa.

Daniel reached out to take the paper from Louisa and realized that his hand was shaking. He'd just seen a ghost, and now he was going to hear what that ghost had to say.

He unfolded the paper and read the note aloud.

To My Dearest Rival,
    If you are reading this, I must congratulate you. Our battle is obviously at an end, and I proved the lesser man, it

seems. While I am saddened that you have refused to join me in defending the world from the very real threat your friends pose, I am nonetheless impressed at the ingenuity that it must have taken to defeat me.

Perhaps you are reading this because you are looking for the photographic evidence that I kept on your friends. Fear not—such evidence no longer exists. I would not want it to fall into the wrong hands. I have spent a lifetime protecting the secrets of this town, and I would not want them exposed even in the event of my death.

I am this world's protector, whether you have chosen to believe it or not.

And now that I am gone, this role is left to you, as I always knew it would be. But before you can bear this burden, you must know the truth. The clues are out there for you to follow, and since you have chosen to spurn my help, you are on your own. The power of the Witch Fire Comet burns in the veins of Noble's children, and it must be kept in check lest it consume us all.

I trust you are up to the challenge.

Respectfully,
Herman Plunkett

"He's crazy," said Louisa after Daniel had finished. "Even after he's dead, he's still crazy."

Daniel nodded, but he didn't answer right away. He was too busy looking at the postscript beneath Herman's signature. At the only words he hadn't read aloud:

P.S.: Have you tried on the ring yet?

"Daniel. Daniel!" Louisa reached out and put her hand on his arm. Reflexively, he folded the paper back in half, hiding the words from her.

"Whatever it is you're thinking about—he's dead, Daniel. This was just his last, stupid attempt to get inside your head."

Daniel managed a halfhearted smile for Louisa's benefit. He did not actually feel reassured in the slightest.

"C'mon," he said. "We'd better get back. There's nothing here but trash."

"Are you okay?"

"Yeah. You're right—he's just messing with my head is all. I'm fine."

Louisa leaned forward then and surprised him with a kiss. It wasn't a long kiss, but it was more than friendly. It was soft and nice, but it was also unexpected. And it was still a kiss. Daniel's first.

When it was over, Louisa blinked at him. She had the prettiest eyes. Flecks of green within the brown.

"Are you all right?" she asked. "You look a little pale."

Daniel nodded. Words weren't working so well right now.

"Why don't you go back first, then," she said. "I'll follow in a minute or two."

He nodded again. Perhaps a bit too emphatically.

"And, Daniel? Take a few breaths before you go back down there. You're blushing like crazy."

111

The grandfather's snores sounded like a hacksaw at work, and Daniel felt suddenly silly tiptoeing down the hallway. He stopped sneaking and tried to think of what he was going to say to Eric and the others about Herman's note, but he couldn't form a plan. His thoughts were still tangled up in the kissing. Or being kissed. Louisa had kissed him, but had Daniel kissed her back? He suspected that he had. And badly, at that.

Why had she kissed him? Did she think they were more than friends? Did she want that? Did he? Suddenly Daniel was filled with an irrational terror that his friends would find out what he and Louisa had done, or more accurately that Mollie would find out. She'd never let him live it down; she'd tease him mercilessly forever, and Daniel couldn't live with that. Mollie could never know. Not Mollie. Not ever.

Daniel turned around and headed back to the study. He needed to explain to Louisa that they were just friends. That the kiss was nice and all, but that was that.

But when Daniel reached the study doorway, he saw . . . something. Louisa was lying on the floor, unmoving, and standing over her was some kind of dark shape. It lacked depth and weight—as if someone's own shadow had peeled itself off the wall and was floating in midair. But it *felt* threatening, malicious. Daniel could practically taste the spite in the air as the creature sucked the light and warmth out of the room, stretching its long fingers toward Louisa's unmoving form.

Daniel's first thought, the only one that made any sense, was that the Shroud had returned. But even as Daniel's stunned brain struggled to come to terms with what he was seeing, he recognized that this was not the same Shroud that he'd fought just months before. This thing was smaller— there was hardly any real mass to the creature at all. And gone was the burning heart of fire that had marked the Shroud's Witch Fire pendant. This thing was solid darkness. A Shade.

The creature lifted its featureless face toward Daniel as it caressed Louisa's head. She was alive but unconscious. She stirred as if she was fighting something in her sleep, as if she was in the grip of a terrible dream.

Daniel looked around for a weapon, but there was nothing in here but books. He reached for the sturdiest one he could find, thinking he could at least lob it at the creature's head, but when he grabbed for it, nothing happened. He couldn't pick up the book! Why couldn't he get a grip on it?

The Shade had abandoned Louisa and was coming for Daniel. It reached for him, its fingers looking more like claws now as they raked at his face . . . and passed harmlessly through him. It didn't miss—it just couldn't touch him. Daniel had become as intangible as a ghost. As Louisa.

Reeling back in fury, the creature came after Daniel with attack after attack, unable to connect. It might as well have been trying to strangle the very air. Then all at once the assault stopped and the Shade cocked its head, as if listening for something.

And like that, it was gone. It blew out of the room like a chill wind, moving so fast that Daniel didn't even have time to see what direction it headed in. It flew past, or through, Daniel and out the doorway in an eyeblink.

Footsteps were coming up the stairs. Someone was running.

Daniel knelt by Louisa's side. She didn't appear hurt, but she was still unconscious. Daniel reached out and watched as his hand passed right through her. He couldn't touch her. He couldn't touch anything.

"Daniel?" a voice called.

Theo was standing in the doorway, out of breath.

"She's unconscious," answered Daniel. Theo knelt down too and gave her shoulder a gentle shake. Her eyelids fluttered open, and she looked at the two of them.

"Hi," she said groggily. "What's everyone looking at?"

The rest of the kids appeared in the hall, Mollie in the front. "What's going on? You guys were gone so long, we got worried!"

With Theo's help, Louisa sat up. Daniel wanted to give her a hand, but he dared not touch her.

"I'm fine, I think," said Louisa.

"You're in my granduncle's study," said Theo, looking around. "Do you know how you got here?"

"Uh, no," she answered, glancing quickly at Daniel.

Theo looked questioningly at Daniel.

"I . . . was on my way back from the bathroom when I

passed by," said Daniel. "I saw Louisa lying there on the floor."

Theo kept his eyes on Daniel for a minute. Daniel knew that look, and he didn't like it. He felt like he was under an interrogation lamp.

"Yeah," said Theo. "I heard something in here. Decided to check it out."

"You weren't with the rest of them?" Daniel asked.

"He was supposed to be getting more soda from the kitchen," said Eric. "We told him we weren't thirsty, but he's too good a host." Daniel understood the unspoken warning beneath Eric's words: Theo had left soon after Louisa, and they hadn't been able to stop him. Eventually the rest of his friends had gotten suspicious and come looking for them.

"I guess I got turned around," said Louisa.

"Well, obviously I'm not that good a host," said Theo. "My guests getting lost, fainting. Daniel here is the real hero. He was already on the scene."

Before Daniel could react, Theo reached out and clapped him on the shoulder. It was a solid, reassuring pat that Daniel could feel.

Daniel breathed a sigh of relief.

"Little jumpy?" Theo asked.

"Just worried about Louisa," Daniel answered.

"I'm fine," Louisa said. "Really. Must've gotten light-headed or something."

They helped her to her feet and one by one filed out of

the study. Theo was the last to leave. As they exited, Daniel noticed Theo's eyes searching the room.

"Strange that she'd end up here," he was saying. "Bathroom's at the other end of the house."

"It's a big old house," said Daniel. "Easy to get lost."

"Yeah, well, we should get back. Dad says this room's off-limits. This was Herman's private space. The old guy sure was a reader."

Daniel nodded, but as he turned to go, he glanced back at the cabinet and saw the door slightly ajar, exposing the wall safe inside. They'd forgotten to close it. If Theo had seen it, then he probably knew that someone had been snooping around in there. Today's strange events would only make Theo more suspicious, not less. Daniel's hand went instinctively to the letter in his pocket.

"After you," said Theo, giving Daniel room to pass. "Heroes first."

Daniel nodded and walked past Theo Plunkett. The situation had changed, and frankly, Daniel couldn't care less about Theo's suspicions. They had bigger problems now.

The Shroud had returned.

Chapter Eleven
Aftershocks

When Daniel told the others about what he'd seen in the study, about what he'd *really* seen, the reaction was silence. He'd expected as much from Rohan, who was thoughtful about everything, but the others were quite honestly freaking him out. He'd just told them that the Shroud had returned, and they greeted the news with open stares.

After leaving the mansion, the Supers had regrouped at the tree fort. Louisa's unexplainable fainting spell gave them a good reason to end the party early and get as far away from that house as possible. Louisa honestly couldn't tell them much. After Daniel had left the study, she'd waited for a few moments; then as she'd started to leave, a black shadow had come lunging out of the hallway for her. She remembered being cold, then nothing at all.

Despite everything, first and foremost on Daniel's mind was what had happened to him during the fight. He thought he finally understood the nature of his new powers, and he didn't like it. When Clay had attacked him, when Daniel's life had been in danger, he'd gotten super-strong and had manifested the power of flight. When the Shroud had attacked, he'd gone intangible so that he couldn't be hurt. Both times he'd been in real danger. Both times he'd been in close contact with a Super. Eric's super-strength and flight. Louisa's intangibility.

Daniel was a leech. A parasite. He was the real Shroud.

"So he's back," Rohan said at last. "Somehow Herman escaped that collapse, and now he's back to hunting us."

Daniel nodded.

"Herman, or something else. It wasn't the Shroud exactly, but close enough. If it is Herman, then he's weaker than before. Smaller, more like a ghost."

"Great," said Rohan. "We're being haunted now."

Rohan was trying to make a joke, but nobody laughed. None of the others said a word. At the very least Daniel had expected Mollie to argue, to tell him he was seeing things and that he should get his eyes checked. Something. But all anyone did was stare at him. They'd gathered around in a semicircle, just like this was any old meeting of the Supers. Surrounding them, all along the walls of the tree fort, were the drawings and posters left by generations of super-kids, all of whom had lost their powers and their memories to the Shroud. Those pictures—here a faded crayon sketch of a boy flying, there a watercolor painting of a girl all in yellow, shining like the sun—they were the ghosts that haunted this place too. They joined his friends in silent acceptance that the Shroud had returned, like they'd been expecting this all along.

Then it struck him that perhaps they had. They had been expecting this. These kids had been living in fear for so long that they had never really believed it could be over. Deep down, the years of terror wouldn't let them. Of course the Shroud had returned. Far more unbelievable was the idea that he'd ever left. He was a part of their lives, and even if they wouldn't admit it, they knew he always would be.

Now all that was left was to figure out what to do next, and for that they were looking to Daniel, the new kid. They were waiting for their orders.

"So first things first," said Daniel. "We need to find out if this is Herman, and if so, what he wants."

"What do you mean?" asked Mollie. "You know who he is, and he wants what he's always wanted—our powers!"

"Yeah, after he attacked Louisa, I think it's pretty clear," said Eric.

"I don't know. What I saw in Herman's study, guys, it was different. Smaller. More like a Shade of what the Shroud used to be."

They thought about this. It was a small piece of good news that this thing wasn't as powerful.

"And why wait until we went into his house?" Daniel continued. "His method in the past was always to come after us when we were asleep, when we were vulnerable. We would've made easy targets up to now; why wait?"

"You said he looked weaker," said Rohan. "Perhaps the collapse at the Old Quarry didn't kill Herman, but it hurt him so much that he couldn't come to us. He was waiting for us to come to him. He obviously knew we'd come looking—he said as much in his letter."

Daniel had told them what they'd found in the safe, about the taunting letter, but he'd left out the part about the ring, and as of yet no one had asked to see the letter for themselves. But it was only a matter of time, and Daniel figured he'd come clean when they did. There would be time for confessions later.

"You've got a point, Rohan," said Daniel. "But I don't know how Herman could hang around that house and not have Theo discover him. Whatever that thing was, I don't think it was waiting—I think it followed us there."

"Maybe Theo's in on it," offered Eric. "Maybe he's a Shroud Junior."

"He did invite us over there," said Rohan. "This was all his idea, and he wasn't with us when the attack happened."

"Yeah," agreed Eric. "He conveniently slipped out."

"But it wasn't his idea to go snooping around the house alone," said Mollie.

Everyone in the room looked at Mollie. It was not like her to defend a Plunkett.

"What?" she said. "I'm just saying."

"And Theo was so concerned," said Louisa. "I think he really was worried about me."

"He was totally acting!" said Eric. "That kid's a super-villain in the making if there ever was one."

Daniel exchanged a look with Rohan, but his friend just shrugged. The issue of Theo's loyalty had suddenly, and perhaps predictably, divided along gender lines.

It looked like Daniel would be the deciding vote.

"I'm going to go with innocent until proven guilty on this," he said. "But I don't exactly trust him either. I think he's got some of his uncle's sneakiness, his paranoia even, but I don't think he's in league with him."

"Whatever," said Eric.

"If it was Herman, I don't get why he would wait to come after us when he did," said Daniel. "Louisa, can you remember anything about the attack? What you were doing when you were in the study alone?"

Louisa shook her head. "Nothing. I was just waiting to return to you guys, like we planned. I might've been thumbing through the bookshelf, but I wasn't really paying attention."

"You think Herman was hiding something?" asked Rohan.

"Maybe," Daniel said. "Or maybe he's just protecting his turf."

"He has other turf," said Mollie. "We can't forget about the cave."

Mollie and Daniel had first discovered Plunkett's Shroud-Cave, his true lair. But that was now buried under tons of limestone rubble. It would be hard getting any clues from there.

"I still say Theo's in on it," said Eric. "C'mon! A new Plunkett shows up in Noble's Green and it's just coincidence that the Shroud returns around the same time?"

"Didn't Theo save your life?" asked Louisa.

"Daniel saved my life," answered Eric.

"All right, that's enough!" said Daniel. He still didn't understand what it was that Eric had against Theo. Other than him being a Plunkett, that is. "I'm not ruling him out, but let's focus on one thing at a time."

"Sounds fair," said Mollie. "So what do we do next?"

"I'll . . . come up with a plan. At some point we should check out the Old Quarry again, just in case. But we need to do that together. It could be dangerous, and there's safety in numbers. In the meantime . . . just give me some time to think it all through. And be careful. Everyone."

It wasn't much of a rallying cry, but it was the best Daniel had to offer. If they were looking for inspiration, or courage, he didn't have any to give. But he was determined that the Shroud wouldn't get the drop on them again. This time Herman would be the one on the run.

As the meeting broke up, Eric took Daniel by the arm and pulled him off to the side.

"Look," he said, "I still think you're being too easy on Theo, but I just wanted to say thanks."

"For what?"

"For treating this like your problem too," said Eric. "You could have walked away from all of this, from us, long ago, but you keep sticking it out."

"Yeah, well . . ."

"And you said *we*."

Daniel looked at him. "I what?"

"In the past, whenever you've talked about the Supers, you've always referred to us as *you*. Daniel and the Supers were always two different things, and I know it's because of the powers. But today you said *we*. That's a big deal."

Powers. The one thing Daniel hadn't told them about. Everyone just assumed that the Shroud had fled when Daniel had arrived, but they didn't know about how he'd defended himself. They didn't know what he'd done.

"Look, Eric," said Daniel, "I need to tell you something. It's happened again."

Eric smiled. "The powers? That's awesome!"

"No!" said Daniel. "It's not! Listen, I—"

But Daniel didn't have a chance to finish, because someone was shouting his name. It was Mollie.

"Daniel! Eric! Come quick!"

The two of them turned. Daniel felt Eric tense up, his friend ready for action. Ready for anything.

No one could have been ready for this. Mollie and Rohan were standing with Louisa at the front door. She looked shaken, but there was no Shroud anywhere. No sign of trouble.

"What's wrong?" Daniel asked. "Louisa?"

"I . . . Sometimes I take the shortcut," she said. "I go through the wall here and it takes me outside. Then I just float down to the ground. I don't really weigh anything when I'm phasing. . . ."

"What are you talking about?" asked Eric.

Daniel watched as Louisa put her hand on the wall and pushed. And nothing happened. Nothing at all.

"She can't phase through," said Mollie. "She's powerless."

Chapter Twelve
The Long Way Home

Daniel took the long way home. He rode his bike alone along Route 20, the Old Quarry road, until he could see the lights of houses in the distance; then he turned off and walked the bike along a twisty footpath that would eventually curl its way onto Elm Lane. The Supers usually avoided this route because it passed by the outskirts of the abandoned junkyard that Clay and Bud had claimed as their territory. But tonight Daniel walked the junkyard's chain-link fence without fear. It was quiet, minus the usual sounds of senseless destruction and Clay's cursing. The two were not around, not that it mattered. What could the pair of super-bullies do to him now? He'd just steal Clay's strength, take away his toughness, and use it against him. What did Daniel have to fear from any Super? He'd just do to them what he'd done to Eric. What he'd done to Louisa.

Daniel squeezed himself through a tear in the chain-link fence and walked through the junkyard until he found the gutted old van that the two bullies used as a hideout. Badly misspelled graffiti covered every inch that wasn't already rusted out, and the floor was littered with empty potato-chip bags and cigar butts. It looked much the same as the last time Daniel had visited—it was a dank, smelly hole. There was only one new addition. In the corner was a carefully stacked pile of rocks. It looked like an amateur's collection, limestone mostly. The pieces were different shapes, and of different Shades, but not one of them was anything special. But it was clear that they'd all come from the same place.

The junkyard sat roughly halfway between the town and the tree fort. But if you dared cross it, you could find another footpath that took you farther up the mountain and curled around to the north face and the Old Quarry road. The path cut across Elm at the precise point where Daniel and Eric had discovered Clay and Bud several nights ago. If you were hauling rocks from the quarry to this junkyard, you couldn't avoid it.

Daniel wasn't sure when he'd started to cry—he wasn't even sure what he was crying about. He wasn't sure if he was feeling sad about Louisa or sorry for himself. He certainly wasn't crying over this latest discovery. He'd guessed what Clay was up to when they'd met on the road: the two bullies were looking for a way to take away Eric's powers. If Clay could, he'd take away all their powers and make himself into the one Super in existence. A super-bully in a world of victims.

Funny. Clay was digging through a mountain of dirt and rubble looking for a power Daniel already had.

Now that Daniel had begun to cry, he couldn't make himself stop. If he'd been as strong as Clay, he'd have twisted metal. He'd have punched holes in cars. He'd have smashed their useless rocks. But he couldn't do that. Such things were beyond him, such *strength* was beyond him . . . that power belonged to someone else, until he took it.

He'd taken Louisa's powers when she'd needed them the most, and he'd left her at the mercy of that Shade creature.

The mountain overhead had never seemed so ominous as it did this night. Daniel wasn't super—he was cursed.

As he left the rusted-out hulks of the junkyard behind and started along the wooded footpath away from the town, he pictured a young orphan named Herman Plunkett walking in those same woods, beneath that very same mountain, on an evening so many years ago. Had it begun like this for him? Plunkett was only a boy when he discovered the terrible power of the meteor stone, and his first victim—Daniel's own grandmother—had been an accident. Did Herman cry too when it happened that first time? Was he filled with regret and shame for what he'd done? And how long did it take before that shame softened into acceptance and, eventually, pleasure? How many children did it take?

He walked his bike along the footpath until he reached Route 20. Then he pedaled away from Noble's Green, away from the tree fort and his friends. He followed the poorly kept road, broken and gravelly in places, as it curled around the mountain's deserted north face.

Daniel hadn't been back to the Old Quarry since the collapse, since their final battle with the Shroud. The limestone quarry had been owned by the Plunkett family, but it had only ever served as cover for Herman's true purpose: the meticulous excavation of the hidden caves beneath the mountain and Plunkett's obsessive search for remnants of the Witch Fire meteorite. Daniel supposed that the quarry technically belonged to Theo's side of the family now, although if Herman was back, that wouldn't last very long. The Shroud wasn't one to share.

It looked just like Daniel remembered. The Old Quarry was a creepy place to begin with, hidden away in the constant shadow of the mountain's north face, but the once-steep walls of the deep ravine had collapsed in their fight with the Shroud, and now the dark caves were buried beneath tons of broken earth and rock. Somewhere underneath all that rubble was Herman's body, or so they'd thought. No Super was especially anxious to visit the Shroud's grave.

In his dreams, Daniel had been reliving that night over and over again. In real life the Supers had won their fight, the Shroud had been defeated. But in his dream, Daniel lost. Or if he won, he did so at a hideous cost. Awake now, and standing on the edge of the rock pile, Daniel looked down at his hand. In the dream his hand burned away, and there were times, even when he was awake, that he was startled to find it there. Snippets of the dream were slipping into his waking world, and Daniel had started to fear for his sanity. What was truer, real life or the dream? And who'd really claimed victory that night, the Supers or the Shroud?

He'd warned the others to stay away from here. He'd said that they'd explore this place together—that if the Shroud had returned, then it was too dangerous to go snooping around his old lair alone. But that had been before he'd learned what he'd done to Louisa. It was too dangerous for him to be around the others now. He had to do this by himself.

Daniel carefully scrambled his way along the rock pile. Though the walls here were not nearly as sheer as they had been before the collapse, the way down was still treacherous, and no one knew that Daniel was even up here. If he fell or twisted an ankle, help wouldn't come. Luckily the loose dirt and gravel had settled over the last few months, so his footing was sure. Nevertheless, it was late and it was getting dark, and when he finally discovered the hole it was only because he nearly walked headfirst into it.

It had looked just like another shadow beneath a large slab of limestone, until he noticed the surrounding piles of dark, freshly turned earth. Someone had been digging here, and beneath the slab was a hole just big enough for a person to climb into. Or out of. Scuff marks were everywhere on the surrounding rocks, a sign that someone had been dragging things out of there. At first Daniel thought he'd found Plunkett's escape route, but then he saw the two pairs of muddy footprints that crisscrossed everywhere. One set looked like they belonged to someone roughly the same size as Daniel, or with the same size feet anyway. The other set left a larger impression—wider, deeper. Whoever had made those had been big and heavy.

Clay and Bud. Of course they'd been here. This was where they'd been digging for all those rocks. Those useless pieces of limestone that Clay had hoped might be meteor stones. Daniel shuddered again to think what Clay would do if he got his hands on one. Clay was as spiteful as Herman, but without any of the old man's delusions of heroism. No one would be safe from him.

Another thought had occurred to Daniel as well. A chilling one. While Daniel was fairly certain that Clay and Bud had failed in their search for the meteorite, there was no telling what they might have uncovered instead. Or more accurately, *who*.

Peering over the side, Daniel saw that the hole was deep, and built up on the sides to prevent a cave-in. The weak flicker of electric light was visible some ways down and Daniel could hear a series of grunts and curses getting closer.

Daniel leaned down and took a big sniff of tunnel air, just to be sure. Sour milk. Spoiled fish wrapped in dirty socks. Bud.

His gut told him to get out of there as fast as possible. Survival in Noble's Green thus far had relied on an inarguable strategy: when Clay and Bud were coming one way, he ran the other. And so Daniel began backing away from the hole. Slowly and quietly at first, then he'd make a run for it once he got to his bike parked up on the road. Neither one of them was very fast.

But Daniel hadn't taken more than two steps backward before he stopped. He just stopped moving. Things were different now. He was different.

Daniel wasn't powerless anymore. He didn't have to *run* anymore. He placed himself in front of the hole and waited.

Bud came out first, huffing and puffing, awkwardly fumbling with a dirty rock. The poor kid could barely squeeze his big body through the mouth of that hole, much less do so while dragging a chunk of limestone. And that's all he had—limestone. It was a slightly odd color, and to someone who hadn't actually been close to a meteorite, it could be mistaken for some kind of extraterrestrial rock; but Daniel saw it for what it was. Of all the Supers, only he'd had the fortune, good or bad, to see the Witch Fire rock up close.

Bud backed right into Daniel, butt-first. He yelled out in surprise and dropped the stone. Then he shouted even louder as it rolled onto his foot.

Clay followed him out of the hole, wearing one of those helmets with a flashlight attached to the front. It was too large on the boy—he had to keep pushing it up above his eyes as he went. Daniel wondered where he'd stolen it from. Clay's mean little eyes spied Daniel right away. Which was fine. Daniel wasn't hiding this time.

"Oww!" said Bud, hopping on one foot and cursing. "Man, Daniel, that's the second time!"

"What do you want?" Clay asked.

Standing there alone with Clay and Bud, a mountain between him and the possibility of help, Daniel nearly lost his nerve. But he tried to picture how Eric would act in this situation. His friend would be calm and confident. Daniel tried to summon up that same bravado.

"I was wondering, um . . . you know . . . How you doing, by the way?"

Not a great start.

"We're doing fine, *Daniel,* how about you?" Clay answered. Whenever Clay said his name, it sounded like he was chewing the word around in his mouth before spitting it out.

At least this time Clay was keeping his distance. He wasn't getting in Daniel's face, breathing on him with that horrible tobacco breath of his (he stole his father's cigars). Clay stayed near the mouth of the hole and was content to leave Bud between them.

"What've you two been digging for?" asked Daniel. "More rocks?"

"It was his idea!" Bud suddenly burst out. "He makes me carry them and I don't wanna."

"Shut up, Bud!" said Clay. "So, New Kid's not so normal

anymore, huh? Now you got powers like the rest of us, and you think you're going to start throwing your scrawny weight around too!"

The air had taken on a more pungent tang. Bud must be getting anxious—his powers were really kicking in.

"But they're not really *your* powers, are they, Daniel? I saw you catch that tree just as your buddy Eric had himself a power blowout. Now isn't that a coincidence?"

Daniel felt his blood rising. He'd hoped to bluff his way through this, but Clay must've guessed how Daniel's powers worked. Clay was as mean as they came, but he was also clever.

Daniel took a deep breath to calm himself—and nearly gagged on the smell. His palms were sweaty, but his mouth had gone as dry as paper. He should have run when he'd had the chance, but maybe he could still defuse the situation by taking a different approach.

"Clay, I have to tell you something," he said. The air around him was thickening into a foul-smelling fog. Why couldn't Bud just turn it off?

"The Shroud's back," Daniel said. "Or something like it. I need to know what you two have been doing up here. What you've seen. Because we're all in danger."

Clay didn't say anything right away. He seemed to be sizing Daniel up, measuring whether he was telling the truth. But it was getting increasingly hard to see. And even though Daniel was trying to breathe into the crook of his arm, he was getting nauseous from the smell of Bud's stink.

"Bull!" Clay said finally. "How could that old Plunkett guy survive that cave-in . . . ? Man, Bud! Knock it off, will you?"

But Bud was shaking his head. "I'm not . . . Clay, I'm not doing it! I'm not doing anything!"

"What do you mean?" asked Clay. "Then where'd all this stink come from . . . ?"

Clay's words drifted away as his eyes settled on Daniel. By then Daniel could barely even see his own feet. The noxious fog was thickest near him, and the smell seemed to be everywhere—cloying, clinging to him like it was sweating out of his very pores.

His pores. Daniel had stolen Bud's super-stink.

Daniel had hoped to take Clay's strength if things got too heated. He hadn't even thought about Bud. And now he was a walking stink cloud.

Bud had his hands on his knees and was getting sick all over the ground. Apparently it smelled worse when it wasn't your own. Clay had pulled his shirt up over his nose and mouth.

"You weren't happy with stealing Eric's powers, so you came up here after ours?" said Clay as he grabbed a basketball-sized hunk of limestone from the pile. More than enough to pop Daniel's head open like a melon.

"I won't let you do it!" Clay shouted, and Daniel barely had time to duck before the limestone rock exploded over his head.

He didn't know what he was doing or how he was making

it happen, but the fog got even thicker. Of this, at least, Daniel was glad. Clay couldn't smash Daniel to a pulp if he couldn't see him.

The problem was Daniel couldn't see now either. A foul yellow cloud loomed around him, and no matter where he went, Daniel was stuck at the center of it. He could hear Clay raging, smashing rocks and throwing whatever he could get his hands on, blindly, at Daniel. Or maybe he was just throwing the world's biggest superpowered tantrum. Either way, it would soon turn deadly if Daniel didn't get out of there.

He managed to feel his way out of the quarry and into the line of trees. Though he still couldn't see, he knew he'd made it that far because he smacked his face on the trunk of a giant pine. The fact that he'd gotten out of the rocks without breaking his head open, and that the trees would provide decent cover from the shrapnel of Clay's tantrum, allowed Daniel a moment to try and calm himself.

As his own heartbeat returned to normal, the stink cloud faded a bit. Had he really created all this smog? Fortunately, the strong mountain winds were already beginning to clear the air, and he could finally see more than five feet in front of him. Daniel wasn't sure how far he'd gotten, but he knew he wanted to get farther. If he made it to the road, he could find his bike and be gone.

A fresh gust of wind stirred up the air, and for just a moment Daniel could see the Old Quarry road clearly through a break in the fog. A boy was standing there, watching him.

Daniel saw him for only a few seconds before the wind died down and the blinding wall of fog returned.

He could hear footsteps as someone ran along the gravel, then a few minutes later the sound of a car pulling away. Daniel kept moving until he felt the crunch of gravel beneath his feet. By that time, the fog had dissipated until it was little more than a few wisps in the copse of trees. His bike was there, leaning against a tree, untouched. Daniel could actually detect a hint of the air's normal pine smell out here away from the quarry.

The boy was gone. Daniel had caught just a glimpse of him, just a few seconds. But it was long enough to recognize that cat-eyed stare. There was no question as to who it was.

The only question now was how long had Theo Plunkett been watching? How much had he seen?

Chapter Thirteen
Stalled

The super-stink wore off before he got home, but Daniel's problems were here to stay. The next day he phoned Theo, but no one picked up. He visited the house, but his knocks went unanswered and the windows were all shut with the curtains drawn. The new school year started, and when Clay and Bud bothered to show up at class at all, they stayed far away from Daniel. Now they were the ones who turned and walked the other way when they saw him coming down the hall. That, at least, was a relief.

But while Clay and Bud seemed to be out of the picture for the time being, a new problem had emerged—Louisa's powers still hadn't come back. When Eric had lost his flight and strength, they'd returned within a day. But Louisa had been powerless for weeks now. Whether her condition had something to do with the Shade creature that had attacked her, or whether this was something Daniel had done, he couldn't be sure. But he was sure of one thing—it wouldn't happen again. He wanted nothing to do with his new abilities, and so he went to great lengths not to find himself in a situation where he might accidentally steal from his friends. That meant he cut out after-school visits to the tree fort, and he kept to himself on the weekends. He didn't want to so much as play catch with the Supers, just in case his new power suddenly decided it needed someone's super-strength just to throw a ball.

Of all of them, only Eric knew about Daniel's new powers, and he had his own problems to deal with. His home life was getting worse. Eric's mother and her boyfriend, Bob, were fighting again, and Bob took it out on Eric when she wasn't around. Although Eric couldn't prove it, he suspected that Bob had sold his bike for beer money. But rather than escape when the arguments started, Eric toughed it out. He was afraid of what Bob might do to his mom if their fighting ever got out of hand, and so he stayed. His mom had her own personal superhero watching over her and didn't even know it.

It was a reminder that the Shroud wasn't the only monster in Noble's Green.

Meanwhile, Daniel's investigation had stalled. The days

dragged on and he just couldn't focus, he couldn't see how the clues fit together. In fact, he couldn't see the clues at all, if there were any. It was hard to chase a villain when you were afraid of becoming a villain yourself. His long days were full of worry, and his restless nights were filled with nightmares. The Shroud dreams got worse, more frequent. Most nights he woke up in a cold sweat, unable to get back to sleep. His parents grew worried at the ever-present bags under his eyes and tried to take him to see a doctor, but a doctor was the last thing Daniel wanted.

One day after school, as Daniel was drifting off with an unread book in his lap, Rohan popped his head into Daniel's attic room. Daniel had taken to stealing his parents' leftover coffee from the morning's carafe, but even with that he must've been too tired to hear the front doorbell, if it had rung at all. Rohan had no qualms about letting himself in.

"Reading anything good?" asked Rohan, squinting at the book in Daniel's hands.

"Not really. It's Conan Doyle, but I like his Holmes stuff better. This one's got dinosaurs living on some forgotten land. Not very believable."

"This from the kid who hangs around with super-tweens," said Rohan.

"All right, you've got a point."

"You don't look good," said Rohan.

"Well, thanks. You look swell yourself."

"Just saying. You should try to get more sleep. You look . . . puffy."

Daniel grunted. Being this exhausted didn't make it any easier to put up with Rohan's characteristic lack of tact.

Rohan took the book from Daniel and looked at the cover. A T. rex chasing a bunch of old men.

"Hmm, *The Lost World*. Ever read *Journey to the Center of the Earth*? In that one the dinosaurs live in the earth's core. Talk about unbelievable."

He handed the book back to Daniel. "It's got a good ending, though. Maybe you should give this one more of a try."

Daniel set the book down on his desk next to his souvenir Holmes pipe and tried to rub the sleep from his eyes.

"So, what's up?" Daniel asked with a yawn.

"A few of us are going over to the tree fort. Since you're reading about jungle dinosaurs instead of doing your homework, I thought you might want to come along."

A trip to the tree fort actually sounded great. Daniel was tired of being indoors. October had arrived and it brought with it a cold snap, but Daniel still longed for some fresh air. He just didn't trust himself around his friends.

"You know, I think I might go ahead and give this book another try," he said. "You guys have fun without me."

"Uh-huh," said Rohan. "I thought you'd say something like that."

"What? What do you mean?" But Daniel knew exactly what he meant. He'd seen this conversation coming.

"I mean that lately you always come up with an excuse not to hang out with us," said Rohan. "You're perfectly fine at school, but you're missing in action the rest of the time. Can't even interest you in a game of basketball."

"You're terrible at basketball."

"Right—I'm the only one you can actually beat, and I can't even get you to do that. It's your only chance to play jock."

Despite Rohan's playful teasing, Daniel felt himself squirm under his friend's stare. Because of Rohan's sensory powers, the boy was often distracted, focused on things only he could see. But when a problem caught his attention, he was relentless. He never gave up and he focused all his considerable powers on solving it. This was a quality that Daniel admired, and it had made the two of them good friends.

It also meant that he was nearly impossible to lie to. Daniel had to be very careful now. Rohan could be listening to Daniel's heartbeat, trying to detect a nervous pulse that might indicate that Daniel wasn't telling the truth. Or he might spy the tiny beads of sweat appearing on Daniel's upper lip. Or then again Rohan might be listening to a family of field mice burrowing a new tunnel beneath the house. With Rohan you never could tell.

"Look," began Daniel, careful to keep his composure. Nice, easy breaths. "The truth is that I've just been a little down. You know, with what happened to Louisa. And the Shroud back in town."

Good. So far, nothing Daniel had said had been a lie. He was just selectively editing the truth.

"Yeah," answered Rohan. "Everyone's freaked out. But we're helping each other through it. Safety in numbers."

Rohan walked over to the bookshelf and looked at the rows of hardback books there. Daniel's mom believed in what she called "substantial books." Paperbacks were rare in the Corrigan house.

"You know," said Rohan, absently fingering a faded copy of *Dr. Jekyll and Mr. Hyde,* "Louisa's taking it kind of personally. She thinks you're avoiding her in particular. I think you hurt her feelings."

"What? Why would I . . . ?" Daniel didn't finish. In truth he did feel guilty about Louisa, and he was avoiding her. But then, he was avoiding them all.

"Daniel, I'm not saying that she's right, but you know she's always had a little thing for you."

"That's not true."

"Come off it—it's obvious. And it's not like you need to be her boyfriend or anything, but you could make an effort to . . . I don't know . . . be nice. She's going through a hard time, and I just thought you might be able to help her with it."

"You mean because I'm the only one of you who knows what it's like to be powerless?"

Rohan shrugged, but he didn't try to deny it.

Louisa had been confusing to start with, even before she'd lost her powers. Daniel didn't really know how he felt about her. At least he didn't have to worry about Rohan catching him lying—he was so flustered and ashamed that Rohan was probably experiencing sensory overload.

"Look, Rohan, I'm not avoiding anyone, especially not Louisa. . . . I'm just . . ."

"A stupid boy?" said a new voice. Mollie Lee.

She was hovering just outside his window, her arms crossed disapprovingly across her chest. Daniel knew that look. He knew it well.

"What are you doing?" said Daniel. "Someone will see you flying outside my window!"

"Relax, will you?" said Mollie as she drifted inside. "I made sure the coast was clear."

Rohan shook his head. "You said you'd be coming by to back me up; you didn't mention you'd be levitating."

"I don't see the big deal," she said.

"You're too careless," said Rohan. "You and Eric both. People have eyes, you know."

"And you're an old woman," said Mollie.

"All right, cut it out, both of you," said Daniel. "And what's all this about Mollie being your *backup*? Is this some kind of intervention?"

"He thought you might need some convincing, so I told him I'd come over and reason with you."

"She promised to beat you up if you didn't come out with us," said Rohan.

"I offered," said Mollie. "I didn't promise."

If Daniel let them, Rohan and Mollie would go on and on like this. Their banter was like a Ping-Pong game—that is, until Mollie tired of the back-and-forth and decided to start swinging.

"Fine," said Daniel. "So you two came here together to force me to get out and have some fun. On threat of pain."

"Seriously, what's up with you?" asked Mollie. "Rohan thinks you're just scared of the Shroud."

"Mol!" said Rohan.

"Well, you do!"

They thought he was hiding from the Shroud. Louisa thought he was somehow repulsed by her, and these two thought he was hiding from the bogeyman like some scared little baby.

For a moment, just a moment, he considered telling both of them the truth. They were two of his best friends, and they would normally support him through anything. But things were different. The Shroud had returned, and how would they look at him now, knowing that he was practically a Shroud himself? That was the ugly truth of it all: if the Shroud didn't get them, Daniel would.

He had to find a way to stop it, but he had to do it on his own. He wouldn't put his friends in any more danger than they were already in.

"I'm just as scared of the Shroud as anybody else," said Daniel. "But I'm not hiding from him. Honestly, guys. I know that Louisa thinks I'm avoiding her and you both think that I'm a coward . . ."

"We don't think that," said Rohan.

"But I'm not avoiding anyone. I'm just . . . I don't feel like going out to the fort today. Seriously. I'll be up for it this weekend."

"Are you sure?" asked Mollie. "You sure you're all right?"

"I'm positive," said Daniel. "No worries."

Daniel didn't look at Rohan, because that last part was a lie, a big fat one. He hoped it went unnoticed.

The three of them said their goodbyes, with Mollie disappearing out the window. It was like she'd forgotten what front doors were for.

Once he was alone, Daniel put his copy of *The Lost World* back on his bookshelf. And for a moment he let his hand linger near the top, only inches away from the black ring's hiding place. Just the tips of his fingers brushed the spine of the ring's hollowed-out book. Just the tips and only for a second, but it was enough for the dream to come crashing back to him. His hand burning away. The Shroud's voice calling his name.

His friends were worried about him. The Shroud had everyone in a state of panic, and Daniel was hurting and confusing them even more. Eric and the other Supers, Daniel, and Theo—even Clay and Bud—they were all living in fear.

The Shroud was out there and Daniel was going to find him.

But first he owed someone an apology.

Chapter Fourteen
Louisa

Louisa and Rose lived in a little white house that looked less like a real house than like someone's picture-perfect dream of what a house should be. The yard was so deeply green as to look unnatural—Astroturf green. The house was ringed on all sides by a flower bed of rich, black soil and a bright painter's palette of flowers. Everything about it was immaculately cared for and lovely, just like the sisters themselves. The only hints of chaos visible were the pair of bikes carelessly leaned against the garage and a lone soccer ball forgotten in the garden—a little reassurance that there were children around to upset the perfectly dull order.

Daniel always grew self-conscious when he came near that house. His day-to-day appearance was anything but lovely. He had a cowlick on the back of his head that had proven comb-proof for as long as he'd had hair. His new pair of sneakers just didn't feel as good as the ones he was wearing now, the well-ventilated pair with the hole near the left big toe. All the things that made Daniel Daniel also made him stick out like a sore thumb next to that house.

He paused at the front door to check his shoes for mud and tried to smooth down his cowlick by licking his palm and patting it down, but he merely succeeded in making the rest of his hair flat. The cowlick only looked worse. At least he had on a mostly clean shirt.

The girls' mother answered the door, with Rose popping up behind her wearing a wide, toothy grin. Because she was only in the first grade, Daniel hadn't seen Louisa's little sister in weeks, not since he'd started avoiding the tree fort. When she saw him, she squealed and did a little dance. Rose was nothing if not enthusiastic.

"Daniel! Daniel! Daniel!" she shouted as she spun in a little pirouette.

"Hi, Rose," said Daniel. "Hi, Mrs. Rodriguez. Is Louisa home?"

Louisa's mother smiled politely at Daniel the way she might smile at a mangy puppy her daughters had brought home. It was cute to look at, maybe deserving of a scratch behind the ears, but she didn't want it on the carpet.

Daniel self-consciously patted at his cowlick again.

"It's nice to see you, Daniel," answered Mrs. Rodriguez. "Louisa's in her room. I'll go get her."

Louisa's mother left Rose with him at the door. At least someone was glad to see him.

"So, long time, Rose, huh?"

"For-eeeever! Where have you been?"

"Oh, I've been busy," Daniel said. "Just real busy."

"Oh! Have you been looking for . . . *him*?" she asked in a loud, conspiratorial whisper, followed with a wink. The Shroud was serious—she understood the threat—but like everything in life, he was also a bit of a game to Rose.

"I'm working on it, Rose," said Daniel. "I'm working on it."

"I know you'll do it. I told everyone! I said Daniel got rid of him the last time and Daniel will do it again. I told them so."

Daniel smiled but said nothing. Poor Rose. She was waiting for him to make the bad guy go away. Like waiting for her father to check for monsters under the bed. If only it was that simple.

"Are you just here to see Louisa?" Rose asked.

"Well, I came to see you both."

"Are you going to make me go and play by myself? Because Louisa always makes me go and play by myself when boys are around."

Daniel remembered the kiss, that little kiss that Louisa had given him in Herman Plunkett's study just before the attack. He was suddenly very keen to have Rose with them at all times. His purpose here today had nothing to do with kisses.

"Of course you can stay," said Daniel, grateful for her presence.

Louisa was also happy to see Daniel, and she greeted him with a smile and an awkward hug. But the tension between them was very real. There was nothing flirtatious about her now—she was all self-consciousness, embarrassment even. Daniel tried to break the tension with a few corny jokes that earned big laughs from Rose, but Louisa was a tougher audience.

The three of them ended up in the girls' backyard, where Daniel and Louisa twirled around on a pair of swings while Rose showed off by doing cartwheels and handstands.

"So how are you doing?" Daniel asked. "Without . . . without the powers?"

Louisa shrugged as she chewed on a piece of her hair. That was a new habit.

"I try not to think about it too much," she said. "But it's hard with Rose. She's so sure that I'll get better."

"You will get better, Louisa!" shouted Rose as she twirled into a hand plant. "Look at me! Look at me!"

"Maybe she's right," said Louisa, clapping for her sister's acrobatics. "But if I don't get better . . . you know, well, I'm okay with it. I really am. I don't feel like a freak or anything."

"I understand," said Daniel.

Louisa looked at Daniel, realizing what she'd just said.

"Oh! Daniel, I didn't mean that you . . . I mean you've always been that way, so it's totally different."

"It's all right, Louisa. I know what you meant."

"Geez, I'm not making things any better, Daniel."

"What? Look, I'm the one who should be apologizing. I haven't been around much outside of school, and I know how you need your friends right now. All of them."

Louisa continued to chew on her hair, gently kicking back and forth on the swing. Daniel could tell that he'd been right—she'd needed him and he hadn't been there.

"I came by today to tell you that I am your friend, Louisa."

"Hey, guys!" called Rose. "Left-handed cartwheels! Left-handed cartwheels are real hard!"

Louisa and Daniel clapped again for Rose, if somewhat less enthusiastically than before.

"Thanks, Daniel," Louisa said.

"And I came by to tell you that I am going to fix this as best I can. I'll get the Shroud."

Louisa stopped swinging. "I was afraid you were going to say something like that."

"But isn't that what you want? Look, we stopped him once before, and we can do it again!"

"Then what?" asked Louisa.

"Yeah, then what?" echoed Rose, but she looked just as confused as Daniel when she asked it.

"What do you mean?"

"I mean," said Louisa, looking Daniel straight in the eyes

150

for the first time, "say you find the Shroud. Say you find it's Herman, who's really still alive, or it's Theo following in his granduncle's footsteps. Or somebody else entirely—then what are you going to do?"

"Well," said Daniel, "I'll figure that out when the time comes, I guess. . . ."

"No, you won't," said Louisa. "You and Eric, Rohan, even Mollie, you all think you are this bunch of . . . superheroes! Like you can have some big fistfight at the end of all this and haul the bad guy away. But what are you going to do, really? Are you going to hit Herman Plunkett until he promises to stop being the Shroud?"

"Well, no. . . ."

"So are you going to turn whoever it is over to the police?"

"They'd never believe us," said Daniel. "And if they did, we'd be in danger of our secret getting out."

Louisa put her hand on Daniel's arm. "Are you going to kill him?"

"Of course not, Louisa!"

"Good. But then what *are* you going to do?"

Daniel opened his mouth to protest, but she was right. They had no plan to make Plunkett stop hurting them, not really. They were a bunch of kids. Even Eric, with everything he could do, was powerless to stop the Shroud.

"I've been thinking about this a lot, Daniel. Ever since what happened to me . . . happened. We got lucky last time with the Shroud. When he came after you and Eric, we didn't have time to think. We just knew we needed to get you both back. That was a rescue mission. But now the idea of *hunting* him down . . . We're in over our heads, Daniel. We always have been."

Poor Rose's face was scrunched up in concentration. She'd lost the thread of the conversation long ago. But Daniel hadn't. Louisa was right: as long as the Supers needed to stay a secret, the Shroud had them. They couldn't expose him without putting themselves in danger. So how would it ever end?

"Daniel," Rose said, "are you going to fix my sister or not?"

Louisa smiled and patted Rose on the arm. "I'm not his responsibility, Rose. This isn't Daniel's fault, and it's not Daniel's job to fix it. Even if he thinks it is."

Rose pulled her arm away from Louisa's touch. "But you have to get better! We all have to be okay."

"We will be, Rose," said Louisa.

"I don't want him to get me!" Rose shouted, tears suddenly welling up in her eyes. "Daniel, I don't want the Shroud to get me too!"

And then she was gone. Rose disappeared and they could hear the sounds of her crying fade into the distance.

"I'd better go and calm her down," said Louisa. "Whatever you decide to do, just be careful, Daniel. I have a feeling things are about to get worse. Much, much worse."

Chapter Fifteen
Halloween

It was Eric's decision to declare mandatory trick-or-treating. There had been far too much moping and feeling sorry for themselves for his taste, especially by Eric himself, and therefore the Supers would go trick-or-treating together this Halloween, en masse. Shroud or no Shroud. No excuses. No passes.

As the weeks went by and Halloween approached, the trees around Mount Noble turned deep orange, like a swath of rust spreading across the mountainside. Mollie said they were getting too old for trick-or-treating, but Eric had his mind set on it. Most of the Supers had picked out their costumes already—Rohan would be a bug-eyed alien (which left him open to any number of Mollie's jokes) and Eric would be, unsurprisingly, a superhero.

Daniel was torn. There was still no sign of Theo. He didn't go to their school but instead attended a private academy over an hour away. The best Daniel could get out of Theo's mom was that her husband and son were involved in some kind of business project together that was eating up all their time. Whether that was the truth or a convenient way for Theo to keep avoiding Daniel, it didn't really matter.

After the disaster with Clay and Bud, Daniel dared not go back to the Old Quarry alone, but he didn't want to put his friends in any more danger by asking them to accompany him. He was stuck. The trail had grown cold and he'd run out of clues.

As for spending Halloween with the Supers, he'd been put on Georgie duty for the evening, and his parents expected him to take the three-year-old out trick-or-treating anyway, but Daniel wasn't sure if he was comfortable around all his friends at the same time. It would be the largest gathering of Supers since Louisa's attack, and that made Daniel nervous. But in the end Eric was just too stubbornly persuasive, and the idea of spending the evening alone with Georgie (who was going dressed as a pink bunny, by the way) was too much for Daniel.

So he set about getting materials for his costume, and for the first time in months he stopped worrying every minute of the day about Shrouds and powers and nightmares and focused on something fun. He scoured the town for the perfect touches—the green deerstalker cap from the local thrift store, the garage-sale brown overcoat—and, of course, there was the long bowl-shaped pipe Daniel already had. For a couple of weeks he was able to be a kid again.

All he was missing was Sherlock's trademark nose. Holmes's nose was thin and hawklike, while Daniel's was short and sort of button-shaped. But there was no changing that, and he thought he otherwise made a pretty impressive master detective, if a bit young for the role. He even worked up a few catchphrases in his best British accent. He'd tried to convince his mom to dress up Georgie as Watson—just stick a fake mustache on him and call it done—but she refused to glue facial hair of any kind on her younger child. Daniel would have to settle for "Elementary, my dear pink bunny!"

When Halloween finally arrived, they assembled outside Daniel's house, all the Supers together at last: Rohan in his alien costume, which made him look more like a grasshopper than an extraterrestrial; Rose as a cowgirl; Louisa as some pop star Daniel had never heard of; and Mollie as Mollie. She had agreed to come along but announced that she was done with dressing up. Rohan commented that if she tried being in a good mood for once, she wouldn't need a costume—she'd be totally unrecognizable.

Eric was the last to arrive. He was wearing a red shirt and black domino mask and black pants. He had the letters *KN* stitched across the front of the shirt. He looked pretty superhero-ish except for the dirty white sneakers.

"Which superhero are you supposed to be?" asked Daniel.

"Kid Noble," answered Eric.

"Kid Noble?" said Rohan. "He related to Johnny? I don't remember him from the comics."

"That's because he wasn't in them," said Eric. "Johnny Noble was a letdown. I'm going to show him how it's really done."

Daniel gave his friend a pat on the back. After they'd learned the truth about Plunkett's Rules, Eric had lost faith in the idea of Johnny Noble—the comic-book hero he had practically worshipped since the day he'd discovered his powers. He said that if Johnny was real, then he was to blame for letting the Shroud prey on them for all those years. Daniel was glad to see that giving up on Johnny didn't mean that Eric was giving up on being a hero himself.

"Nice shoes," said Daniel, pointing to Eric's out-of-place sneakers.

"Can't fight crime in loafers," Eric answered. "And what are you supposed to be, anyway? Middle-aged Man?"

"Smoking's bad for you!" said Rose, pointing at Daniel's pipe.

"So are guns," answered Mollie, looking at the bright-orange squirt guns holstered at Rose's side.

"These only squirt water!" Rose said.

"It's okay, Rose," said Louisa. "Mollie's only teasing. And Daniel's not smoking his pipe. It's just part of his costume."

She smiled at Daniel. "I think he looks great. He makes a very handsome Sherlock Holmes."

"Oh, brother," said Mollie, and Eric snorted. Daniel really wished Louisa wouldn't say those things out loud.

"Tricks or treats!" shouted Georgie, waving his empty candy bag around. "I want candy!"

"Well said, Georgie," said Rohan. "Since we're all here, we should get a move on. We'll start on Elm Lane, and then we'll hit the houses on Maple. I'm anticipating quite a haul this year, so we'll need to do this in phases. Collect, then return to drop off. Then collect again."

"We should go to Cedar!" said Rose. "There are big houses there!"

"Those big houses are always stingy with their candy, Rose," said Daniel quickly. Cedar Lane was the Plunketts' street, and they wanted to stay as far away as possible.

"Good point, Daniel," said Rohan. "We'll steer clear of Cedar and surrounding streets."

Daniel nodded appreciatively at Rohan. Better safe than sorry.

"Also, um," continued Rohan, "let's all remember that there's no rush. There's plenty of time to hit plenty of houses, so there's no need to, ah, exert ourselves."

At first Daniel didn't understand this last bit, but then it dawned on him. Rohan was talking about powers. With Georgie along, they needed to be careful not to take any superpowered shortcuts. Daniel's little brother was only three, but he was old enough to know that kids couldn't fly. Or at least he knew enough to know they *shouldn't* be able to.

As the streetlights blinked on, Noble's Green began to swarm with all manner of costumed beings. Werewolves, vampires, and axe-wielding maniacs walked side by side with princesses and fairies. Mollie might not be wearing a costume, but that didn't stop her from going up to each and every door with her bag open. While Daniel believed that trick-or-treating without a costume was a hanging offense, most of the people handing out candy didn't seem to mind. The few who did question her laughed when she told them she was dressed up as herself. Then those same people scolded Daniel for carrying around a pipe. Life wasn't fair.

Georgie, being a three-year-old pink bunny, made out like a bandit. Pretty soon Daniel was carrying Georgie's bag for him in addition to his own. By the weight alone, Daniel estimated that his brother had at least twice his haul. He'd have to even out their candy a bit before they got home.

As the night wore on, the Supers began to drift apart, splitting into twos or threes to cover more ground. And eventually it became a kind of race to see who could get the most. Since Daniel was still responsible for Georgie, he found himself lagging behind the others, but since Georgie the bunny was a candy-attracting machine, they were still in the lead loot-wise. Eric and Mollie were hitting the most houses, but Daniel suspected they were using their powers to cheat when no one else was around, so that didn't count in his book.

Eric had just shown up to check in with Daniel when the first shadow appeared.

They'd come to a lonely stretch of street on the outskirts of Briarwood, where Eric lived. This was the border between the two major neighborhoods, so the houses here were more spread out, and that meant traffic was sparse. Daniel and Georgie plopped down on an empty patch of grass just to get a breather. Georgie's little bunny legs were tired from all the walking, and he wanted to be carried the rest of the way, something Daniel was not about to do.

"Looks like we've got the street practically to ourselves," said Eric, waving at the two of them. "But most of the houses here don't even have a porch light on. I think it's a bust."

"Just as well," answered Daniel. "Georgie's wiped out and I can't carry another candy bar. I think we're going to head back."

"Yeah, since we're almost to my house, I think I'll call it a night. . . . Wait, did you hear that?"

"Hear what?" Daniel listened for a moment. Then he heard it too. Someone was calling Daniel's name, and they sounded frightened.

Daniel scooped up Georgie, and the three of them ran toward the sound of the voice. They hadn't gotten far before they found Louisa holding a shaken and crying Rose in her arms. Mollie, of course, was already there, and she was wiping tears from Rose's face.

Louisa was trying to quiet her sister.

"What happened?" asked Eric.

"Rose just saw her own shadow, and it spooked her," answered Louisa.

"It wasn't *my* shadow!" said Rose between sobs. She threw her arms around Daniel. "I saw the Shroud, Daniel! I saw him!"

At the mention of the Shroud, Daniel looked at Mollie, but she just shrugged. She obviously hadn't seen anything.

Daniel patted Rose on the back, trying to comfort her, as Eric scanned the dark trees around them.

"Tell me what you saw, Rose," said Daniel. "Be specific and take your time."

"I was walking behind Louisa and . . . and I saw a black thing come out of the dark. It stopped between me and Louisa, and then I disappeared!"

"And she started screaming," said Louisa. "That's the only way I could find her."

"And you didn't see anything?" asked Daniel.

"No," said Louisa.

"He went back into the dark!" said Rose. "He . . . faded away."

"Maybe it was just another kid trick-or-treating," said Mollie. "Maybe he was dressed up."

"He just faded away!" said Rose. "Like a ghost!"

Georgie grabbed hold of Daniel's hand. He didn't understand what was going on, but he could sense that something was wrong. "I wanna go home now, Daniel."

"I think that's a good idea for everyone," said Eric. "We've done pretty well anyway, and it's getting late."

"Hey, where's Rohan?" asked Louisa.

"Oh, he was with me," said Mollie. "When I heard Rose calling, I flew as fast as I could, but he should have been right behind me. We were only a few houses away. . . ."

No one said anything for a second, and then, faster than anyone could blink, Mollie was gone.

A moment later they heard her shouting for help. They ran again, all of them this time, toward the sound of Mollie's voice. Eric could've gotten there sooner, but Daniel guessed that his friend must be staying close to the group to protect them.

Soon Mollie became visible beneath the glow of a streetlamp. She was kneeling over Rohan, who was lying on the ground unmoving.

"Help me!" she cried.

Daniel had just begun to run toward them when Eric put his hand on Daniel's chest.

"Look," he said, pointing at the streetlamp.

The shadows around the lamp *moved*. They peeled off from the darkness like a spreading ink stain and formed into a manlike shape. A shadow as tall as Mollie, and it was reaching out for her.

But Mollie was faster than an eyeblink as she veered away from the creature. The shadow brought itself up to its full height and stalked toward Rohan, claiming its prize.

"No!" shouted Mollie. "You can't have him!" Then Mollie

was fighting back—flying and punching at super-speed. She was a blur, and the shadow fell back away from her blows.

Only Daniel knew what this creature was capable of. He knew what she was up against. Not even Mollie Lee could hold out for long against it. They had to get her and Rohan away.

But then another shadow formed out of the darkness. There were two of them now.

"Mollie! Get out of there!"

"Daniel!" Louisa was shouting his name. "Daniel!"

He turned and saw what Louisa was pointing at. Behind them was a new figure all in black. Another man of shadow. Another Shroud, and it was coming for them.

"Eric, do something!" said Daniel. He could feel the panic rising up in him, could hear his own heart beating in his ears. "Rose, disappear!"

"I can't!" shouted Rose, crying and hysterical. "I'm trying but I can't!"

"What do you mean?" asked Daniel.

"She can't use her powers," said Eric. "And neither can I."

Daniel stared at his friend, at first not comprehending. Then his heart broke inside him as he understood.

"Oh no, Eric!" Daniel said, his voice a whisper.

"No time!" said Eric. "You know what you have to do!"

Daniel nodded. He did know.

"Then go! I'll get Georgie and the girls out of here!"

"Daniel?" Georgie was crying as Daniel put his little brother into Eric's arms.

162

"It'll be all right, Georgie," Daniel said, then turned to Eric. "Head for the first house with a light on. Don't stop and don't look back. No matter what!"

The four of them—Eric with Georgie, and Louisa with Rose—ran into the dark. A shadow drifted toward them like it was going to follow, but Daniel got there first, putting himself between it and his retreating friends.

The thing turned its eyeless head toward Daniel but said nothing. For a moment it quivered, seemed to stretch and expand, until it tore in two and another was standing next to it.

Daniel stood his ground, took a deep breath, and balled his hands up into fists.

Four. There were four Shrouds.

Chapter Sixteen
Night Battle

The powers came to him just like before—he didn't feel any different at first. If anything, he felt worse, sick and weak at the knees, but that was from sheer terror. Yet as Daniel reached within himself, he found something just below that fear, something *powerful*. It was his if he focused on it. Strength. Flight. Eric's powers, now Daniel's own.

He'd stolen them from Eric again without meaning to, without even knowing how he did it. But there wasn't time to feel guilty now. He was facing down four of these shadow creatures, and his friends were in trouble.

The last attempt at flight had nearly ended in disaster, so this time he resolved to keep his feet firmly planted on the ground. With his friends depending on him, he couldn't afford to get lost in the clouds.

Mollie was managing to keep just out of reach of her pair of creatures, weaving and ducking their attacks while keeping them from the unconscious Rohan. These things were slower than the Shroud. Slower and smaller, but still dangerous, like shadows of the old villain. *Shades*. In his mind, that was the name he gave them.

Daniel wondered how long Mollie could keep up the fight. She had to be getting tired, and though she could fly to safety at any time, he knew she wouldn't. She wouldn't abandon Rohan. She would go down fighting. And so would Daniel.

There were two Shades stalking him, moving in to strike. Besides being smaller than the Shroud, these Shades possessed another, perhaps significant, difference. Daniel had noticed that the first Shade, in Herman's study, lacked the green glowing heart of the Witch Fire meteor. Plunkett's power came from the meteorite pendant he wore, which in his Shroud form burned brightly at his chest. Daniel had defeated him last time because he'd aimed for that heart and torn the pendant from the Shroud's throat. But these Shades were solid black shadow; there were no hearts to target, at least nothing he could see. Whatever they were, Daniel didn't think he'd be able to beat them the way he'd defeated Herman.

But maybe he wouldn't have to. Daniel wasn't the same ordinary boy he'd been the last time. For better or for worse, Daniel had changed.

The first Shade swiped at Daniel with a long, thin arm, its fingers searching for Daniel's throat. Even with Eric's powers Daniel wasn't a natural fighter, and he didn't manage to dodge in time. Cold fingers of shadow wrapped around his neck, and where they touched his bare skin, he burned from the unnatural cold. These things might be made of shadow, but they were real enough to squeeze the life out of him. He grabbed the creature's arm around the wrist, thankful at least that there was something solid under there to get a grip on. He tried to tear the creature's hand away from his throat, but it was like trying to bend iron. Spots began forming on the edges of his vision as he struggled for breath that just wasn't there.

The Shade leaned in close, like it was mocking him. It watched Daniel claw uselessly at the iron fingers as it squeezed even harder. Daniel Corrigan could never bend iron, but Eric could.

The power answered his call. It flowed over his muscles like a hot bath, tingling his skin with warmth, beating back the thing's frigid touch. He felt so strong. This was what it was like to feel strong. Daniel tightened his own grip on the Shade's hand, plucking the creature's fingers from his throat one by one. The Shade's iron grip had seemingly turned to rubber. Daniel inhaled a few lungfuls of air to clear the spots away from his eyes, then pulled.

The Shade's hand came away easily, but Daniel didn't stop there. He lifted the creature over his head and flung the Shade into a nearby bench, causing it to explode into splinters as the two collided. The Shade picked itself up but seemed dazed, unsteady. Drips of shadow ran along the ground in rivulets, like blood trickling from a wound. These things could be hurt, at least, and that was something new.

Unfortunately, the fight had drawn the attention of Mollie's opponents too. They left off their futile attempt to capture her and stalked toward Daniel, their hungry arms clutching and grasping at the air as if they were rehearsing Daniel's death scene.

But there wasn't time to worry about them yet. Daniel still had another Shade of his own to deal with. The second creature was nearly on him. A mouth formed where its face should be, opened in a silent scream of rage. Daniel raised his arms to protect himself as he was tackled backward. As the two of them wrestled on the ground, Daniel tried to free himself. But like vines, the blackness grew out of the creature's own body and wrapped around Daniel's arms and his legs. Despite his struggles, the freezing strands crept along his body, inching toward his throat.

Again Daniel felt the heat, the surge of borrowed strength, but this time it took all his effort to break away. Tentacles snapped off like rotten sticks as Daniel wrenched himself free, and the Shade reared back in pain but let out no sound. The ground around them was dotted with drops of black.

Daniel pulled himself to standing as the Shade retreated to join its companion. Behind him the others were hovering—preparing to strike, but hesitating. They were clever, and they'd given up on attacking Daniel one on one. Like a pack of predators, they were waiting to rush him all at once, and Daniel knew he couldn't fend off four of them at the same time, no matter how strong he was.

He heard Mollie's voice, but he didn't look for her. He didn't dare take his eyes off the Shades.

"Daniel! What's going on? How are you . . . ?"

"Stay back!" he shouted. "Don't come near me!" He didn't know how close was too close, but he couldn't risk accidentally stealing Mollie's powers too. "Get Rohan out of here!"

The two Shades he'd wounded seemed to have recovered. The four of them had taken to the air, circling him like vultures around a dying animal. They were getting ready to move in for the kill.

"Daniel, you can't fight them all alone!"

She was right, of course. He had Eric's strength, but he didn't know how to use it the way Eric did. He could try to fly away, but they would probably catch him. Even with all these powers, he just didn't have any experience being super.

Then it hit him. *All* these powers! Eric hadn't been the only one whose powers had failed him this night.

He looked up at the four circling shadows and smiled at them. All he had to do was remember not to giggle.

"Come and get me!" he said. Then he willed himself to not be there. To disappear, just like Rose.

It worked. Daniel looked at his own feet and they weren't there. He held up a hand in front of his face. Nothing. The

Shades were already looking around frantically for him, flying here and there. Daniel sidestepped the first one as it passed, then grabbed it as it sailed by. He yanked the creature out of the air and slammed it as hard as he could into the solid pavement. Once, twice. This time it didn't get back up. It quivered a bit before dissolving into a pool of blackness, an oily stain on the road.

The other three rushed into the fight, but they didn't know what they should be attacking. Swinging blindly, they missed Daniel entirely. Invisible, he began hitting first, then sidestepping away before they could counterattack.

It didn't take long for the three remaining Shades to begin their retreat. Back into the shadows they melted, one by one, until Daniel was left on a suddenly quiet street, his blood still pounding in his ears. His arms and legs had gone wobbly, and so he put his hands on his knees and stood there, panting. After a few minutes he thought to make himself visible again but realized he already was. The borrowed invisibility was gone, and so was the strength. He was lucky that the Shades had chosen to run away when they had—a few more minutes and he would have been totally vulnerable. Like last time, as the power faded he was left exhausted.

"Daniel?"

Mollie was watching him. Rohan was awake and standing next to her too. Thankfully, neither appeared physically hurt.

"Rohan, are you all right?" Daniel asked.

"He's fine," said Mollie. "The Shrouds didn't get him. He just . . ."

"I fainted," said Rohan. "I'm not ashamed. That Shroud was very scary, and when it jumped out of the dark, I had a perfectly normal, albeit ineffective, response."

"It's a Shade," said Daniel. "These things, whatever they are, aren't Shrouds. . . . I don't know what they are exactly, but it's safe to say Herman can't divide himself into fours. So I'm calling them Shades."

"Shades, then," said Rohan, nodding. "Fits."

"And I'm glad you're okay," said Daniel.

"Thanks to Mollie, I am," said Rohan. "I owe her one."

"Whatever. No big deal," said Mollie.

"Yes, it was," answered Rohan. And Mollie let it go, but she looked pleased.

"But you, Daniel," she said. "I saw what you did. You . . . you have powers."

Daniel looked at his friends standing in front of him and he felt his heart break all over again. They had such expectant, hopeful faces. Joyful, even. Despite all that had just happened, they were happy for him. Even after the attack, they had room in their hearts to feel something good and positive. They hadn't yet guessed the truth about Daniel's new abilities. But they would sooner or later.

It was time to stop fighting it. Daniel gave in and sank down to the ground, his head on his knees. "They weren't my powers," he said. "I stole the strength from Eric and the invisibility from Rose."

There. The truth was out at last.

"What are you talking about?" asked Mollie. "What do you mean, 'stole'?"

"I do have one power," he said, looking up at her. "It happened the first time, I think, at the Tangle Creek Bridge, the day of the accident. It happened again later when I was alone with Eric, but we promised each other not to tell you guys. It happened recently when I had a run-in with Clay and Bud. And it happened with Louisa, on the day she was attacked."

"What? What happened, Daniel?" Mollie looked confused, and because she was confused, she was getting angry. Rohan wasn't saying anything.

"I stole their powers. That's what I do now. I steal powers and use them for myself. Like I stole Eric's and Rose's. I can't help it—I don't even realize that I'm doing it. But that's why I've been avoiding you. I can't be trusted."

Daniel looked down at the dark stain on the road. It had a grimy sheen to it, like spilled gasoline. So that's what it looks like when a Shade dies, he thought.

"When Eric needed his powers the most, I took them away," said Daniel. "And poor Rose was so scared. . . ." He closed his eyes. "I don't know what those creatures are," he said, "but I'm the real Shroud."

Chapter Seventeen
Recriminations. Confessions.

Eric got Georgie home safely, and it was just dumb luck that Daniel's little brother hadn't gotten a good look at the Shades. Convincing him that the shadow creatures were really just kids in Halloween costumes felt wrong in a way, but how do you explain the truth of such things to anyone, much less a three-year-old? And it was a simple lie for Daniel's parents to believe. They had no problem believing that masked bullies had stolen their sons' candy. It was an easy thing for a parent to buy into the casual cruelty of childhood.

Georgie woke up several times that night with nightmares, but his mother always rocked him back to sleep with a lullaby. Little Georgie was a true child of Noble's Green now—his dreams were haunted by real-life monsters.

Daniel's father wanted to call Sheriff Simmons and complain about the local "bullies," but Daniel was able to talk him out of it. Next year, his father promised, they wouldn't be allowed to go out on Halloween night alone. Dad would keep the bad kids away. He would keep them all safe.

Safe. Daniel had seen four Shades tonight. No one was safe anymore.

Like Georgie, Daniel was scared to close his eyes. He was afraid of what he might see. But in time exhaustion overcame him and he fell into a deep, and thankfully dreamless, sleep.

Early the next morning his friends showed up at his door, looking only slightly better than they had the night before. They managed a bit of small talk before retreating to Daniel's room to talk in private.

"I touched Rose last night when she hugged me," said Daniel. "And then she couldn't turn invisible."

"And I put my hand on your chest when I spotted the Shrouds," said Eric. "But we've tried out touch before and it didn't work. . . ."

"It must not be all the time," said Daniel. "But until I figure out the trigger, we'd better have a hands-off policy whenever I'm around."

Rohan and Mollie weren't saying much of anything. And Daniel noticed they kept their distance as well. Probably smart.

"Well, I'm back to normal this morning," said Eric. "So part of our theory is true—you don't steal powers, you borrow them."

"What about Louisa?" asked Rohan. "Her powers haven't come back."

"Do you have them?" asked Eric. "I mean, can you walk through walls and stuff now, Daniel?"

"No," said Daniel. "I could during the fight with that Shade in Herman Plunkett's study, but it faded fast."

Rohan wiped his glasses on his shirt. "So Louisa's an outlier."

"A who?" asked Eric.

"An outlier," said Rohan. "It means she's something that breaks the statistical trend."

Daniel walked over to his bookcase and pulled down the copy of *The Final Problem*.

"There's one last thing," said Daniel. "Something I never told you. When we fought Herman last year, he gave me something. A ring made of the same meteorite that he used to make his pendant. I haven't worn it. . . . I don't know why I kept it. To make sure it stays safe, I guess. I meant to tell you all, but . . . I didn't.

"This black ring," Daniel said. "I've had it hidden here since the night we beat the Shroud."

They didn't say anything right away, but they didn't have to. Daniel could imagine the feelings of shock and betrayal that they must be going through. He'd hidden more than a ring—he'd hidden a piece of the Shroud. It was a symbol of all the years of terror that they'd lived through, and here it was in Daniel's safekeeping. Secret. Still, it felt better to say the words, to get it all in the open at last. It had been sitting on his heart like a stone for so long now.

"Have you touched it since you started developing this . . . power?" Rohan asked.

"No," said Daniel. "I'm afraid of what would happen. A power thief touching a power-stealing ring."

"Maybe you'd become superpowerful," said Eric. "Like a double-negative-makes-a-positive type of thing."

"I don't think that's how it works," said Rohan. "It could be bad. Really bad."

Daniel set the book on his desk and reached for the cover.

"Don't," said Mollie. "I don't want to see it. I don't want to even look at it."

"Huh?" asked Daniel.

"Never mind that you two jerks didn't tell us about these powers, why did you hide this ring, Daniel? Honestly."

"I don't know. I thought I was keeping it safe, and keeping you guys safe, but . . ."

"You kept it around as a weapon in case any of us got out of line, is that it?"

"No!" said Daniel. "Not you guys! But Herman Plunkett said that comet—the Witch Fire Comet that started all this—was coming back. I just . . . Could you imagine what could happen if there was a whole town of Supers?"

"So you kept it to keep the town safe," said Mollie. "Just like Herman?"

"No!"

"Well, you don't need to worry about it now," she said. "You don't need the ring—you're a Shroud already!"

There was a gust of wind and, like that, she was gone. The window was open and the curtains were blowing in the sudden breeze, but there was no Mollie.

"I'll find her and calm her down," said Rohan, going to the door. He paused there for a second and looked at Daniel.

"She didn't mean it, you know," he said. "But you still should have told us. It was wrong not to."

Then Rohan jogged down the steps, chasing after Mollie. Once they were alone, Eric let out a long whistle.

"Boy," he said. "You really screwed up this time."

"I thought it would be like tearing off a Band-Aid," Daniel said. "Hurt less if I did it quick."

"And?"

"That was a heck of a Band-Aid. Still, I'm glad it's over with."

Eric nodded. "So lemme get a look at that big bad ring of yours."

Daniel opened the cover. "Don't get too close, though. I don't really know what it can do. . . ."

Daniel's words trailed away as Eric looked down at the book and then back up at Daniel.

"This a joke?" asked Eric.

Daniel shook his head as he felt around in the book's

hidden compartment. In the perfectly hollowed-out, *empty* space. This was no joke. This was a disaster.

The ring was gone.

In the following days Daniel saw Rohan and Mollie only at school, and while they didn't exactly avoid him, they didn't really talk to him either. As a rule, the Supers didn't speak of anything "super" on school grounds. There were too many ears in the hallways, and so it was understood that powers talk was off-limits. But now Daniel was lucky if his friends complained to him about the cafeteria food. No one besides Eric was saying much of anything at all, at least not to him. A chill had descended over their little group of friends, and Daniel was to blame.

Eric broke the news to the others about the missing ring, and of course Theo was immediately his prime suspect. Everything that had happened thus far—Daniel's powers, the black ring, the Shroud attacks—was just a part of Theo Plunkett's master plan to replace his uncle. Never mind that Eric couldn't explain how these things connected, or what Theo would gain out of all of it, or how he'd managed to split himself into four Shrouds, or that there wasn't a single piece of solid evidence that pointed to Theo other than his name. Eric wasn't about the details, and he felt it in his gut that Theo was their man.

That was theory number one, and Eric practically shouted it in Daniel's ear whenever he had the chance. Theory number two, however, Daniel caught only in whispers. It was spoken of when Rohan and Mollie thought he wasn't around, and it went like this: What if there never had been a ring? What if Daniel was having some kind of breakdown? Herman's power had driven the old man at least slightly mad. At the very least he'd been seriously delusional. What toll might all this be having on Daniel?

It was that theory that worried Daniel the most. Even more than the missing ring. The dreams, the sleepwalking. Ever since that morning at Tangle Creek Bridge, Daniel hadn't felt himself. And it was deeper than just the powers. It was like he'd forgotten something important. He walked around feeling as if he'd tied a string around his finger and couldn't remember why. There was this itch in the back of his brain. . . .

This went on for about another week, until one day Daniel, Rohan, and Mollie got off the school bus at their home stop and found Eric waiting there for them. Daniel had spotted him through the window as the bus pulled up. Eric was smiling up at the bus driver and stepped aside as Mollie and Rohan walked right past him, as if he wasn't even there. Daniel, at least, stopped to say hi.

Eric waved away the exhaust fumes of the departing bus as Rohan and Mollie disappeared down the lane.

"They're even madder at me than they are at you," said Eric as he watched them go. "They're ticked off because I knew and didn't say anything."

"That's silly," said Daniel. "They're just scared. Scared that I'm losing my mind."

"You're as sane as they come, Daniel."

"I don't know anymore."

"Listen to me," said Eric, stepping in front of Daniel. "Things have gotten all tangled up. These Shades, your powers, the ring disappearing. Someone is messing with us bigtime. Everyone's scared, and we've been knocked back on our butts, but we'll get up again and figure this all out! There's a villain out there behind all of this, but he's not *you*. Got that?"

Daniel nodded, but in his heart he wasn't sure if he believed it. He had once been too quick to suspect Eric of being a villain, too easily fooled by Herman's manipulations. But Eric was just as guilty of being too trusting of his friends. Eric's world was still based on comic-book versions of good and evil, white and black. He left no room for gray.

Daniel watched as Eric dug his hands into his pockets and hugged his arms close against the cold. These November days had turned downright frosty, but Daniel knew from personal experience that Eric didn't feel the cold, not the way normal people felt it. He was just shivering out of habit, because that's what everyone else did.

"I've been thinking about your powers," Eric said. "How sometimes they seem to be touch activated but not always. For argument's sake, let's say this started back at the bridge. On the day of Theo's accident."

"Okay."

"On that day, when Theo's car lost control, did we touch?"

"I don't remember. I might have grabbed you, to get your attention."

"Good," said Eric. "I thought so." Eric was rubbing his hands together as he spoke. He was animated, the way Daniel normally was when confronted with a mystery. But Daniel had lost his zest for puzzle solving.

"Now when we fought Clay and Bud, I know we touched, because I tried to push you out of the way. So I could clobber Clay."

"Yeah."

"And on Halloween Rose hugged you, and I held you back from running to help Rohan. Double touch, double powers!"

Daniel thought about it. Eric did have a point. He'd touched all the Supers he'd stolen powers from; even Bud had backed into him before Daniel had turned into a moving stink cloud. Even . . .

"So that leaves Louisa. Did you guys, you know, touch before she was attacked?"

"Yes," said Daniel quickly, remembering the kiss. In some ways that had been scarier than all the rest.

"And each time, there was some kind of danger. Something exciting or threatening was going on."

Daniel thought for a moment. "Maybe."

"It's instinct! Fight-or-flight response!" said Eric, clapping his hands. "Look, did I ever tell you how I discovered my powers?"

"No," said Daniel. "I don't think so."

"When I was eight, my mom hooked up with this sales-
man named Ted. He seemed nice at first, but he had a temper. Bob's bad, but he's just a drunk. Ted, it turned out, was a
hitter."

"Wow, Eric. I'm sorry."

Eric held up his hand. "That's not why I'm telling you
this. I'm telling you because I discovered my powers the day
I threw Ted through a window."

"Oh."

"Yeah. He was trying to record a big basketball game on
our TV and I messed it up by playing with the remote. Mom
had run out to get pizzas, and Ted, well, he came at me with
a belt. A big metal buckle too. So he swung at me with the
belt and I just shoved him away. Didn't realize what I'd done
until the dust had settled and Ted was outside in the driveway with a broken arm and bunch of cracked ribs. I could've
killed him without even meaning to."

"But, Eric, he came at you! And you were just acting
out of—"

"Instinct?" interrupted Eric.

"I was going to say self-defense."

"Same thing," said Eric. "And you're right—I don't
blame myself for what happened to Ted. But I am careful about how I use my power now. I have to keep a lid
on my temper. Ted had it coming, but when a simple shove
can put someone in the hospital, you have to watch yourself.

"You've been acting out of instinct, Daniel. You can't tell

someone not to flinch when you clap your hands in front of their face."

Daniel threw up his arms. "So you see? It's not something that I can turn on and off!"

"Not yet," said Eric. "But with practice, maybe you can. Maybe you can learn to control it. To be more careful."

Daniel wished that was the case. But how could he even begin when he had no idea when it was happening? It wasn't like he had any warning.

"It just happens," Daniel said, shaking his head. "Whenever there's danger, I just do it without thinking."

"So it's a response to something physical. Great. That's something to start with."

"What do you mean?"

"Think about what happens when a person's in danger," said Eric. "Our bodies release adrenaline, the heart speeds up. Maybe it's one of those things that activates your power."

"So what? The next time there's danger I should take a nap?"

"Not too far off, maybe," said Eric. "I think you have to practice not being scared."

Daniel laughed. Now Eric really was trying to be funny.

"I can't help it when I get scared! I can't change it!"

"If I clapped my hand in front of your face enough times, you'd stop flinching. You'd train yourself not to," said Eric. "Maybe you have to teach yourself not to be afraid. In the meantime, think about your power like this: it works on touch plus fear. If you're afraid, make sure you don't touch anyone."

Daniel kicked a pebble and watched it roll down the road.

"It's controllable," Eric said.

The two of them stepped onto the shoulder as a small caravan of work trucks came barreling by. Dump trucks, flatbeds carrying bulldozers and cranes. As Daniel watched, the pebble he'd kicked was thrown up and battered around by the passing tires. He felt like that pebble now, being tossed about by forces well beyond his control.

"The truth is we don't have time for this," said Eric. "I know you're worried and Mollie and Rohan are scared and angry, but we've got problems to deal with. Real problems."

"Four Shades," said Daniel. "And the missing ring."

Eric nodded. "Yeah. Well, *three* Shades now. Mollie said you let one of them have it."

"I don't know if it really matters. I watched one split itself into two; there could be more. Maybe it really is Herman behind all this. Maybe he's still alive."

"Eh, I'd still put my money on Plunkett *Junior.* He's just clever enough to be involved but not show his hand. I'm telling you."

Eric was right about one thing—whoever the villain was, he was devious. Herman had been crazy enough to believe that his relationship with Daniel was that of teacher and pupil, but the only lesson Daniel had learned from the old man was that Herman Plunkett was the most twisted human being he'd ever known. No sort of trickery was beyond him. Even an army of shadow creatures to do his bidding.

"The one thing I know," said Eric, "is we'll never find out for sure if all we do is sit around and mope."

Daniel allowed himself a small smile. "The League of Pouty-Pants?"

"The Society of Whiny-Whiners! Doesn't that strike fear into the hearts of evildoers everywhere?"

Something rumbled in the distance, and Daniel looked to see a second convoy of trucks heading their way. That was odd. Noble's Green was not exactly a boomtown; there were no new suburbs being built that he knew of. But here came more and more trucks loaded with machinery, hauling it up the mountain. This time as they passed, Daniel made a point of getting a better look at them, more specifically at the logo branded on the sides.

PCI: Plunkett Construction Industries.

"Eric," Daniel said, pointing to the passing vehicles.

"I see it. They're headed up the mountain. To the Old Quarry road. . . ."

"Go get Mollie and Rohan," said Daniel. "Tell them . . . I don't know, tell them they can come after me with torches and pitchforks later, but we need them now. I'll meet you all in the woods next to the quarry. Near the road."

"Now you're talking. What are you going to do in the meantime?"

"I'm going to get a head start on you all. It's too risky for you to try to fly me, so I need to run home and grab my bike. I'll get there the old-fashioned way."

Eric smiled and saluted before soaring off into the sky. "See you there!"

Daniel waved back. Things were moving fast, and Eric was right that they'd lost valuable time being angry and distrustful of each other. Something big was happening, and Daniel had one memory in his head that he couldn't shake. The memory wasn't Herman or even the Shades. It was of Theo Plunkett standing there at the edge of the quarry, watching him. The look on that boy's face.

The new kid.

Chapter Eighteen
Back to the Old Quarry

Trucks continued to speed by Daniel as he pedaled his way up Route 20, yard by agonizingly slow yard. He wished he could simply hop on the back of a bulldozer and hitch a ride, but he didn't think it would be a good idea to show up with the very people he was planning to spy on.

When he was about a quarter of a mile away, Daniel steered his bike off the road and cut through the trees on foot, unseen. As he approached the quarry, the rumble of machinery could be heard echoing through the forest, and the sweet smell of pine was tainted with the tang of motor oil and gasoline. This wasn't Clay and Bud snooping around anymore. These people were gearing up for a full excavation. But did they even know what they were looking for?

He searched the woods for a few minutes before he spotted the others. The steady roar of engines meant that Daniel didn't have to worry about making noise as he tromped through the fallen twigs, but the leafless trees of late autumn provided poor cover, and he worried about being seen. Luckily, his friends had found a thick patch of evergreens on the edge of the quarry that made the perfect place for spying. Once he was inside the safety of the trees, Eric waved at him, Rohan nodded a curt hello, and Mollie didn't say anything. But she also didn't fly away or throw a rock at his head, which Daniel took as a good sign.

The four of them peered through the branches of their hiding spot and looked out over the quarry, which had transformed seemingly overnight. The trucks Daniel had seen back on the road were there, as were the usual vehicles you'd expect to see at a working quarry—dump trucks and a couple of excavators. But there was more going on here than digging for limestone. A number of large, semipermanent tents had been erected on the outskirts. When the canvas doors were pulled back, Daniel could glimpse tables of men working at laptop computers or unpacking boxes of sophisticated equipment. This was a very high-tech operation.

"This is bad, right?" Eric asked.

Rohan nodded. "I think this is very bad."

"Can you hear what those nerds in the tent are talking about?"

"Watch it—you're talking about my people," said Rohan. "But let me try." He closed his eyes and concentrated. "There's . . . there's too much background noise. I can't make out much. But they sound excited about something. The word *awesome* is being tossed about way too much, I can tell you that. And someone keeps talking about caves."

"What are they doing here?" asked Mollie. "Why now?"

"I think I can answer that," said Daniel. "I was up here a few weeks ago, and I found Clay and Bud digging around in the rocks."

"More secrets?" said Mollie.

"Go on, Daniel," said Rohan.

"It was after we learned about Louisa's . . . condition. I was just kind of wandering around and I found myself up here. Clay and Bud were searching for meteor rocks."

"And you were alone?" asked Rohan.

"I wasn't scared of them," said Daniel. "I thought my . . . powers would protect me."

"And how'd that work out for you?" asked Mollie.

"Not so good. Clay tried to pound me and I ended up with Bud's stink powers."

There were a few moments of silence as Daniel's friends seemed to be digesting this. Nothing but the sounds of trucks rumbling in the distance as they looked at him. Judged him.

Mollie was the first to go. She snorted once. Then again.

Then exploded into a full belly laugh. Within moments Daniel's friends were holding their sides as they practically cried with laughter.

"Oh, man! What I would've given to see that!" said Mollie.

"Not me," said Rohan, wiping tears from his eyes. "I don't need the real thing."

"Okay, okay," said Daniel. "It's not *that* funny."

Daniel acted embarrassed, but in truth he was relieved. Listening to his friends laugh again, even if it was at him, was a wonderful feeling. It was like he'd been holding his breath for days and just now let it out.

"So your super-stink won out over Clay's strength?" asked Eric.

"Well, it bought me enough time to get away, I guess," said Daniel. "But as hilarious as this all is, my stink power is not the point of the story. I saw Theo Plunkett up here, and he saw me. He saw everything."

"Well, that settles it then," said Eric. "We know who's behind this. Theo asked his super-rich daddy to dig up the quarry!"

"But why?" asked Mollie. "It still doesn't explain why! What's there worth digging for?"

"He's after the same thing Clay and Bud were—the meteorite," said Eric. "He stole the black ring—he must've snuck in while you were at school—and now he's helping his old uncle out and looking for the rest of the meteorite so they can continue the family business of being total jerks."

"I agree that it doesn't look good," said Daniel. "But we still don't know for sure."

"Why don't we just ask him?" said Rohan.

"It's not that easy," said Daniel. "I tried calling, I tried going by his house, but he's avoiding me."

"No, I don't mean you should call or stop by," said Rohan. "I mean ask him. Now."

Rohan pointed through the trees, and they all watched as one of the tents opened and out walked Theo Plunkett. He was with his father and another man they'd never seen before.

"There's your proof," said Eric.

"Maybe," said Daniel. "Rohan's right, though. Only one way to know for sure."

He stepped out of the trees and into the open.

"What are you doing?" whispered Eric.

"I'm listening to my friends for once," Daniel whispered back. "I'm going to ask Theo what's going on. You guys stay here and watch my back."

"We're on it," said Rohan, nodding.

"You're nuts," said Mollie, but she nodded as well.

It felt good to know they were there with him. He'd been trying to do this all by himself, and look where it had gotten them. He'd forgotten what it felt like to be part of a team.

Because of all the trucks coming and going, Theo didn't even hear Daniel approach. It was Theo's father who spotted him first. Mr. Plunkett tapped his son on the shoulder and pointed. When Theo saw Daniel, there was a moment of obvious shock, even alarm, on his face. But he quickly recovered and stowed his surprise away behind his usual cool smile.

"I saw the trucks," Daniel said.

Theo nodded. "I'm glad. It's good to see you."

"Daniel," said Mr. Plunkett, "this is Dr. Lewis. He's from the university archaeological department."

The other man, one of Eric's nerds, shook Daniel's hand.

"Technically, this is a closed site," said Dr. Lewis, peering down at Daniel over the rim of his glasses. "But if you're a friend of the Plunketts', then I guess we can make an exception."

"You're an archaeologist?" asked Daniel. "I thought this was just an old limestone quarry."

"Well, it was," said Dr. Lewis. "But before that it was a site of significant importance. The university has been trying to get access to it for a very long time. There've been some very interesting finds in the surrounding areas—some of which date back hundreds, if not thousands, of years. But all this land is private property and, well . . ."

"Granduncle Herman didn't care much for archaeology," said Theo. "But now that we own this land, things have changed."

"Theo's being modest," said his dad. "He found out that the university had an interest here, and so he pestered me to let them dig. I had my people verify that there really wasn't any money to be made in limestone and then gave my okay. Looks like Theo's the Plunkett family philanthropist!"

"It's a very generous donation," said Dr. Lewis. "We're already very excited about the site."

"Dr. Lewis said that the original people here on Mount Noble were cave dwellers," said Theo. "But no one's been able to find their actual caves."

"This would actually predate even the Native American tribes that lived here," said Dr. Lewis. "We are talking about true prehistoric people. The first humans who migrated here from Asia, across what is now the Bering Strait—the very first human beings to settle this area. We've gathered enough evidence over the years to get an idea of what happened to them. I believe some catastrophic event—an earthquake or perhaps even a meteor strike—covered their caves. But there still might be some remaining tunnels under there somewhere. And if we find the tunnels . . . well, who knows what they might have left behind?"

Daniel nodded as Dr. Lewis lectured him, feigning interest and even surprise. But Daniel already knew what was in those caves—he'd seen them. And they were wrong about Herman's interests. He *was* obsessed with the archaeological finds here and around Mount Noble. The difference was that he'd been determined to keep those secrets for himself. He'd shared them with Daniel and no one else. He'd allowed Daniel to see the cave paintings those prehistoric people had created, and he'd told him the truth of what had happened here. There had indeed been a catastrophe brought about by a meteor strike. But it wasn't the impact of the strike itself that had destroyed those people. What had destroyed that tribe was the very first generation of Supers ever, thousands of years before the meteor strike that burned down the St. Alban's orphange. That group of prehistoric young people used their powers to fight among themselves until they'd destroyed their entire tribe. And it was all painted on the walls of those caves still hidden beneath the mountain, just waiting to be discovered.

And what of Herman's meteorite pendant? Was that still down there as well? Were there still fragments of the original buried deep beneath the earth? Herman had spent a fortune excavating enough to forge the black ring, but what if they dug deeper? What might they find?

None of this made sense. If Theo was in league with his uncle, he wouldn't have involved the university or its team of scientists. Herman had worked too hard to keep those caves secret; he was too paranoid to share his discovery with anyone else. There was no way Herman Plunkett would let any of this happen.

No. In that instant Daniel made a judgment call about the youngest Plunkett. Theo was spoiled and reckless and he'd very nearly killed himself on that first day in Noble's Green. But he'd also saved Eric's life. He hadn't hesitated, and because of that Daniel had been betting that deep down at his core, Theo Plunkett was a better person than Herman. Maybe even a truly good person. What Daniel did know was that Theo was a new kid looking for answers, and Daniel could relate to that.

It was now or never.

"This all sounds very cool," said Daniel. Dr. Lewis visibly flinched at Daniel's choice of words to describe what the professor considered a historic discovery. Little did he know that his own team of scientists was probably inside the research tent high-fiving each other and shouting "awesome" even now.

"Theo, are you going to be here for a while?" asked Daniel. "I thought you might want to hang out." Although Daniel kept his voice casual, he gave Theo a look that he hoped the older boy would understand. They needed to talk.

"Well, I don't think Dr. Lewis really needs Theo here, do you?" asked Mr. Plunkett.

"Oh, no. Of course not," said Dr. Lewis.

"Just the Plunkett checkbook," added Mr. Plunkett with a wink.

Dr. Lewis blushed and smiled awkwardly.

"Do you two want a ride back?" asked Mr. Plunkett.

"Well, I've got my bike a ways down the road," said Daniel, "if Theo doesn't mind walking me back. It's not too cold."

"Sure," said Theo after a moment. "Why not?"

"Suit yourselves," said Mr. Plunkett. "As long as Theo's not behind the wheel of anything with a motor, I'm happy to let him out for a bit."

The two men left the boys alone, with Dr. Lewis continuing to lecture about the history of the site and Mr. Plunkett nodding and offering the occasional, bored "Mm-hmm."

Once they'd gotten out of earshot, Theo turned to Daniel.

"Surprise," he said, gesturing to the quarry and the twenty or so university scientists and grad students swarming about. "So I got your attention, and all it took was a few hundred thousand dollars of my dad's money and a small army of archaeologists."

"My attention?" said Daniel. "I've been trying to talk to you for weeks. You went missing in action!"

Theo looked at Daniel for a long minute. The two boys were having a showdown of sorts. They weren't friends, exactly, and they weren't yet enemies. Daniel became keenly aware that these next few minutes were vital if he was to have any hope of winning Theo over.

"I'm interested in mysteries," said Theo at last. "I've been going through Herman's study, examining his papers, and it became obvious that he'd been doing more up here than simply digging for limestone. He was paying specialists all over the world to examine stuff he found up here, but he was too good at hiding the results. Lots of clues, but no answers. But they all lead here."

"So you're a detective," said Daniel.

"I'm no detective, I'm just rich," answered Theo. "I don't even know what it is I'm looking for."

The smile finally disappeared from his face. "Or for that matter what I'm looking at."

That stung. Daniel didn't like the implication that he

might be something other than what he seemed. But then again, he supposed he'd earned Theo's suspicion. They all had.

"You need to convince your father to call off the dig," Daniel said.

"Why? I'm the one who convinced him to start it in the first place."

"You don't know what you'll find in there. It . . . it could be dangerous."

Theo laughed. "Dangerous? There's *something* in there that *might* be dangerous? Man, even now you won't be straight with me, will you? It's all vague warnings!"

"Look, Theo, I can't explain, but you have to trust me—"

"Trust you?" Theo said. "Like you haven't been lying to me from the moment I first met you, Daniel! You and your friends."

Theo leaned in, his eyes narrowed in anger. "My car didn't magically float in midair! Something happened at that bridge. And I saw you fighting with those other boys here at the quarry. I saw stuff . . . stuff that's just not possible!"

At the sound of Theo's raised voice, his father and Dr. Lewis glanced over in the boys' direction. Theo caught himself and smiled back. That practiced, smooth smile. There wasn't even a hint of anger left on his face.

"My uncle was obsessed with something in this mountain," Theo said. "You and your friends obviously know what it is, but you don't feel like sharing. Fair enough. I'll find it my own way."

For a tense moment neither one of them said anything. Daniel knew that if Eric had been in this situation, the time for negotiation would have been over. The gauntlet had been thrown, and Theo Plunkett was now a threat. But Daniel wasn't Eric, and as much as he looked up to his friend, Daniel believed there had to be another way of dealing with this problem. He often wondered if there had been a time in the past when Clay and Bud could've been reasoned with. It was too late for them now, but it might not be too late for Theo.

The last thing the Supers needed was another enemy. But more than anything, he needed to convince him to stop the dig.

"So now what?" asked Theo. "Am I your arch-nemesis? Just like in the comic books?"

"No," said Daniel. "I thought we'd take a little walk together."

"Where to?" asked Theo.

Now it was Daniel's turn to smile. He remembered an afternoon just over a year ago when, bewildered and frustrated and desperate for answers, he'd asked Eric the very same thing.

"We're going to a tree fort."

Chapter Nineteen
The Supers of Noble's Green

"**M**ollie's a flier, and super-fast," said Daniel. "I mean super-super-fast."

Mollie snorted, but she didn't deny it, and she might even have liked the compliment. It was hard to tell with Mollie. Next up was Rohan, who was using his shirtsleeve to scrub at a stubborn spot on his glasses.

"Rohan here's got super-senses," said Daniel.

"Super . . . senses?" asked Theo.

"It's not as lame as it sounds," said Rohan.

"Yes it is," said Mollie.

"And lastly," said Daniel, "there's Eric."

"And what can you do?" asked Theo, glancing over to the window where Eric been sulking for the last ten minutes.

"Strong. Tough. Flier," he answered without looking up.

Theo gave an impressed nod. "Lucky you."

"He's the one who caught your car at the bridge," added Daniel.

"Well, thanks for that," said Theo.

Eric shrugged his shoulders without answering. He didn't even bother to glance away from the window. And no one missed the fact that Eric should've been the one thanking Theo for performing the CPR that probably saved his life. Eric had been firmly against bringing Theo inside the tree fort in the first place, but he'd been outvoted. Daniel had been able to convince Mollie and Rohan that this was the smart move. That for once, honesty was actually the best policy. In the end it was three for, one against. And the one against had taken to sulking.

"So that's it," said Daniel. "The Supers of Noble's Green."

Theo sat there for a moment, studying them, his face impossible to read. Daniel could imagine what must be going through his mind right now, because he'd been there himself not long ago. The tree fort, the faded posters and yellowing old comics that littered the place like relics. This whole place was a museum of super-kid history. In many ways it was their only link to a past that had been stolen from them by the Shroud. But for someone like Theo, who'd arrived in town speeding in his dad's stolen sports car, it probably all seemed like kiddie stuff. Only these kiddies could fly.

"Okay," said Theo. "So what about you?"

"What?" asked Daniel.

"What do you do? What's your superpower?"

Daniel had forgotten about that part. He was now a Super too. As much as he might wish it otherwise.

He could feel his friends' eyes on him. "I steal other people's powers."

"Well, how about that?" answered Theo after a moment.

"He *borrows* them," said Eric, pulling himself away from the window at last. "It's temporary."

Theo nodded and smiled. "Got it. So where are your costumes?"

"We don't wear costumes," said Rohan.

"Eric sometimes wears a costume," said Mollie.

"Only on Halloween!" said Eric.

"Well, you really need costumes," said Theo. "Isn't it against union rules not to wear a costume? Won't they expel you from the fraternal brotherhood of crime fighters?"

"He's making fun of us," said Mollie.

"What?" said Theo, looking around the tree fort. "You're telling me that you all get together here and fight rampant neighborhood crime without costumes? I mean if I woke up one morning and discovered I was a superhero, I'd certainly take on the diabolical bad guys of the safest town on earth. Isn't that the Noble's Green slogan?"

"The situation's more complicated than that," said Daniel. "Nobody here thinks of himself as a superhero."

"Well, some of us . . . ," said Mollie, looking sideways at Eric.

"We help people," said Eric. "Call it what you want."

"Do you have superhero names at least?" asked Theo. "Like Super Smell Boy? Or Talks Too Fast Girl?"

"How about Super-Kid Who Drops Smart-Alec Rich Boy into the River?" said Eric, standing. "How's that?"

Theo laughed. "I don't know what I was expecting, coming here, but I thought you'd have a better story than this load of bull."

"We're telling you the truth," said Daniel. "I know it's hard to believe—"

"Look," said Theo. "I know there's something . . . strange going on. I've seen enough to understand that. But if you actually expect me to believe that the nerd king here—"

"This nerd king has a name, thank you very much," said Rohan.

Theo continued as if Rohan hadn't spoken at all.

"If you expect me to believe the nerd king can smell a flower on the other side of the mountain, and that girls and boys can fly, then you *are* crazy. You might get your tweener friends to buy this, but I'm not."

"Believe it or not, Theo, for generations there have been super-kids in this town," said Daniel. "And we can prove it to you. No one knows exactly how it happened, but your uncle believed that it was caused by a meteor crash over a century ago. The quarry where your dad's men are digging is ground zero of that crash. Herman excavated the site for years in secret."

"Why?" Theo asked. "What was he looking for?"

Daniel looked around at his friends' faces. Eric's eyes were full of warning. He did not want Daniel to continue; he did not want Theo to hear what came next. But Daniel couldn't think of any other way to stop the dig without telling the boy everything. If the university discovered those caves, they might discover the Witch Fire meteorite, and that kind of power would be a risk to the world. In that, Herman had been correct. It was best left buried under the mountain, forever.

Confiding in Theo was a risky move and Daniel might be courting disaster, but it was their only shot. Daniel didn't exactly trust him, but he was convinced that the only way to keep the secrets of Mount Noble safe was to get Theo Plunkett on their side.

"The meteorite that landed here gave the children their powers. But it could also be used to steal them away too. As Herman did for years and years."

Daniel left the comment dangling there, but instead of watching for Theo's reaction to the news that his relative was really a villain, he watched Rohan. Rohan was Daniel's secret weapon in all this. He'd decided to come clean with Theo, but if his friends had any lingering doubt as to whether Theo was in league with the Shroud, then Rohan's job was to watch Theo for signs that he was being less than honest himself. If the news was truly shocking, if he was as innocent in all of this as he claimed, then Rohan's sensory powers should be able to detect it. Theo's reaction would, hopefully, tell them all they needed to know.

They never got the chance. No sooner had Daniel glanced in Rohan's direction than his friend's eyes grew wide with alarm. He was hearing something that had nothing to do with Theo. And it wasn't good.

To Daniel's ears it was little more than a scratch at the door, like an animal pawing at the boards. One scratch . . . two.

"They're here! Get down!" shouted Rohan an instant before the door exploded open, ripped from its hinges, and clattered to the floor. In flew two long black shadows. The Shades had found them again.

Eric was the first to react, throwing himself in their path and tackling the first one straight out the window. Daniel could hear the crashing of branches outside as the two carried their fight out among the trees. Daniel saw what Eric was doing—he was getting far away from Daniel. He wanted to put enough space between them that he wouldn't accidentally bump into him and risk losing his powers. He'd try to take care of the first Shade as fast as he could, but he'd do it outside. Then he'd come back for the second. Unfortunately, that meant they still had a Shade to deal with by themselves.

Mollie was already in the fight. Using her speed, she

dodged around the creature, hitting and retreating in the same instant. But here in the tree fort she couldn't use her flight to maneuver, and the Shroud was already starting to box her in. Her punches were little more than a distraction, and still it just kept coming, driving her into the corner where it wouldn't matter how fast she was. It was just a matter of time.

Daniel forced himself to close his eyes and take a deep breath. He needed to find calm. He was careful not to touch anyone, for fear of what his power might do. But what help was he if he just stood there?

He nearly shouted when someone grabbed him by the shirt collar. It was Theo, pale and shaking. Daniel had never seen the boy so afraid. Not even when his car had careered off the Tangle Creek Bridge.

"What's going on?" he was shouting. "What are those things?"

"Shades," answered Daniel. "We have to get out of here!"

"Daniel," said Rohan, "another's coming. I can hear it slithering through the trees."

The trees?

"Eric!" said Daniel. "He's alone out there!"

There was a scream then as Mollie came hurtling toward them, skidding to a halt at their feet. She looked up at them with dazed, unfocused eyes.

"Wasn't quick enough . . . that time," she said weakly.

The Shade was coming toward them, stretching itself to its full height. It filled the room, robbing it of its light. It might be midafternoon, but it was darkening to full night inside.

The creature reared up like a wave of shadow, but just as it seemed ready to envelop the four of them, it paused. Then it leaned close to Theo. And sniffed.

"What . . . what's it doing?" whispered a terrified Theo. The Shade's featureless face was just inches away from Theo's own.

"I don't know," said Daniel. Why wasn't it attacking? What was it waiting for?

"It recognizes him!" said Rohan.

"I've never seen one of these things in my life!" said Theo. "How can it recognize me?"

"Herman's your granduncle," said Rohan. "Maybe it smells him on you."

"I smell like Herman?" asked Theo, eyes wide.

"You smell like a Plunkett!" answered Rohan. "All families have different smells, if you have the nose for it."

That gave Daniel an idea.

"Theo, tell it to go away," Daniel said.

"What?" Theo asked. The Shade was moving its "nose," if it had such a thing, all over Theo's body. It seemed confused by him, but it wasn't attacking. At least not for now.

"Do it!" said Daniel through gritted teeth. The Shade was obviously confused about whether this young Plunkett was actually a threat, and they needed to act before it made up its mind.

Theo swallowed. A long, thin tendril of Shade stuff was

now flicking in and out of the creature, like a snake's tongue. It couldn't figure out Theo's smell, so now it was resorting to taste.

"Ugh," said Theo, shrinking away from it. "Go . . . get!"

The Shade paused, but it didn't retreat.

"Harsher," said Daniel. "Treat it like . . . treat it like a servant!"

"You get out of here," said Theo. Still the creature did not move. "I said GET OUT OF HERE!"

The Shade suddenly shrank back, like a dog who'd been threatened with a rolled-up newspaper.

"Good," whispered Daniel. "Keep it up."

"Go on," said Theo, growing more confident. "I told you to go!"

The Shade turned and started to slink off toward the door, but it had just reached the exit when there was a crash from above and Eric came bursting though the ceiling. He was covered in some kind of oily black stuff, like the stain Daniel had seen on the street after he'd destroyed one of the things. Eric must've won his fight with the first Shade, but another of the creatures had already appeared on the roof, peering over the jagged hole at the scene below. Eric managed to pull himself up onto his elbows, but just barely. He was struggling to get a second wind.

At the sight of the looming battle, the retreating Shade reversed direction and began closing in on Eric. Now there were two Shades ready to pounce on him. He wouldn't have the strength to defend himself.

If Daniel tried to borrow Eric's power, would he also borrow Eric's weakness? Would he take on his friend's wounds and leave both of them defenseless?

There wasn't time to consider. The two creatures were closing in, like sharks after blood. Daniel had no choice. He started forward . . .

"STOP!" shouted a voice.

Daniel looked over at Theo, who was now standing tall, his finger pointed at the Shades.

"I told you to get away. I told you to disappear. . . . Now, for the very last time, you miserable sacks of garbage, you empty pieces of *nothing . . . BEGONE!*"

Daniel had never heard such command in a voice before, such authority. It was the voice of someone used to giving orders. It was the voice of someone used to being obeyed.

One minute the Shades were crouching, ready to attack, and the next they were gone. It was like a sudden dark cloud had passed over the sun, but now the light had returned. The tree fort was a wreck. There was a gaping hole in the roof, and papers and comics were everywhere. The door was destroyed. But there were no Shades.

Daniel looked at Theo. The boy still looked pale and shaken, but he had also broken into a huge grin.

"Now, just how awesome am I?" he asked.

Theo Plunkett had told the Shades to disappear and they had.

Chapter Twenty
A Late-Night Visit

The Supers agreed to reconvene the next day. After the attack on the tree fort, no one felt safe there anymore. What had once been their sanctuary was now far too isolated, too vulnerable—the doors had literally been blown off. They needed to be around people. And the more, the better.

Examining the facts so far, Daniel began to suspect that for whatever reason, the Shades were drawn to attack when the Supers were all together but isolated from crowds. Although Louisa had been alone in Herman Plunkett's study during that first attack, there had been four other Supers present in the house. The second attack had come when everyone was together on Halloween. And the last at the tree fort. Three attacks. Maybe they'd had it backward, maybe there really wasn't safety in numbers. Small comfort that their enemy was unafraid to face them as a group, but maybe it meant they were safe alone in their beds at night.

Not that anyone really expected to get any sleep. When he got home, Daniel put on his usual brave face for his parents (he'd become good at it since moving to Noble's Green) and sat through dinner and pretended that he hadn't just been attacked by shadow monsters — again. After the meal was over, his parents chased Georgie through his usual bath-time routine while Daniel tried to find some distraction in his homework. He'd hoped to lose himself in the equations of his pre-algebra book, but it was a hopeless battle from the start. He was doodling pictures of Shades in the margins without realizing it. Startled, he tried erasing the frightening scribbles; but the pencil marks just smeared together into one great, messy blob, and no matter how he looked at it, he still saw monsters. Without meaning to, he'd turned his math book into a twisted Rorschach test. If the Shades didn't get him, Ms. Daehler, the pre-algebra teacher, would.

After a little TV with his parents, Daniel washed up and slowly, reluctantly, put on his pajamas. He was just climbing into bed when he heard Mollie's secret knock at the window. Although flying around alone at night was a very dangerous, very foolish, very Mollie Lee type of thing to do, Daniel was glad for the company. In the dark, he could just see her silhouette as she perched on the edge of his bed, her knees hugged tightly to her chest. For a while neither of them said a word. They were just content not to be alone.

After a few minutes she whispered his name.

"Yeah?" he answered.

"Do you think we'll win?"

Daniel let out a deep sigh. He'd been asking himself the same thing, and he had only one honest answer to give.

"This time . . . I don't know," he said. "We're not even sure what we're up against. Not really. Herman might be behind it all, but those Shades are definitely something new."

"I've been thinking about Theo, those Shades, and your . . . powers. They can't all be coincidences, can they?"

Of course Daniel had wondered about this himself, and Eric had said as much. Daniel had looked for a catalyst, a single event to tie all these various disasters to, but the only thing that seemed to link it all together was Theo. He was the common factor in all of this. The only problem with that line of thought was that Daniel's *gut* told him Theo was not behind this. The evidence was stacked against him, and Theo's spoiled-rich-kid persona wasn't helping him any. But Daniel had followed the evidence rather than his instinct once before, and he'd ended up falling into Herman Plunkett's carefully laid trap. While Daniel admired his idol, Sherlock Holmes, for his reliance on deductive reasoning, his own experience had taught him that real life was about more than logic. Daniel chose to go with his gut this time. He chose to trust Theo Plunkett. For a while, at least.

Which left him struggling to come up with an alternative theory as to what the heck was going on.

"I've been turning things over and over in my head, Mollie. And the only thing I know is that someone is trying to keep us off balance. Those attacks that keep coming when we're all together, it's like whoever's behind this doesn't want us to sit around and compare notes. Or maybe when we're all together, it's like putting pizza in front of a starving person—we're irresistible."

"Great," said Mollie. "We're pepperoni."

Daniel smiled, then realized she probably couldn't see him in the dark. But she wasn't waiting for him to respond to her joke—she was already talking.

"The thing is," she was saying, "you should have told us about your powers, Daniel. And you should've told us about the ring."

"I know."

"No, I don't think you do. You are sitting there thinking that you should've told us because that would've been the best way to keep *us* safe. But that's not it at all. That's not even close to why Rohan and I want to stick your head in a toilet and flush it."

Daniel swallowed. That was not a pleasant image.

"Okay, why do you want to flush my . . . why are you upset with me?"

"Because you were hurting and you didn't let us help, you idiot. If we are going to be friends, really truly friends, then you need to stop trying to be everyone's dad."

"I'm not trying to be—"

"Yes, you are. First it was because of the powers thing. You didn't have powers, so you were always, I don't know, trying to prove yourself. To us. To yourself, maybe. And now you've got these new powers and they're scary and you're doing the same thing. You won't let anyone help you. And that's not what friends do, Daniel."

Daniel thought about what she'd just said. He was glad that she couldn't see his eyes in the dark—that way she couldn't see the look on his face. He was in pain. He was scared. Scared of his new abilities, and what they might mean. And he was scared of the Shades. He'd been dealing with all this on his own. He'd believed he could. But he'd been wrong.

"Sorry," he whispered.

"Apology accepted. But only because you're a boy and can't help but be mostly brain damaged to begin with."

Daniel wiped his eyes. Because of the dark, he couldn't be sure, but he thought Mollie was doing the same thing.

"So, tomorrow," he said, "when we see the others, can I get your help?"

"Help with what?"

"I'll need your help convincing them what needs to be done next."

"Okay," said Mollie. "Your ridiculous schemes worked out the last time we faced the Shroud, so I'll give you the benefit of the doubt. What's the plan?"

"We take the fight to them. Theo's scientist buddies are

bound to discover those caves, so let's beat them to it. We go back to the quarry. All of us. The Old Quarry was the Shroud's lair, and it's the only lead we have, so if there's something there, I want to find it before those scientists do."

"And if the Shades come after us again?"

"I'm counting on it," said Daniel. "That's why we're bringing Theo along. He was pretty useful against them this time."

"So he'll just order them to shoo again?"

"No, this time Theo tells them to take us to their leader."

"And if they decide they don't want to take orders from Junior?"

Daniel didn't have an answer for that possibility. The truth was they would be taking a terrible risk, but Daniel was tired of sitting around and waiting for the Shades to attack again.

Mollie sighed. Daniel could just picture her rolling her eyes and shaking her head at his usual stupidity.

"That's your plan?" she asked. "Walk us back into the one place in all of Noble's Green we don't want to go, and offer us up to the Shades on a silver platter?"

"Yep. I guess it is."

"Cool," she said, and Daniel could hear the smile in her voice. "I'm in."

Chapter Twenty-One
The Master of the Shades

The town library seemed a safe place to meet. It was private enough that they could make plans without being overheard, but it was still public enough that the Shades would be unlikely to try another attack. Daniel, Eric, Rohan, and Mollie met there after school to finalize their plans. Theo had agreed to meet them at the quarry.

The Supers assembled beneath the statue of Johnny Noble overlooking the library entrance. This Johnny was depicted as the town folk hero, and instead of the domino mask of the comics, he wore a coonskin cap and full beard. In his arms he carried a small child, one of the St. Alban's orphans he'd rescued from the historic fire. In its own way,

Johnny's story as town hero was as sensationalized as the comic-book fictions Herman Plunkett had dreamed up all those years ago. Local legend had it that Johnny had charged into the burning orphanage again and again, heedless of the dangerous smoke and flames. The statue captured that strength, that bravery, well. But in the photos Daniel had seen, the few actual pictures of the real man himself, he'd been gaunt and haunted-looking. A poor, scared trapper who'd been caught up in big events. Too big for a simple mountain man. It was no wonder Johnny disappeared even as his fame spread and his legend grew.

The only things about that statue that seemed genuine to Daniel were the eyes. Whoever had created the sculpture, he'd gotten that one detail right. Johnny had a piercing stare in the old photographs. Even in Herman's comic books. Even here, carved in stone.

Daniel's plan was simple. Theo had informed them that the excavation project always wrapped up before sundown. This being Noble's Green, after-hours security was light— just a single guard who did a drive-by check every few hours or so. Theo used his dad's email account to give the guard an unexpected night off so they were guaranteed not to be bothered. The Supers would draw out the Shades, and with Theo's help the creatures would lead them to the real villain behind all this. Whether it was Herman or something entirely new, they'd find out tonight.

As they were setting out from the library rendezvous, Louisa and Rose showed up. Louisa came walking up the steps, while Rose materialized out of thin air. They were lucky that no one seemed to be paying attention.

"We're going too!" said Rose. "Mollie told Louisa and Louisa told me, and so we're going with you to fight the bad guys."

Daniel shot Mollie a look.

"What?" asked Mollie. "Louisa asked what I was doing tonight and I told her the truth. I didn't invite the invisible girl along!"

"Look, Louisa," Daniel said. "This might be really dangerous, and . . . well, now that you don't have your powers . . . I mean, you don't have to come."

He knew this sounded ridiculous coming from him, but he wanted to give Louisa an out. An excuse to say no. She'd stuck with them all out of friendship, but she'd never really wanted to be a Super. She shouldn't feel obligated to put herself in danger now.

But she said nothing. She just stood there, staring at her shoes.

"Louisa?" said Daniel.

"Go on," said Rose. "Tell them!"

"Tell us what?" asked Rohan.

"I never . . . I didn't know it was Daniel," she said. "Otherwise I wouldn't have. I thought I could blame it on the Shroud."

"Blame what?" asked Daniel.

"She fibbed!" said Rose. "She told me so!"

"I lied, Daniel," Louisa said. "I lied to you all."

Then Louisa looked around to make sure no one else was looking and put her hand into the statue of Johnny Noble. *Into* the statue. Then she pulled it out again as easily as if she'd been dipping her hand into a sink full of water.

"You do have your powers!" said Eric.

"I didn't at first!" said Louisa. "At the tree fort, that was for real. But the next morning they came back. I just . . . I don't like being this way! I thought I could be normal. At least everyone would think I was normal."

She looked up at Daniel and her eyes were glistening with tears. They were such pretty eyes.

"I'm sorry, Daniel," she said. "I didn't know you'd blame yourself. I really do hate lying, but it just . . . seemed so much easier this way."

Daniel didn't know what to say. He'd felt such shame about Louisa. He'd been carrying it around with him for weeks, and to learn now that she'd been lying all along . . .

Just as he'd lied. She'd had her reasons just as he'd had his, misguided though they might have been.

"It's all right," said Daniel. "I understand."

"Well," said Rohan, "that explains our outlier. That's good, because with such a small sample, even one statistical anomaly can be—"

"Can it, Rohan," said Mollie. "We get why you did it, Louisa. But why are you here now?"

"I don't like my powers. I hate them. But I don't want those . . . creatures coming for Rose. If I can help you, I will."

217

"Of course," said Daniel. "You're one of us. Always."

"Can we go now?" asked Rose. "'Cause if we wait much longer I'm gonna have to pee again."

True to his word, Theo was waiting for them at the quarry. He joined them as Daniel opened his backpack to reveal flashlights, rope, and other pieces of equipment. It paid to be prepared when you were planning a late-night expedition to an abandoned quarry haunted by shadow monsters.

"So, you guys do this sort of thing often?" asked Theo. "Like a tween spelunking club?"

"Well, only . . . ," Daniel began. "Yeah, I guess we do."

"And I thought I was living dangerously taking my dad's car for a joyride."

"You were," said Daniel.

"And what do you think we'll find? Old Uncle Herman in his super-villain's hideout?"

"I know it sounds crazy, Theo. But yes, I do. Him or something else. It's possible we're facing something we haven't seen yet."

Theo took a deep breath and let it out slowly. "I gotta tell you, I know those things, those shadows, weren't human. I mean I saw them with my own eyes, but I'm still having a hard time wrapping my head around all this. How'd you handle it? When you first found out about all this . . . stuff?"

"I handled it worse than you," Daniel answered. "You're holding it together much better than I did."

The older boy smiled at him. "That's it. Appeal to my ego. I think you've got me figured out, Corrigan."

The Old Quarry didn't look abandoned anymore. The layer of loose, broken rubble had been cleared away and a complex scaffolding of support struts had been erected to shore up the unstable sides. As the sun went down and the temperature dropped, small trails of steam started to rise from the diggers and dump trucks that sat cooling near the edge of the quarry pit.

Soon the scientists would begin delving into the mountain proper, and Daniel knew what they'd find there. The only thing standing between Dr. Lewis and the Shroud's lair was a few more feet of dirt and rock. Daniel was determined to get there first.

They stood at the edge of the pit, seven children on a monster hunt. Eric out front, Mollie by his side. Rohan wasn't even looking down at their destination—he was scanning the line of trees or perhaps looking for something even farther away. Behind him stood Louisa, who looked like she might be holding her sister's hand. Rose had turned invisible before they'd even reached the mountain, so it was hard to tell for sure. Theo and Daniel brought up the rear several yards back from the others, maybe because they were the ones least trusted, though each for very different reasons.

Eric gestured to the far side of the newly excavated quarry. "The caves were over there someplace, right?"

Daniel nodded and pointed to a tree on the far side of the pit's edge. "See that split oak? Train your eyes on that and then follow it down all the way to the bottom. I used it as a landmark. The cave's almost directly underneath."

"Something's moving around down there," said Rohan. "It's muffled beneath the dirt and rock, but I definitely hear it."

"You sure you aren't just eavesdropping on a family of moles?" asked Mollie.

"I hear voices," he answered. "Whispers. I can't make out what they're saying."

Theo gave Daniel a look. "Can he really hear that?" he asked softly.

"Don't underestimate him," said Daniel. "If Rohan says someone's down there, then someone's down there."

"So Mollie and I will go first and check it out," said Eric. "Rohan, you keep a watch; the rest of you wait here."

"Aye-aye, Captain," came a little voice out of nowhere. Rose.

"And you," said Eric, turning to Theo. "Are you up for this?"

"I'm not along for the scintillating conversation," answered Theo. "I'll do my part."

Eric nodded. Then he and Mollie began floating down to the quarry floor. As they went, snippets of their conversation echoed back to Daniel and the others.

"What the heck's *scinti-whatever* mean?" Eric was saying.

"Just drop it," answered Mollie.

The two flew slowly, doing cautious circles around the quarry's perimeter. The last time they'd come here to fight the Shroud, the whole place had been overgrown with years of underbrush, even a few small trees. Now at least the area was freshly cleared. There was no place for anyone to hide. Or so they thought.

Rohan, of course, spotted them first. The shadows that were too long, that were moving on their own. They snaked across the quarry floor and up the walls until they began pooling together in Mollie and Eric's path. If Rohan hadn't shouted a warning, the two of them would've been caught surprised. As it was, they had only a few seconds to pull up before flying into a pocket of darkness that had assembled in front of them.

Mollie and Eric sped away from the sudden ambush, but another group of wriggling, menacing Shades had formed on the opposite wall. And another, and another. Every shadow in that pit was now moving of its own accord. Groups of them were peeling away from the walls now, fluttering about the quarry like a flock of panicked birds. Eric and Mollie were in the middle of it all.

"Get out of there!" Daniel shouted. They weren't prepared for this: there had to be hundreds of them down there. Hundreds.

"No! Leave them alone," shouted Theo, pushing his way past Daniel. "Stop! I command all of you to stop!"

Theo's voice echoed across the empty quarry and the shadows heard him. In an instant they stopped swirling about Eric and Mollie, but they didn't retreat either. Daniel's friends were boxed in by Shades, but at least they'd broken off their attack.

Theo looked over his shoulder back at Daniel and chuckled. "Looks like I've still got the touch!"

Daniel joined Theo at the quarry's edge. A couple of the Shades had drifted off from the main pack and were hesitantly approaching, but they appeared submissive, even docile, in the presence of their new master.

"Easy, boys," said Theo as two of them got a bit too close for comfort. "That's far enough. Now, I guess, take us to your master."

In answer came the sound of wind rustling through dried leaves. It might have been their voices, but there was no way they could make it out. Even Rohan shook his head in confusion.

"Too many at once," he said.

"Theo, on second thought this might not be a good idea," said Daniel. He'd expected a handful of these creatures to deal with, not an army.

But Theo waved him off. He was too busy getting into the part.

"This isn't decision by committee!" he shouted down at the Shades. "I said I wanted something done and I want it done now!" Theo turned and winked at Daniel. "That's my dad's corporate-speak."

It seemed to be working. One by one, the Shades drifted away. The two nearest to Theo turned and flew down to the base of the quarry and began to dig up the earth directly below Daniel's split oak tree. The rest of the creatures formed a semicircle around the Supers, urging them down the sloping trail that led to the quarry floor. They weren't being attacked, but the Shades weren't ready to let them run free either.

By the time Daniel and the other walkers made it to the bottom, the Shades had finished with their hole, exposing a half-buried cave entrance beneath. Eric and Mollie were waiting for them on the floor, nervously eying the Shades that stood nearby, observing—or more likely guarding—the two kids.

The Supers stood at the bottom of the Old Quarry, surrounded by an army of Shades, and prepared to enter Herman Plunkett's Shroud-Cave. Surrounded by a hundred Shades, Daniel thought again that maybe his plan wasn't so sound, but they had no other choice but to follow it through. These Shades were obeying Theo, but only up to a point. They hadn't relaxed their guard, and though Theo was ordering them around like a pack of whipped dogs, to Daniel's eyes they looked more like hounds straining against their leashes. He was afraid what would happen if they broke free.

This time Daniel went first. He flicked on his flashlight and peered into the freshly dug hole. Several feet down he spotted the giant stone door that marked Herman's Shroud-Cave. It was split down the middle, one half of it missing. A moist breeze blew out of the darkness beyond. Daniel remembered that breeze. He remembered the smell of these caves, the chalky air, and what it felt like to be held prisoner in the darkness, bound and helpless. With an effort he willed himself to relax. He took a deep, calming breath and pushed that terrifying memory away. They had a purpose to focus on, and he needed to stay calm.

The hole in the door was just big enough to squeeze through. A grown man probably wouldn't have been able to manage it. Once upon a time this door had rolled on hinges, but that mechanism had been destroyed in the cave-in. The tunnel was wider on the other side, and two people could comfortably stand side by side, but Daniel was still startled when Mollie appeared next to him. He'd expected Eric to take the lead, but Mollie must have beaten him to it.

"Just like old times," she said. They'd been the ones to first discover this cave together, although the memory didn't exactly inspire confidence. They'd barely escaped with their lives.

Eric came through next, followed by Rohan.

"Theo's barking orders out there, and those Shades seem less and less happy about it," said Rohan. "He's getting a little *too* into his role."

"Then we'd better hurry," said Daniel, and they began creeping along into the darkness.

They'd traveled only a few yards when Daniel heard movement, a kind of shifting sound, and his first thought was that the tunnel might be unstable after the cave-in. But then he realized that the sound was actually coming from shapes that were moving alongside them. Shades were tracking them, escorting them farther into the darkness. They were pulling him and Mollie along but seemed to be slowing Eric and Rohan down. The Shades were keeping them a safe distance apart from each other.

Whispers as soft as rustling sheets echoed around them as they went.

"They're saying my name," Mollie said, her eyes wide.

"Don't be silly," said Daniel, although he too thought he heard someone calling to him. But he wouldn't admit it. Their minds were just playing tricks on them.

They were nearly to the first chamber, the wide cave where Herman Plunkett had held Daniel captive, when Mollie cried out. She was pointing at the dark and saying something, but she was speaking so fast that her words were little more than buzzing to Daniel's ears.

"Slow down! Mollie, what's wrong?" Daniel shone his light at the Shades, but they continued to float harmlessly by. They kept pace with them, but there was nothing new or threatening that he could see.

Mollie was crying. Daniel wanted to reach out and reassure her that everything was okay, but he dared not risk touching her. Even a gentle pat on the shoulder could leave her powerless.

"Mollie?" he asked.

"One of them . . . got close," she said as she struggled to pull herself together. "Oh, Daniel! It showed me its face! I saw its face!"

Daniel aimed his flashlight's beam directly at the nearest Shade. Nothing but indistinct blackness.

"Mollie, I don't see anything."

"I did! The Shade . . . it was the one saying my name. It was Michael!"

Michael. Michael had been Mollie's best friend before the Shroud had stolen his memories. Daniel had spoken to him. He was a sad case, a little lost perhaps but physically fine. Daniel even shared gym class with him, and he'd seen him that very day and he'd been perfectly normal. Michael wasn't a Shade.

"Look, Mollie . . ."

"Don't say it!" Mollie wiped her nose. "Don't you dare say that I'm imagining things, because I saw Michael! Somehow . . . he's one of them. He's out there!"

She meant it. Whatever else was going on, Mollie wasn't prone to hysterics — she believed what she'd seen. Daniel nodded slowly. Whether she was mistaken or not, there was nothing they could do about it now. The Shades were gathering around them, urging them on, deeper into the cave. Behind them, Eric and Rohan were calling ahead, asking why they'd stopped. Obviously, they hadn't seen anything either.

The tunnel opened into the Shroud-Cave itself. An eerie green glow shone through the opening, causing real shadows to dance among the slithering Shades. This large chamber was left over from the prehistoric people who'd made these caves their home — the large wall of cave paintings was proof of that. But Herman Plunkett had colonized it, adding his own pictures to the ancient mural. The cave paintings were a history of a people who'd been seduced and then destroyed by the power of the Witch Fire meteor—a hunk of the same comet that had passed by Noble's Green when Herman had been just a little orphan child. Herman's contribution to this ages-old mural was to record his own history with a photo of every child he'd ever robbed. Picture by picture, it was a wall of shame and terror.

Now, as Daniel entered the room for the second time in his life, he saw a new addition to the mural wall. Tied up in a web of what looked like solid darkness—Shade stuff—hung Herman Plunkett. He was bound up like a fly, dangling helpless in a web of shadow that stretched the length of the large chamber's ceiling. Herman's beady eyes squinted against the glare of the pulsing green pendant around his neck as he tried to focus on Daniel and his friends.

He spoke, his voice croaky and broken, like someone desperately in need of a drink of water. "Help me," he said.

Herman wasn't the Shades' master. He was their prisoner.

"Daniel, what . . . what is that?" Mollie whispered, but Daniel didn't have the words to answer. After all, what they'd found deep inside the Shroud-Cave was an entirely new kind of horror.

And somewhere in Daniel's head another voice was saying his name. It was the memory of a dream. Or a nightmare . . .

"Daniel, what are you doing?" asked Mollie. "Daniel, stop!"

But Daniel didn't stop. He couldn't. He wasn't even sure

why he was moving, why he was walking toward that web. It had something to do with the voice, with that nagging itch in the back of his brain.

The voice was talking to him. Telling him to take something out of his pocket, something he'd been carrying for a long, long time.

Out of curiosity, he looked down. There in his palm was a small ring of black rock. The emerald light of the cave caught the polished stone and danced along its edges like firelight. It was beautiful.

Chapter Twenty-Two
The Black Ring

Herman Plunkett was alive, but that looked to be small comfort for him. His normally thin face was almost skeletal now, and his eyes burned feverishly inside their sunken sockets. The rest of his body was bound up tight and dangled in the middle of a web of the Shades' making. Even without the benefit of flashlights Daniel would have been able to see here in the cave, because of the sickly glow that spilled out of the meteorite pendant dangling from Herman's neck. The Shroud pendant was split down the middle, and from that crack oozed forth the grainy light and something else — Shades. The shadows were drifting in and out of the stone, flitting about here and there along the web, testing and strengthening parts of their trap. They were intent on keeping the Shroud, and his stone, around for a long, long time.

"And so . . . we meet again, my dear Mr. Holmes," said Plunkett, a tired half smile forming on his cracked lips.

Plunkett's words seemed even weaker now compared to the other voice Daniel was listening to. The Shroud was in his head.

"Bring me the ring, Daniel. Bring it to me."

"What the . . . ? No way!" said Eric as he and Rohan stumbled into the chamber. Behind them, Daniel could hear, Theo was still back in the tunnel, barking orders at Shades. Daniel found himself getting annoyed. Why couldn't everyone just shut up and let the Shroud talk?

As he started forward again, Mollie appeared in front of him. She put her body between him and Herman, blocking his line of sight.

"Daniel!" she said. "What's wrong with you? Why do you have that ring?"

"I . . . I've had it all along," he said. "I've been carrying it around in my pocket. Funny I couldn't remember until now."

"Use it," said the Shroud in his head. *"All you have to do is touch her. Take her speed and free me!"*

He reached out a hand toward her.

"Daniel!" Mollie shouted. "Snap out of it before I give you a bloody nose!"

Daniel hesitated for a second, his hand outstretched. What was he supposed to do?

"Huh?" he said.

Herman's pendant flared bright, illuminating the cave like a lightning flash. When the spots in Daniel's vision cleared, he was back in the nightmare, caught in the throes of his wrestling match with the Shroud. The flesh of his fingers was blackening in the flame; he could smell his skin burning. The Shroud was shouting in his ear.

Then, just as quickly, Daniel was back in the cave, only he was flat on his back and staring up at the ceiling. His nose throbbed and his eyes were tearing up from the pain. Both Mollie and Eric were standing over him.

"Sorry about the nose," said Mollie. "But I warned you."

Daniel gently examined his nose. It smarted, and there was a tiny spot of blood on his fingers. The black ring was on the ground next to him. How did that get there?

"You were freaking us out," said Eric. "Like a zombie boy. Mollie smacked you in the face with your own backpack."

Daniel sat up and saw the Shades hovering in a circle around them . . . waiting. For what, Daniel didn't know. It reminded him of animals gathering for a feeding.

The black ring gleamed green in the dark. Daniel pointed at it.

"How did . . . ?" Daniel asked.

"You pulled it out of your pocket," said Eric. "Don't you remember?"

Daniel looked at Herman, hanging there so helpless, so weak and frail. But his eyes were powerful. They were hungry eyes, and they were focused on that ring like it was a last meal. That look scared Daniel more than all the Shades.

"Mollie, give me my backpack," he said.

Mollie handed him his backpack, her eyes still wary.

"It's okay," said Daniel.

He threw the backpack over the ring and managed to scoop it up, careful not to let it touch his skin before he zipped it inside. With the ring buried in the deep folds of his backpack, he felt immediately better. The pain in his nose actually helped him clear his head, focusing on it helped to drown out the Shroud's whispers. He dared to face Plunkett's stare.

"What . . . what did you do to me?" asked Daniel.

Plunkett didn't answer. Instead the old man shifted his gaze to let it drift over them all. His skinny bald head used to remind Daniel of a turtle's, but now it looked more like a snake weaving back and forth, ready to strike at any second.

"So, you've brought the whole gang," said Plunkett. "The super-kids and my watery little wisp of a grandnephew, eh? Is that him I hear back there? What a joyous reunion we'll all have. You, me, and *them*!" Herman cocked his head to indicate the gathering shadows.

"The ring," said Daniel. "I've been carrying it all this time. The sleepwalking . . ."

"You're strong, I'll give you that," said Plunkett. "You fought me at first, never fully giving in, but I am stronger. It was only a matter of time.

"Use it, Daniel!" he continued. "Together we can stop them! You can free me!"

"What did you do to me?" Daniel shouted, his voice echoing through the cave.

Herman finally dropped the forced smile—it looked as if he hurt too much to keep it up for long—and locked eyes with Daniel.

"I'm losing strength by the minute, Daniel," said Herman. "They keep me alive yet weakened. But I'm not totally powerless, not yet, and I've always been particularly good with dreams."

"Daniel?" said Mollie. "What the heck's he talking about? Why were you carrying that ring in your pocket?"

"Nightmares," said Daniel, realization slowly dawning on him. "In my nightmares I'm still fighting the Shroud."

"Our battle never ended," said Herman. "You only thought you'd won."

"Daniel," said Eric, "what's going on?"

"He's been in my head all this time," said Daniel. "In my dreams. He manipulated the memories of Supers for generations, and somehow he found a way into my head. Maybe he did something to me when I was his prisoner; I don't know. But he's been controlling me, making me use the ring without even knowing I was doing it. . . ."

They were interrupted by Theo, emerging from the tunnel with Louisa. The Shades were crowding the two of them, mobbing Theo like a pack of fawning admirers. But there was something menacing in their attention too.

"Hey, not so close, okay?" Theo was saying to the Shades as they pressed in around him. "I'm getting claustrophobic here."

When Theo spotted Herman dangling from his web, the boy's bluster instantly vanished. Despite what Eric had said about Theo, the young Plunkett was not dumb. He was as clever as they came, and he understood the new situation immediately. He saw what the Shades had done to his relative and he realized the danger that put him in as well. Daniel saw that the trick was to keep him from panicking.

"It's okay, Theo," Daniel said. "Just stay calm."

But Theo wasn't listening. He was already trying to back out of the cave, only to find the way blocked by Shades. He shouted at them to move, to clear a path, but they weren't obeying, and his voice had lost the deep bass of command that he'd been using. A sharp edge of fear crept in as he began insulting them. He shouted obscenities as they closed in, cutting off his escape.

"It's the powers," said Herman. "Powers make them angry, and having you all here, together, in their home, it's only a matter of time. . . . But Daniel can stop them now! He can save you all by giving me my ring!"

Herman Plunkett was right—the Shades were getting agitated. The dark corners of the cave were alive with roiling shapes, and Daniel could spot the faces now as the Shades revealed themselves to them: a chubby boy with braces; a little girl with her hair done up in ringlets and bows, her expression a snarl of rage. The Shades pulled back their shadowy disguises to expose the faces of children twisted with hate.

"They're just kids!" said Louisa. "How can they be kids?"

"Let's back up," said Daniel. "Slowly."

Daniel and the others began moving backward toward the tunnel entrance, careful not to make any sudden movements. But Herman saw their retreat and began squirming, pulling against his bonds and trying to wiggle his way to freedom.

"No!" he cried. "You can't leave me here with them!"

One of the Shades—the one with the chubby boy's face—pounced on him. The boy used a long black claw to rake Herman across the face. Although the attack drew no blood, the old man shrieked in pain and was left whimpering, the last of his energy expended.

"The ring, Daniel," moaned Herman. "Give me the ring. . . ."

The cave exploded into chaos. Theo was already making his dash for the tunnel leading out when the Shades attacked. Like a swarm of rats, they closed in on the Supers.

The battle would have been over then if it hadn't been for Eric and Mollie. As soon as the Shade children began to surge forward, the very instant they started to peel off the walls, the two fliers went into action. Eric shouted something at Mollie that sounded like "Spin and sweep!" In the close-quartered cave they couldn't really get airborne, but Mollie had just enough room to twirl, which at super-speed turned her into a girl-sized twister. The force of her minicyclone blew the Shades into the rock walls or bounced them off each other. Those that weren't stunned by Mollie's sudden attack looked up to find they were being punched in the head. Eric's brawn and Mollie's speed. For the moment, at least, the Supers had the advantage.

But it couldn't last. They were far too outnumbered. They had a few seconds at most before the Shades could regroup and overwhelm them. Rohan was already leading Louisa and Rose out through the tunnel, following Theo. If they moved quickly, they had a chance of making it out before the Shades counterattacked. They had a chance, which was why Daniel was so surprised to find himself running *away* from safety. In the opposite direction, toward the Shades. Toward Herman Plunkett.

But this time he wasn't listening to the Shroud's voice. He was in control.

The Shroud stuff was not sticky, like he'd expected, but it was thick, and Herman was wound up tight in a web of it. Herman watched as Daniel pulled at the black strands, his face ghastly in the green ghost light of his cracked pendant. Daniel shoved the backpack with the ring in it over his shoulder, careful to keep it out of the old man's reach.

"Always the hero," said Herman.

"Shut up," replied Daniel as he yanked at the webbing. It was coming loose, but slowly.

"What are you doing?" shouted Eric, appearing at his side. He kicked at a Shade with the face of a red-haired boy with glasses.

"I need Herman!" said Daniel. "I need answers!"

Eric didn't argue. There wasn't time. He grabbed the web with both hands and yanked. The cave split with the sound of tearing, and that was followed by a loud, wailing moan issuing from the mouth of every Shade at once. It was the first time Daniel had heard their voices clearly, and the sound of it made him want to curl up in a ball and hide. He wanted to cover his ears or pull out his hair. A hundred fingernails on a chalkboard.

But Eric had succeeded in freeing Herman, throwing him over his shoulder as easily as he would a sack of potatoes—and about as gently.

"Now can we go?" asked Eric as he eyed the Shades closing in.

Daniel didn't even have time to nod, because the next thing he knew, he was being dragged/pulled out of the cave by Mollie Lee.

"You can't even run away when you're supposed to," she was saying as she yanked him backward, his butt skidding along the rocky floor. "We are leaving!" she shouted as the two of them came flying out of the hole and into the cool night air. It felt good against his face for about two seconds before he was deposited, rather roughly, onto the leaf-strewn forest floor. The smell of fresh pine air was quickly buried beneath a noseful of dirt.

But he was free of the cave, and for the moment, at least, he was safe.

Chapter Twenty-Three
Night Terrors

The first thing Daniel did was to get a head count of his friends. Mollie, Rohan, Louisa, Theo . . .

"Rose?" he asked.

"Here!" said the empty air.

"Where's Eric?"

In answer came the sound of rocks breaking in the distance. A lot of rocks. Then Eric appeared above the trees with Herman in his arms.

"I closed the tunnel behind us," he said. "Though I doubt that'll hold them for long."

Eric tossed Herman onto the ground, then wiped his

hands on his pants. He looked like he'd just finished handling a snake.

Herman lay in the dirt, gasping for breath and watching them all. The green light bleeding off his broken pendant had dimmed to a weak glow, little brighter than a firefly. But it was enough to catch Plunkett's glassy eyes. They shone like narrow mirrors in the dark. He was worse than a snake, Daniel thought. So much worse.

Theo broke the silence.

"So, you're not dead?" he said, arching his eyebrows at his granduncle.

"No," answered Herman.

"And those creatures back there . . . those Shade thingies, they're because of you?"

"Your side of the family always had a knack for stating the obvious," said Herman, his mouth turned up in a sneer.

Theo nodded and thought for a minute. "You know what?"

"What?"

"You're a real jackass."

Herman Plunkett snarled at the comment but barely glanced in his grandnephew's direction.

Daniel stood, brushing himself off. He held the backpack with the ring far out of Plunkett's reach.

"All right, I need answers," Daniel said. "You used something on me, some kind of mind control."

"Some days you wouldn't let me in," said Herman. "You fought me, but in your dreams you were most vulnerable. Even from my prison, I could reach into your dreams. I have a lot of experience with those." Herman smiled. "And your dreams haunt you, don't they? Your subconscious is at war with itself because you won't accept what you are!"

"Was it the ring?" asked Daniel. "I slept just a few feet from that ring for all those months—maybe that allowed you access to my dreams. Allowed you to get into my head!"

"Wouldn't you like to know?" said Herman.

"Hold on, hold on," said Eric, stepping between the two of them. "So when you took our powers, Daniel, it was the ring all the time?"

Daniel nodded. "I don't have any powers. I'm not a Super. Never was."

"And never will be!" said Herman Plunkett. "Accept it! But you can still be special. You've had only a taste of that ring's power! I spent a lifetime's fortune scraping together enough meteorite to forge it, but it's still just a fragment, an imperfect piece of the whole. Unlike my pendant, its power-stealing effect is only temporary, but with time and the proper training, we might be able to—"

"Can I just punch him now?" asked Mollie.

"No," said Daniel. "Don't bother. He's desperate. His own meteor stone is broken, useless. If he had any power left, he'd have freed himself from those Shades. I think he used up the last of it messing with my head."

Herman glowered at them even as he seemed to curl in

closer to himself. Herman was free, thought Daniel, but he still wasn't in control. This had to be an intolerable situation for the almighty Shroud.

"Now what?" asked Louisa. "Do we just wait here or—"

Louisa's words were drowned out by a new sound, the rumble of shifting earth and stone. The resulting explosion was far away, much farther away than Daniel had expected, which meant that Mollie and Eric had gotten them all well clear of the quarry. But it was close enough for Daniel to still feel it in his teeth, and his ears rang with the sound. He started to say something, to suggest that they run or hide, when Rohan motioned for him to be quiet. He was pointing up at the sky.

Even against the night sky they were visible—a swirling flock of Shades twisting and turning like a funnel reaching to heaven, blocking out the stars. As the Supers watched, they spread out overhead, flying back and forth, high above the treetops.

"The Shades!" said Louisa.

"Oh, yes," said Plunkett. "When my pendant was damaged, they began to escape. One by one, they drifted free. Shadows given substance by the power of the Witch Fire meteorite."

"But what *are* they?" asked Louisa. "They're more than just shadows. In the cave they showed us their faces. Children's faces!"

"Every child he's stolen from," said Daniel. "That's what they are. You've stolen the memories and powers of how many kids over the years, Herman? Hundreds? You took their powers, but what happened to all those memories?"

Herman Plunkett looked again at Daniel, and for a moment there was nothing but cold, calculating clarity in those reptilian eyes.

"Why, the memories lived on in the pendant, of course," he said. "Kept safe for years and years inside my beautiful meteor stone. Echoes. Just Shades of who they once were, but each one as black and hard as the stone itself. As black as my broken pendant."

"Somehow the meteor stored all those memories, and they became like ghosts or something," said Daniel. "They were trapped for all those years, but after the pendant cracked . . . they got loose."

"He's right," said Mollie. "I saw Michael in the cave. He was one of them."

"Michael?" asked Eric.

"But it's not him," said Daniel. "Not really. Michael is alive and well. Mollie saw a part of who Michael used to be, maybe. She saw Michael's shadow."

"Corrupted by the power of the Shroud," said Rohan.

"Well, they can't find us," Eric said, pointing to the twirling mass of shadows disappearing into the distance. "We must've been hidden by the trees."

"They weren't looking for you anymore," said Herman.

"Well then, what are they doing?" asked Eric. "They're your little monsters, so where are they going?"

But Daniel knew the answer before Herman even spoke.

They were headed south, to the other side of the mountain. Toward civilization.

"They're going to Noble's Green, aren't they?" asked Daniel.

Herman nodded slowly. "Your visit was a reminder of the lives they once lived. And to a Shade a memory—any memory—is painful. Your powers just made the memory worse. Up to now only a few have been bold enough, angry enough, to haunt the town. But tonight you shook the hornet's nest. They're coming home, and they are angry."

"They're going to attack Noble's Green?" asked Louisa.

"Undoubtedly," answered Herman. "I'd hoped to prevent all this." He turned his eyes on Daniel. "I knew Daniel wasn't up to the task by himself. So I urged him to bring me the ring. It can stop them. Trap them again. That's why I visited his dreams. I needed his help whether he wanted to give it to me or not."

"You controlled me!" shouted Daniel. His anger welled up in him so quickly that he couldn't contain it. He didn't want to. "You manipulated my memories! You made me use that thing like a puppet! I didn't know what I was doing!"

"You didn't know? Or you didn't *want* to know?" Herman sat upright now and had regained a bit of his old menace. The look he shot at Daniel was pure contempt.

"It was an easy thing," Herman said. "Little Maggie Johns was a twelve-year-old girl with the power to enter dreams. Not a terribly threatening power at first glance, until you realize that dreams are the keys to the subconscious.

243

Control dreams and you can control a person's mind. Plant suggestions, influence decisions. In her hands it was a dangerous thing. But I took her power, and it has served me well over these many years.

"We have a bond, Daniel, whether you want to admit it or not. I found that I could connect with you, reach out to you from my prison, to your sleeping self. Then it was an easy thing to plant suggestions, to set up mental blocks in your mind to make you forget what you were doing. Just carrying the ring in your pocket was enough to let you access its power, and I knew you'd bring it to me eventually. Your own pathetically guilty heart kept you from seeing it. You lied to yourself, Daniel. You hid from your true potential just like you always do."

"You tried to make me into a monster," said Daniel. "Just like *you* always do."

Herman sighed and closed his eyes. "And that brings us to the here and now. We've both played our parts, *hero*. I've revealed my grand plans, my diabolical schemes, like a good little super-villain should. . . ." His eyes popped back open and he glared at Daniel. "Now, what are you going to do about it? Do you have the will to do what it takes to save your friends? To save Noble's Green?"

"All right," said Eric. "We don't have time for this. Herman's bad, Daniel's good, and I think we can all agree on that. Daniel, is this old guy still in your head?"

"No. At least I don't think so," said Daniel. The Shroud's whispers were silent. The itch in the back of his brain was

244

gone, for now. He held up the backpack. "Now that I'm on the lookout for it, I think as long as the ring's in here and I don't go to sleep, I'm okay."

"Good," said Eric. Then he turned to Herman. "And you said this ring *could* stop the Shades?"

"Yes," answered Herman. "I believe so. My pendant is too damaged to be of much use, but the ring is an unbroken fragment of the meteor stone. It's not nearly as powerful as mine was, but it should be able to trap them again."

"Guys, it's starting," said Rohan, listening. "The Shades have reached the town."

No sooner had Rohan spoken than they all heard the distant sound of an explosion. Something bad was happening.

Eric nodded. "Time to go. I can carry Daniel and Rohan, but that's it."

"I can take Rose," said Mollie.

"What about Louisa?" asked Rose.

"I can take her," said Theo. "Louisa *and* my dear old uncle."

"You?" said Louisa. "How?"

Theo smiled at her as he held up a ring of shiny car keys. "What? You didn't think I *walked* here, did you?"

Chapter Twenty-Four
The Ambush

It was obvious something was wrong as soon as they cleared the trees. Mount Noble had always been a bit fearful, a craggy spike in the middle of the gentle Pennsylvania hills. But for Daniel the mountain was always tempered by the pleasant sight of the town nestled beneath its shadow. In the evenings, the lights of Noble's Green shone like a warm patch of stars against the black forest.

But not tonight. Except for the glow of some traffic along the main roads, the town was completely dark. It was hard to tell where the forest ended and the lightless houses began.

Worryingly, they did spy a number of glowing fires. On

the outskirts of town they flickered orange and yellow, and a parade of red flashing fire trucks was speeding toward them.

"Electrical transformers," Rohan shouted against the wind. "The Shades must've blown them up to knock out the town's power."

As Eric flew them into town, Daniel hugged his backpack to his chest, mindful of the terrible weapon inside. He still couldn't believe that he'd been using the ring all this time, his subconscious under the influence of the Shroud himself. The thought of the old monster creeping around inside his head made Daniel physically ill. He'd manipulated Daniel into bringing the ring right to him, hoping it would give him the power to escape the Shades. But he hadn't counted on Daniel's showing up with all the Supers in tow. Once again he'd tried to drive a wedge between Daniel and his friends, and this time he'd nearly succeeded. Divide and conquer was the Herman Plunkett way.

Daniel cringed to remember the night he'd visited the quarry alone. It had been dumb luck that he'd found Clay and Bud there. If they hadn't been in the way, if he'd gone on to explore the quarry alone and actually found Herman . . . Perhaps the Shades would have gotten him. Perhaps Herman would've. He wasn't sure which would've been worse.

Eric set the two of them down just outside Daniel's neighborhood. Now that they were closer, they saw tiny lights flickering in otherwise dark windows. People were lighting candles and going about their business in the same way they would normally do in the event of a blackout.

Daniel thought about his own family and the times they'd waited for the power to come back on by sitting around telling ghost stories by flashlight. How many families were going through the same routines right now, oblivious to the very real ghosts that were coming for them?

They regrouped in the woods behind Daniel's own backyard as Mollie and Rose joined them. There, in the pitch-black copse of trees that bordered his house, they made their plans. The fliers would take Rohan and search the town for the Shades. No one felt comfortable just waiting for the shadow creatures to come to them—this time they would be proactive. When they found the Shades, they'd return for Daniel. Everyone agreed that it was too risky flying around with Daniel and the ring any more than they had to. While they searched, he'd wait behind for Theo to arrive with Louisa and Herman. Until then, Daniel was to stay hidden and keep the ring safe.

"We should go," said Rohan.

"Right," said Daniel. "Good luck!"

It was a familiar sight, the Supers soaring off into the air to attend to some emergency while Daniel stayed behind. But this time it was different. This wasn't a house fire or some kind of random accident. This time they were fighting monsters. An army of them.

And when they actually found the Shades, Daniel would . . . what? Brandish the ring? Speak the magic words? Their plan fell apart there. Daniel had a weapon that he had no idea how to use. He'd fought the Shades before, but that

248

was with Eric's strength and Louisa's intangibility and Rose's invisibility. How could he actually use the ring against them? They had to trust Herman to help them with that, and trusting Herman, everybody knew, was the worst possible plan. Ever.

But even bad plans are better than no plans at all. Daniel cursed softly under his breath as he crept through the trees toward his house. The old villain might actually be willing to help them, but only if it served his purposes as well. Daniel felt confident that Herman wanted the Shades gone just as much as they did, but what then? It was the afterward that troubled Daniel. He resolved that if they all survived this, he would destroy the ring once and for all. In the meantime he'd just have to muddle through and figure it out as he went.

The neighborhood still seemed so quiet, so peaceful. Daniel remembered what Herman had said about the Shades: that they would be drawn to the reminders of their old lives. For some of them who were almost as old as Herman, those reminders might be hard to find. But more recent victims of the Shroud's power would still have families here. Some would still have *themselves* here—the real boys and girls who'd lost their powers, lost their shadows, and had no idea what was out there hunting them. Daniel thought of the ones he'd known, of Simon and Michael. Were they being haunted tonight by their Shades? Had they been all along?

It seemed like there would be no end to the Shroud's legacy of terror.

Daniel had just stepped onto the grass of his parents' lawn when he heard a voice speak to him from the darkness. The wind had been blowing in the wrong direction or else he would have caught the smell of rotten fish sooner. He might have had a chance then.

"Hey, New Kid," said an ugly voice Daniel recognized instantly. "Been looking for you!"

Daniel turned just in time to see Clay Cudgens's fist appear out of nowhere.

He wasn't unconscious—he was aware of voices talking and of hands wrapping something around him. He felt the soggy grass and leaves scraping along his face as he was dragged into the trees. He knew about these things, but after being hit in the head, he found it just impossible to focus on them. The ground roiled like waves whenever he opened his eyes, and stars exploded in his vision whenever he closed them.

"Man, Clay," a voice was saying. Bud's voice. It was small and whiny for such a big kid, and impossible to mistake. "You really clocked him. Coulda killed him!"

"Nah. That was just a tap. Kid's a wuss when he's not stealing someone else's powers."

When Daniel's world finally stopped spinning, the two bullies came into focus a few feet away. Though he could see again, he now had a headache that hurt so bad, it made him squint. He was tied to a tree with some kind of thick cord that had been wrapped around his waist, pinning his arms to his sides. He could already feel the pins and needles stabbing his fingers as the circulation was squeezed off.

Clay and Bud. They'd pulled him back farther into the woods behind his house, out of sight. Daniel panicked when he didn't immediately see his backpack, with the black ring inside, but neither of the two boys was carrying it, so he must've dropped it on the lawn where they'd jumped him. Clay and Bud were keeping their distance from him now that he was awake, apparently afraid he'd steal their powers if they came any closer. But he couldn't have if he'd wanted to. The ring was too far away.

What were they even doing here? They must've come to his house to take advantage of the blackout, to get a little revenge. Maybe they were going to trash his bike. Or just egg his house. But they didn't have the faintest clue about what was really going on. They hadn't seen the Shades. They didn't know that the Shroud was still alive or about the ring. They were just bullies looking for a little payback.

"Have . . . to let me go." Daniel wanted to say something more urgent, to explain the terrible danger they were all in and how each second that passed put his friends and the whole town in more and more peril, but he just couldn't get all those words in the right order. His head hurt too much.

"What'd he say?" asked Bud.

"I don't know. He's mumbling."

"What if you gave him a repercussion?"

"That's *concussion,* you fat moron. And I told you I didn't hit him that hard."

"Maybe we should check on him."

"You check on him," said Clay. "I ain't getting any closer to that stinkin' power stealer than I already am. I don't like Shrouds."

Shrouds. They thought Daniel was just like Herman. Maybe they were looking for more than just payback after all.

It hurt too much when Daniel tried to focus on the boys standing so far away, so he concentrated on what was closer, his immediate surroundings. He was tied up with a frayed length of rope. The bullies must've snatched it from their junkyard. The knot wasn't tied well, and given time, Daniel could probably wiggle his way out. That is, if the two of them hadn't been standing there watching his every move.

He didn't have time for this.

"You guys don't understand," Daniel said slowly. It still felt like he was talking through a mouthful of cotton. "The whole town's in danger!"

"No? Really?" said Clay. "Like we didn't know that! Here you and the rest of those fakes are marching around acting like you're a bunch of superheroes, while you're the real monster! Your loser friends know what you are?"

"Yes! I mean they know about the powers," said Daniel. "But I'm not a monster. It was Herman Plunkett, the real Shroud. He's back and—"

"Oh, save it," said Clay. "I'm tired of your talking. Bud, gag him."

"Me?"

"Yes, you tub o' lard! Use one of his socks or something— just shut him up."

Bud took an uncertain step toward Daniel. The air took on a freshly pungent reek.

"What about all the lights?" asked Bud, looking at the darkened neighborhood. "What if there is something bad happening here?"

"That something is sitting right there all tied up!" said Clay. "The blackout's probably because of him anyway. Knocked out the lights so he could sneak up on us and steal our powers."

Clay stepped up to Bud and shoved a thick-knuckled finger in the boy's face. "You know what he is. He took your powers up there at the Old Quarry, and you got lucky it wasn't permanent. It's starting all over again! I thought we were free and clear after that Plunkett guy bit the dust, but now here's another one. He tricked us into helping him off the old man so's he could take his place!"

Bud let out a whimper and started to back away, but Clay grabbed the bigger bully by the shirt collar and held him fast. He started shouting at Bud like a barking dog. Flecks of spittle foamed at the sides of Clay's mouth.

"You want that? You want to go back to the way things were?"

Without warning, Bud shoved Clay. It wasn't a very strong push, not where Clay was concerned, but the shock of being shoved by Bud—for what was probably the first time ever—must've thrown Clay off balance. He let go of Bud's shirt as he tumbled backward onto his butt.

"Yes! I want it!" Bud was crying, his face wet with tears and snot. "I want it!"

"What are you talking about?" asked Clay.

Bud didn't answer. Instead, he stomped over to Daniel and plopped down on the ground next to him, his stink cloud drifting along behind him. Daniel couldn't lift his hands to cover his nose, so he tried to bury his face in his shoulder to escape it. Bud didn't seem to notice or care. He just sat there in the fallen leaves crying, trying to muffle the sound of his blubbering with his own hands.

"Can you do it, Daniel?" Bud asked after he'd quieted a bit. "Can you take my powers away? Only this time can you take them away for good? Please?"

Daniel didn't answer. A few months ago he wouldn't have dared to imagine that there was something worse than being powerless, but here it was. It was being shackled with powers you despised. Louisa hated her powers so much, she'd lied to all her friends. And now here was Bud begging Daniel to take them away. Daniel couldn't have understood until recently. Now he understood all too well.

"No," said Daniel finally. "I'm sorry, but I can't."

Bud nodded.

"I really am sorry, Bud," said Daniel.

"Of course you don't want my sucky power," Bud said. "'Cause then you'd be just like me."

"That's not what I meant. . . ."

Bud stood up and wiped his face along his jacket sleeve. He looked over his shoulder at the lightless street.

"Doesn't matter," he said. "Something bad's happening out there tonight, and I'm going home."

Clay didn't try to stop him. He didn't call him names or threaten him. He didn't even watch his only friend march away into the night. Clay's eyes were fixed instead on Daniel, and they were cold and cruel. Daniel hoped he looked brave in the face of that stare, but that was hard to do all tied up and at the mercy of Clay Cudgens. That fact alone would normally have been enough to terrify Daniel, but the Shades were out there somewhere too.

Daniel heard the distant sound of voices shouting. It might have been Eric and Mollie, but he couldn't be sure. Whoever they were, they sounded afraid. Bud was right— something bad was happening. It had already started.

Clay heard it too. He glanced in the direction of the voices, but he didn't move.

"Clay," said Daniel, "they're in trouble. We'll all be in trouble if you don't let me go."

"This is some kind of trick, right?" said Clay.

"It's no trick!"

But Clay was no longer listening. He was looking at something coming down the street toward the two of them. Daniel followed his eyes and saw a black shape drifting toward them in the night. Daniel recognized it at once—a Shade. Clay, unfortunately, didn't.

"Bud?" called Clay. "That you?"

The Shade paused and cocked its head. Then it changed direction and began coming their way, drifting away from the houses and closer to the woods where Clay held Daniel captive. As it drew near, it became obvious even to Clay that this wasn't Bud. When two more Shades appeared next to the first, Clay began backing up. They hadn't yet spotted him through the trees, but they would soon. They were a pack of dogs on the hunt.

"What are those things?" Clay whispered.

"They are the real enemy," answered Daniel. "Now quick, get me loose!"

For a moment Daniel was actually hopeful that Clay would untie him, that he'd at least give Daniel a fighting chance, but Daniel was always overestimating the heartless bully. Leaving Daniel tied up and helpless, Clay turned and sprinted deeper into the woods. It wasn't a stealthy retreat, though, and one of the Shades peeled off from the group to pursue Clay as he crashed through the underbrush. But that still left two more for Daniel. And they were getting close.

He'd gotten one hand nearly free, but the Shades were already at the edge of the trees. He wouldn't make it in time.

"Stop wriggling!" a tiny voice whispered. "I can't see what I'm doing!"

Daniel stopped moving. He was alone with the dark, but

something was tugging at the ropes. As he watched, the knots began untying themselves.

"Rose?"

"Shh!" answered the dark. "I'm staying quiet. I didn't giggle! Not once!"

The rope loosened around his middle and then went slack. Daniel's arms were numb and practically useless from the lack of circulation, but luckily his feet worked just fine. The Shades had already begun snaking through the woods.

Daniel gestured for Rose to follow him, and since he didn't really know where she was, he hoped she was watching as he slipped silently out of the trees and onto the grass of his own backyard. He was careful to tread lightly on the crackling leaves, but once his feet hit the grass, he made a dash for the house. On the way he scooped up the fallen backpack, nearly tripping over himself in the process.

His parents kept a spare key hidden in the rock garden next to the patio door. The key was where it was supposed to be, beneath a weathered old garden gnome. As Daniel retrieved it, he whispered into the darkness.

"Rose?"

"I'm here," answered a breathless voice. "But my shoes got all muddy."

Daniel glanced down at the concrete patio floor and saw a pair of size six footprints leading from the yard to the door. Another glance told him that the Shades hadn't followed them onto the lawn. Not yet. Perhaps the two of them could get inside without being seen.

Daniel gritted his teeth as the door creaked open—the patio door always squeaked terribly. He felt Rose squeeze by him through the doorway; then he shut and locked the door behind them. The patio door was mostly glass, but it gave Daniel some sense of security nonetheless. As they slipped into the basement, Daniel took a deep breath for what felt like the first time in hours.

"Rose, you all right?"

"Yeah. These were new shoes, though. My mom's gonna be mad."

Daniel smiled in spite of everything. Rose had a six-year-old's perspective on the world, and nothing, not even shadow monsters, could change that.

"I'd forgotten about you, Rose."

"I know. Mollie did too. She flew off to fight the monsters, but I wanted to stay with you."

"I'm glad, Rose. Thank you."

"Welcome," said the empty air.

"You know," said Daniel, "you can turn visible now. They can't see you inside here."

There was silence for a moment; then, "I don't wanna."

Daniel nodded. "Right. I understand. That's probably smart."

Daniel looked down at the backpack in his hands. There were two Shades out there in the woods somewhere. Wasn't that what he'd been waiting for? He had the ring, and he'd found the enemy, but now what? He had no idea what to do with it.

And even with Rose by his side, Daniel felt alone. He was worried about his friends. He was sure that had been Mollie and Eric shouting.

Outside the glass door, the trees looked so much darker than normal, especially without any ambient light to see by. There wasn't a hint of movement out there. No wind, nothing. Everything was as still as a statue.

"All right, Rose. I want you to stay put. Keep hiding."

"I wanna go with you!"

"It's not safe!" said Daniel.

The door to the upstairs sat atop a long stairway almost directly above the spot where Daniel and Rose were arguing. Therefore, when it was thrown open, Daniel was almost immediately blinded by the sudden flashlight beam being shone directly into his face. He couldn't see, but the voice was recognizable enough, as was the tone. Daniel was in trouble.

"Daniel Corrigan," his father said. "You. Are. Grounded!"

Chapter Twenty-Five
Grounded

Daniel had escaped a pair of superpowered bullies and a cave full of shadow monsters, only to be trapped in his living room by his parents.

This was bad. This wasn't a go-to-your-room kind of grounding—it was a total-surveillance, we-won't-let-you-out-of-our-sight kind of grounding. Daniel's father, his mother, and Georgie sat on the couch watching Daniel squirm. Lit by one of his gram's old candelabras, they looked like some kind of medieval inquisition waiting to pass judgment. Where had he been for the last several hours? Why was he a dirty mess? Where were his friends, and didn't he know that with the blackout their parents would be worried too?

Daniel and his friends had disappeared like this before, last year in fact. And although they'd been saving the town's children from the Shroud, they hadn't been able to tell their parents that. That night had led to long, long punishments and deep suspicions.

"Do you know what a *recidivist* is?" Daniel's father was asking.

"Dad! I can't stand here and—"

"It's the term they use for a criminal who cannot stop committing crimes. A repeat offender."

"Dad—"

"Let's let him talk," said his mother. "Where were you, Daniel?"

"Daniel's in big trouble," said Georgie.

Daniel swallowed. He needed to think carefully about how to answer. His friends were out there. The Shades were out there. But his panicking would just make him look more guilty than he already did. He needed to calmly and rationally explain to his parents where he'd been, and why he'd been acting so secretive lately. In short, he needed to come up with a whopper of a lie. He needed something that would get him off the hook, at least temporarily. If they sent him to his room, he might be able to sneak out the window and deal with the consequences later. He'd be grounded for life this time, but that was a small price to pay. As it was, he was worried about making it through the night.

Daniel delivered the biggest, most bald-faced lie he could think of.

"I've got a girlfriend," he said.

It had the desired effect. His father looked like he was going to say something, but his mouth just opened and closed without any sound coming out. It was as if he'd forgotten the important part of talking. Daniel's mother looked equally shocked, but she handled herself much better. She hadn't lost the ability to produce language.

"Oh," she said. "Well . . . what's her name?"

Her *name*? Now it was Daniel's turn to be speechless. He hadn't thought it through that far. Should he make up a name? He quickly scanned his brain for every girl's name he could think of, but his mind was a blank. What were girls called? All he needed was a name! Why was that so hard?

"Louisa," he said. He blurted out the word so quickly that he even surprised himself, but the minute he said it, there was a muffled little squeal from the empty air. Daniel bit his lip so hard, he brought tears to his eyes.

"What was that?" his father asked.

"I didn't hear anything," answered Daniel quickly.

"Louisa," said his mother. "That's that nice girl with the little sister? Rosie, right?"

"Rose," Daniel said, correcting her before the empty air had a chance to. "But yeah, Louisa's my . . . girlfriend. We were hanging out with Rohan and Mollie and everyone, and I guess we all lost track of time. When we got back, it was already dark and the lights were out everywhere, so I walked her and Rose home."

Daniel put on what he hoped was his most earnest, truly

repentant face. "I knew I was late, so I snuck in the back. I'm really sorry."

"And who were you talking to?" asked his father. "I heard voices."

"That was . . . Louisa."

"Louisa?" said his mother. "I thought you said you walked her home."

"I did. Then she walked me home. I mean, we both walked her little sister home, then Louisa walked with me back here—"

"Daniel," said his mother, standing over him with her hands on her hips. "Did you let that nice young girl walk home alone? In the dark?"

"Uh," said Daniel.

Daniel's torture was then interrupted as the room lit up with the bright glare of a car's headlights pulling into their driveway. Peeking through the window, Daniel recognized the sleek sports-car silhouette.

Theo.

Daniel's mother beat Daniel to the front door.

"Wait, Mom!" Daniel said. "It's my friend Theo."

"Theo?" asked his mom. "The boy from the car accident? But there were headlights. . . . Did he *drive* here?"

Daniel stopped in midstep. Even in the darkened house, Daniel recognized that look as her shoulders stiffened. This was bad.

"Did he *drive* over here? Did he dare *drive* over here in a *car*?"

"Mom . . ." Daniel tried to think up an excuse, but his voice sounded weak and pathetic in his own ears. How could Theo have been so stupid as to park in their driveway?

There was a knock on the door.

His mom unlocked the door and swung it open.

"How dare you," she began. ". . . Oh!"

It wasn't Theo at all. Involuntarily, Daniel took a step backward, clutching the backpack close to his chest. Standing in the doorway was Herman Plunkett, looking considerably healthier than before. He was straight-backed, and his mean eyes shone in the dark. The green glowing pendant still hung about his neck, letting off trailing wisps of light.

At his feet were the limp bodies of Eric and Rohan.

"Mrs. Corrigan," said Plunkett, "I've come for Daniel. He has something that belongs to me, and I'd appreciate it if you'd kindly step aside and allow me to reclaim what is mine. I'd hate to see anyone else get hurt."

Chapter Twenty-Six
The Shroud

Herman Plunkett. The Shroud. Daniel had turned his back on him, again. He'd underestimated him, believed the old man was as weak as he looked. And now Daniel was paying for it. His friends, and now his family, were in danger because he'd let the snake slither free.

"I should have left you in that cave," Daniel said. "I should have left you there."

"Ah, but you couldn't, could you?" said Plunkett. "You don't have the stuff. I was wrong about you, Daniel. You are not the one to follow me. You aren't strong enough to keep this world safe. If you'd shown *half* the backbone I thought you had, I could've expired in peace. But you're weak-livered, Daniel, and so it's left to me."

"Daniel, who is this man and what's he talking about?" asked Daniel's mother. She'd put her body in between Daniel and the door. She was being protective, instinctual. She didn't have any idea who she was facing.

"Mom, get back! Don't—"

It was too late. Herman flicked his wrist, and a tendril of shadow lashed out at her from the pendant, wrapping itself around her throat and forcing her to her knees.

Daniel's father came running in from the living room, but he barely had time to process what he saw there, because no sooner had he entered the hall than Herman swallowed him up in a cloud of blackness. Daniel's father disappeared behind a wall of dark mist, but Daniel could still hear him gasping and gagging on the noxious stuff.

His mother's face, meanwhile, was turning blue.

"Now, isn't there a baby brother somewhere?" said Herman. "What shall we do to him?"

"Stop it!" cried Daniel, running forward. He reached for the glowing pendant, but it was useless. Herman was ready for him and pinned him beneath a slithering tendril of Shade.

"This gives me no pleasure, Daniel."

The old man leered as he plucked the backpack from Daniel's fingers. Plunkett was stronger than before, and the source of his new power was obvious. Eric lay on the floor next to Rohan. Neither stirred. Plunkett was wounded, his weapon damaged, but he'd managed to overpower Daniel's friends. There was a cost, however. His face betrayed the strain. Even now, Plunkett's stolen power was leaking away; through the crack in the pendant it spilled out and vanished into nothing. That was why he needed the undamaged black ring.

Plunkett kept Daniel pinned on the floor even as he released Daniel's mother and father. But neither of them moved.

"They're not dead," said Plunkett, seeing the worry in Daniel's eyes. "Though I would have killed them if necessary, it's not something I wanted to do. I have no wish to wipe out your grandmother's bloodline. She was special to me.

"But I have too many secrets that need protecting. It's bad enough what's happening out there tonight. It's going to be years before I can calm this town's nerves and make them forget the things they've seen. But your parents, at least, won't remember any of this, I'll see to that."

Herman yanked open the backpack, wincing at the effort. His forehead was beaded with sweat, but he maintained his hold on Daniel, pressing him tight to the floor. Plunkett's face broke into a pleased grin when he opened the pack and gazed upon what was hidden in there.

"Your parents won't even remember what happened to you, their oldest son," Plunkett said, still staring at the ring. "I really am sorry, Daniel, but you've had me in your mind for too long, it seems, and you've built up something of a resistance to my mental powers. I can't erase your memories, not permanently at any rate. Therefore there's really only one way to deal with you. I'm sorry," he repeated.

Plunkett didn't look at Daniel. Perhaps he couldn't. The old man was a villain and a thief, but he was no murderer. Daniel would be his first. The black tendril began to snake its way around his throat.

"Momma? Daddy?" Georgie wobbled into the room looking frightened and small. "I'm scared of the dark. . . ."

When he saw Herman, he started to cry.

Plunkett reached out with another tendril of blackness. It split off the one pinning Daniel, like a vine creeping across the floor.

"Time to sleep, little baby," Herman said. "You don't need to see this."

Then Rose appeared in the tendril's path, materializing in front of Georgie and shielding him from Plunkett. She could have stayed hidden. She probably should have.

"You leave us alone!" she shouted at Herman, and for a moment he did. He was so surprised by her sudden appearance that his concentration slipped for just a second, and Daniel felt the weakening of his power. The tendril coiled about his throat loosened, allowing him a bit of air.

With all his strength, Daniel pulled, but it still wasn't enough. Without the ring he was just ordinary Daniel, and all he could do was watch as Herman reached for his baby brother.

"Run, Rose!" Daniel managed to gasp between stolen breaths. "Get Georgie out of here!"

But Rose didn't have a chance, as Herman's shadow tendril swatted her to the ground and wrapped itself around Georgie.

Georgie cried as he watched the black thing slither along his body.

"Stop it," Georgie cried. "STOP IT!"

Georgie's voice rose into a high shriek, a wailing panic, even as his face turned a bright, angry red.

Georgie launched into a full tantrum brought on by fear, and he grabbed the tendril of shadow with both of his chubby three-year-old hands and yanked. Hard.

The tendril went taut for an instant before snapping entirely. Plunkett stumbled backward as his grip on Daniel loosened. The Shroud's shadow creations were harder than steel, and Georgie had just torn one of them apart.

Plunkett looked shocked, but not half as shocked as Daniel.

"Run," Daniel shouted. "Run, Georgie, run!"

His baby brother was crying again, scared of what he'd just done. Daniel shouted to him, but his words were lost in the sound of a distant whistle getting louder. Something was approaching the house—the terrifying sound of a bomb being dropped.

A bomb named Mollie Lee. She crashed in through the front door and hit Plunkett with something solid—a baseball bat, judging by the shower of splinters—and sent the old villain flying. But Mollie didn't let up. She kept hitting him, driving him through the house. Their fight tumbled out of the living room and down the hall, ending in a crash of shattered glass.

Daniel pulled himself to his feet. It was hard to breathe and it felt like his chest had been slammed with a hundred-pound weight. Rose and Georgie ran up and hugged him. He caught his little brother in his arms as Rose wrapped herself around his waist.

"Georgie, are you okay?"

"I pulled hard!" Georgie said between sobs.

"You sure did, buddy," said Daniel. "You sure did."

It still hurt to breathe, never mind carry Georgie, but his brother wouldn't let go. Together they went to his mother's unmoving form.

"Momma!" cried Georgie.

Daniel leaned in close and saw that she was breathing. She was even snoring, very softly.

"She's sleeping, Georgie," Daniel said, squeezing his brother's hand. "Mom and Dad are just sleeping."

"Wake her up!" said Georgie, but Daniel doubted that would be possible. Whatever Plunkett had done to them, he'd made sure they'd stay that way for a while.

Mollie reappeared in the hallway, looking beat-up and ragged. There was little light to see by, just the glow of his mother's flashlight, which had fallen on the ground. But even in the dark Daniel could see that Mollie was in rough shape. Her clothes were torn and filthy, and she had a nasty-looking cut across her chin. But worst of all was the look in her eyes. Distant, unfocused. She bent down over Eric and

Rohan and talked to Daniel even as she held their unmoving hands.

"Herman surprised us," she said. "The Shades came after us over by the Madisons' house. You know Mr. Madison, the fire chief? He must've been a Super once, because there was a Shade that looked just like him, only younger and skinnier. . . ."

"Mollie," said Daniel.

"Theo pulled up in his car. I think he really wanted to help, Daniel. I think you were right about him. But Herman surprised us all. We were distracted, and while we were focused on the Shades . . . he got Rohan. First Rohan, then Eric. Then he came here after you."

"What happened to them?" asked Daniel, but he was afraid he already knew the answer.

"He took their powers, but worse . . ." Mollie blinked, fighting back tears. "Right before he blacked out, Eric looked right at me. And he asked who I was. I think Herman erased them."

Eric and Rohan were gone. For all intents and purposes, it was like they'd never known them. But there wasn't time to dwell on their losses now. The whole town was in trouble.

"Where's Herman now?" Daniel asked.

"I knocked him out the back window."

"Did you see the ring? It was in the backpack. He was holding it when you started hitting him."

"I don't know."

Daniel set Georgie down as he picked up his mother's flashlight. Georgie held on tight to Daniel's leg.

"Help me look for it," Daniel said as he scanned the hallway floor with the flashlight. "But if you see it, don't touch it!"

They looked through the scattered debris, but it was hard to see much of anything, even with the flashlight. As they searched, they began to hear sounds coming from outside—shuffling scraping sounds at the windows, the door. Mollie looked out the front window and sped away in a flash.

"Shades!" she said. "They're here, Daniel! Surrounding the house!"

"Rose!" said Daniel, looking at the fragile windows. Shapes were gliding back and forth outside, some already pressing against the glass. It wouldn't be long now. "Can you get Georgie out of here? Take him downstairs and find a safe place to hide."

"I can disappear him!" she said.

"What? Are you sure?"

"I make my clothes disappear with me whenever I do it, so if I touch him, I can make him disappear too," she said, as if it was the most obvious thing in the world. In fact, Daniel thought, it probably was.

She put her arms around Georgie, and both of them vanished.

"Daniel?" said Georgie's worried voice. It had to be frightening when you could no longer see your own shoes.

"It's okay, Georgie," said Daniel. "Go with Rose. Hide and seek!"

Daniel turned to Mollie. "They've come for Herman. Maybe the Shades will leave us alone if they get him."

"Oh, but they won't get me. You, on the other hand . . ."

Daniel froze. He knew that voice. It was the whispery, throaty growl that had haunted his nightmares for months.

The glow of his flashlight seemed to weaken as the room was overtaken by the enormous shadow that had drifted in. It filled the space from floor to ceiling, a billowing undulating blackness far stronger than any mere Shade. At its center still pulsed the weak greenish glow of Plunkett's ruined pendant, but one hand, clothed in shadow, held a ball of bright green fire. The ring burned like a hungry star in the Shroud's void. The shadow threw back its head and laughed as Daniel heard the sound of glass breaking behind him.

"Come, my children," it shouted. *"Bow down before me once more! Bow before the Shroud!"*

Chapter Twenty-Seven
The Ghosts That Haunt Us

Herman had the ring. He'd managed to keep hold of it even as Mollie knocked him through a window. With it, he was no longer bleeding power. Worse, Daniel could tell from the way the ring flared and burned that it was hungry for more. The green flames spread out before it, licking the air. It was happening all over again. The Shroud was reborn.

"What to do first?" said the Shroud. *"Shall I gather up my Shades, my wayward children, or should I deal with the last of my foes?"*

"You always sound like a bad comic book," said Mollie, sticking her chin out in defiance, but she looked tired and afraid. She'd given her all in that last attack, and she was exhausted now. Daniel could see it in her face. If there was to be another fight, it would be a short one.

The cracking of glass behind them gave way to shattering, and Daniel watched helplessly as a Shade forced its way inside the house. The shadow creature stretched itself toward Daniel, readying itself to pounce.

The Shroud laughed. *"Of course! I'll let my Shades have a little fun with you first. Let one problem solve another. Eh, Daniel?"*

Beneath the veil of shadow Daniel could see this Shade's face. It was the little girl with ringlet hair he'd caught a glimpse of back in the cave, her child's features made gruesome with loathing. Despite the monstrous appearance, there was something familiar about her. A blurry photograph on the edge of Daniel's memory.

"No," said Herman suddenly as the Shade turned its face toward him. "Not you!"

That was the old man's voice, not the crackling whisper of the Shroud. He'd dropped part of his own shadowy disguise, and Herman's own face was now visible beneath the folds of blackness. He recognized the little girl too.

"Eileen," Herman whispered.

Eileen Stewart. In Gram's scrapbook he'd seen a photograph, blurry with age, of the original orphans of St. Alban's, standing outside the charred ruins of their orphanage home. Among those grimy faces had been young Herman Plunkett, looking so frightened. And standing next to him, her hands resting protectively on his shoulders, had been the little girl with her hair done up in ringlets. Eileen Stewart, Daniel's grandmother.

Daniel was only dimly aware of the sounds of chaos outside—the not-so-distant roar of a fire-engine siren, someone shouting even closer by—but inside here everything went as quiet as a breath. Gram was dead, but here was something left of her, a twisted Shade of the little girl she once had been at the exact instant Herman had stolen her away. Of all the countless faces of all the countless victims, this was the one Herman would have avoided. Of all of them, she might awaken something resembling guilt in the old man's leathery heart. And she'd found him again.

The attack was sudden and savage. Gram had been a gentle soul right up to the day she'd passed away, but this thing that the Shroud had created was more animal than person. He'd said that the Shades were drawn to their former selves or to pieces of their long-gone lives. Gram's Shade had come back to the house she'd been raised in, only to find it occupied by the object of all her pent-up hate, her escaped tormentor and her former master.

The Shade must have taken Herman by surprise, because he didn't even fight back. He crumpled underneath her assault, dropping the Shroud disguise entirely as she wrapped herself around him, binding him again in her own shadow. All he could do was cower beneath her anger. She put her hand around his throat and leaned down until her face was barely inches from his own. But there she stopped, and as Daniel watched, she drew close to the cracked pendant around Plunkett's neck. With a finger all of shadow, she reached out to touch the soft green glow of the meteor stone, only to shy away at the last second.

"What's she doing?" whispered Mollie.

"I don't know," answered Daniel. "She seems focused on Herman's pendant . . . but why? It's broken, it's useless. Unless . . ."

The Shade that had once been Eileen Stewart turned to Daniel and whispered a single word.

"Free."

Daniel nodded, understanding at last. "You lied," he said.

"What?" asked Mollie.

"Not you," said Daniel, limping over to where Herman lay on the floor. "You," he said to Herman. "You lied. It's all you ever do."

"I didn't lie! The ring can stop them!"

"But there's another way," said Daniel.

"Please," said Herman, pulling the ring from his finger. "Take it. I can't do it. Use the ring. You can trap them again. . . . I can't. I can't do it to her, not again."

Herman was whimpering, great beads of sweat pouring down his face as he stared up into the dark eyes of the creature that had once been his only friend in the world. Or perhaps they were tears, but Daniel had trouble believing Herman Plunkett had tears left in him.

Daniel bent down and scooped up the ring. Gram's Shade made no move to stop him, just as Daniel had known she wouldn't. He understood now what she really wanted.

"You could've stopped the Shades at any time," said Daniel. "But you don't just want to stop them—you want to *control* them again. And for that you need the ring. You need it to be the Shroud again."

"Please, Daniel!" begged Herman. "Use the ring!"

"I should've listened to them instead of you."

"Daniel," said Mollie, "what are you talking about? Those things will tear the town apart! Use the ring!"

"The Shades are angry children, Mollie. Hurt, angry children. They are throwing a temper tantrum because they don't know what else to do. They tried to tell us, but we wouldn't listen."

Daniel reached down and wrapped his hands around Herman's pendant.

"No!" the old man cried, trying to bat Daniel's hand away, but Gram's Shade held Herman down. The hate was gone from her face and she watched Daniel with impassive eyes.

"It's the pendant," Daniel said. "The pendant is broken but not destroyed. And they will never be free until it is."

"NO!" shouted Herman.

The old man's voice echoed in Daniel's ears, and suddenly he was back at the quarry, in the grip of the Shroud. Back in the nightmare. Herman was reaching through the ring into Daniel's mind again.

Daniel's hand was aflame. He could smell the charring flesh, taste blood in his mouth where he chewed his lips in pain.

"Use it," commanded the Shroud. *"Use the ring. Steal the Shades' power and you steal the Shades themselves. You can save us all...."*

The ring was consuming him—soon there would be nothing left. It was better to simply give in, make the hurt go away. He could sense the power outside him, waiting to be taken. He could see it in the figures standing in the landscape of his dream—Mollie, Rose, the Shades. Even Georgie. The Shroud was right: He could take it all for himself. He could stop fighting it at last.

He could save them all from themselves. Protect the world. He could be the hero.

He started to slip the ring onto his finger but was stopped by a smaller hand closing around his own. A small hand, a girl's. A girl with her hair done up in ringlets. She smiled at him.

And then Daniel was back in the living room. He held the ring just inches from his finger. The Shade with his gram's face watched him, frowning. Herman's eyes grew wide with anger.

"No! I am the Shroud!"

The cord snapped easily as Daniel ripped the pendant from the old man's neck. It came apart at the same place, the original break where Daniel had torn it from him nearly a year ago. Herman had tied it back together with an imperfect knot.

"Daniel," said Herman, "you don't know what you are doing!"

"Yes, I do."

"Then please tell me!" cried Mollie. "Because I'm freaking out here!"

"The Shades led us into Herman's cave because they wanted us to do something for them, Mollie. They can't touch the pendant, so they wanted us to destroy it. It's what they've wanted all along."

Herman's eyes narrowed into slits again, like a snake's. "Do that, and you unleash chaos. There will be no going back—you understand? You will change Noble's Green forever! You'll change the world!"

"You can't keep them prisoner, Herman. It's not right."

"What about your gram?" he cried. "She's gone, and there's nothing for her Shade to go back to! At least my way there's something left of her! My way she will be with us forever."

Daniel looked at the old man. "My gram is dead. It's time to lay her to rest."

With that he walked over to the fireplace. He set the pendant down on the mantel and picked up a wrought-iron poker. Finally able to examine the pendant up close, he could see the network of tiny cracks that ran throughout it. It was already broken; it wouldn't take much to shatter it. Even an ordinary thirteen-year-old boy could manage it.

For just an instant he hesitated. Herman was right about one thing: there would be no going back for any of them. But he thought about Eric and Rohan. About Louisa. Michael. He thought about Gram.

He brought the heavy poker down on the pendant, and it shattered into a hundred tiny pieces. The weak greenish glow flickered for an instant, then died.

The girl with the ringlets let Herman fall to the floor and floated toward Daniel. For a moment it looked as if she was opening her mouth to say something; then she was gone. Vanished into nothing.

"C'mon," said Daniel, grabbing Mollie by the arm. "I have to see this."

"See what? Darn it, Daniel Corrigan, will you stop a minute and tell me what the heck is going on?"

Daniel just smiled and pulled her outside. There were Shades still out there, but they didn't scare him now. Before his eyes they started to disappear, one by one, released from the hold that the Shroud's pendant had had on them for seventy years or more. Some—the oldest ones, like Gram—vanished altogether. Others returned home.

He knelt down next to Rohan and Eric, who were stirring.

Eric's eyes fluttered open. "Mol?" he said.

Mollie reached out and held on to Daniel for support. He didn't comment on it.

"Eric," she said. "Are you . . . I mean, you know me?"

"Stupid question," he said. "Did we get him?"

"Yeah," said Mollie. "I think so."

Theo and Louisa appeared in the street. Theo shrank back as Shades darted past him.

"Where are they all going?" he asked.

"Back where they belong," said Daniel.

"Daniel," said Rohan, adjusting his glasses, "what did you do?"

"I freed them," said Daniel. "I destroyed Herman's pendant once and for all. And I set them all free. Truly free."

Rohan watched as the last of the Shades vanished. He looked at Daniel, understanding dawning on his face.

"Then that means . . ."

"Yeah," said Daniel. "I think so."

Just then a window opened on the top floor of the Madison house a few doors down. Mr. Madison leaned out, dressed in pajama bottoms and a white T-shirt that did little to hide his middle-aged potbelly. As Daniel and his friends watched, he took a long, deep breath of night air and giggled.

"I remember!" he cried. "I can fly!"

With that he jumped from the window and flew. Not gracefully and not well, but he flew. A wobbly man in his pajamas was flying over Noble's Green for the first time in forty-something years.

"Whoa," said Mollie.

"Welcome to Noble's Green," said Daniel. "Welcome to the new world!"

Chapter Twenty-Eight
The New World

Janey Levine, age nineteen, was on her way home from the movies with her boyfriend when she suddenly remembered she had the power to move small objects with her mind. She'd accidentally dumped her bag of hard candies all over the floor of his car, so she spent the next twenty minutes picking them up one by one and putting them back in her bag—without ever actually touching them. Her boyfriend never even noticed. Alan Masterson, a fifty-year-old plumber, was out walking the dog when he remembered that he could breathe underwater. He leapt the neighbors' fence and spent the rest of the night in their swimming pool.

He might've stayed there longer if it hadn't been for his dog's constant barking.

And Michael woke from the last of his night terrors to find Mollie and Eric waiting for him outside his window. Together the three of them flew to the top of Mount Noble and back again. And again. He won every race.

The blackout had changed everything. When the lights went out, Noble's Green was the sleepy little village it had always been, but when they came back on, Noble's Green was already the most famous town on earth.

Daniel had gambled big and he knew it. They'd always lived in fear of discovery. A small group of Supers, say five or six kids, would find themselves hunted and in danger if people ever learned what they could do. It had been imperative that they keep hidden from the rest of the world, and as Louisa had pointed out, that made them vulnerable. But a town full of Supers? Young, old, and everything in between? Police officers, fire chiefs, teachers, and plumbers? When the newspapers and Internet caught wind of that (which they did by sunrise), no government, no corporation, no military, no men in black suits anywhere would have the power to harm them. You couldn't kidnap an entire town.

At least that was Daniel's hope.

And it wasn't just Noble's Green, though that had the highest concentration by far and was the ground zero of what would become known as the Blackout Event. After that night Supers appeared all over the globe, but each and every one of them could be traced back to that lonely little

Pennsylvania town. All of them had spent a part of their childhood there. Noble's Green became home to the world's superheroes.

Of course the scientists showed up. Biologists, archaeologists, physicists—academics of every stripe came to Noble's Green to study the phenomenon. Some of the Super townsfolk even volunteered for their tests, though very little actually came from it. The source of their powers, as well as how they worked, remained a mystery. Now that the Shades were gone, Theo and his father let the university continue its archaeological dig, but other than the very impressive cave paintings that Daniel already knew about, nothing interesting was discovered. Herman had been thorough in his own secret excavations, and every bit of meteor rock that could be found had been. The fragments that had once been his pendant now were no more remarkable than simple limestone. Daniel's ring represented the sum total of all the Witch Fire meteorite rock that was left on earth.

For now.

"I've thought about dropping it into the bottom of Tangle Creek, but who's to say it wouldn't wash up again?"

Daniel was standing in the middle of the tree fort—the newly rebuilt and improved tree fort complete with a second floor connected by a climbing ladder—addressing the Supers. Standing in a circle watching him were Eric, Rohan, Mollie, Louisa, Rose, Michael, and Simon. Separate from the group, leaning on the rebuilt door, stood Theo.

And on the floor in front of them, resting on a flat rock the size of a dinner plate, was the ring. Everyone kept their distance from it, even, or perhaps especially, Daniel.

"So that's why I settled on the sledgehammer," said Daniel, gesturing with the heavy mallet in his hands. "I'm sure it's perfectly safe to get close enough to destroy it, and you won't have to actually touch it."

"We don't want to destroy it," said Rohan.

"I'm sorry . . . what?"

Rohan took a step forward and pushed his glasses farther up on his nose as he studied the ring.

"Everyone knows how you feel about this," he said. "Your . . . relationship to this ring. And everyone agrees that it's dangerous—"

"It's the most dangerous thing on the planet!" said Daniel.

"Maybe," said Rohan. "Or maybe Noble's Green is."

"Wait a minute!" said Daniel. "What are you talking about?"

Eric placed his hand on Daniel's shoulder. "We knew this would be hard for you, which is why we already met in private. We talked it over, the Supers with . . . superpowers."

Daniel scanned the faces of his friends.

"So you had a secret meeting and decided what?" asked Daniel. "I mean other than to go absolutely crazy?"

"For the record, I didn't get a vote," offered Theo.

"Hear us out," said Rohan. "For years there was only a small group of Supers, a manageable group. But now, as of last count, there are two hundred and three people in the entire world who possess superpowers, and most of them live right here. Now, it appears that many of them have faded in strength over the years, along with many of their stolen memories. So you are looking at the most powerful Supers standing right here—"

"And Georgie!" said Rose. "He's stronger than Eric! I saw it!"

"Only sometimes," said Daniel. "Hopefully it stays that way for a while."

Georgie's super-strength that he'd displayed in the battle with the Shroud hadn't returned since, but Daniel knew it was only a matter of time. He was big brother to a powerhouse toddler.

"And Clay," said Simon. "Forgetting about him was the only good part of being Shroud food."

"And Clay," agreed Rohan. "Bud too—although not as obviously powerful, he's still potent."

"I'll say!" said Simon, waving his hand in front of his nose.

Mollie punched him in the arm. "Let him talk."

"The point is," continued Rohan, "that most of the adults and teenagers out there with powers are weaker than us, but we still don't know what they are going to do with those powers."

"I heard Janey Levine is shopping around a reality TV show," said Simon. Mollie glared at him, but he threw up his hands in protest. "Seriously! No joke. Just contributing useful information to the discussion like a useful Super should!"

Daniel took a deep breath. It hadn't taken long to get sick of Simon all over again.

"So you guys want to keep this ring around as a . . . weapon?" asked Daniel. "Your own personal contingency plan?"

"No," said Eric. "We want *you* to keep it. And don't think of it as a weapon. Think of it as insurance."

"Yeah," said Louisa. "We trust you to make the right choice. Only you."

Daniel wanted to argue the logic of this, but the truth was that he'd had some of the same thoughts. It was why he'd kept the ring in the first place. Why he hadn't told anyone about it, and why the very idea of keeping it now made him sick to his stomach. It was all too familiar.

"Things didn't turn out so well last time," he said.

"That was because Herman manipulated you," said Rohan. "He used his powers to influence you. But his power's gone. With his pendant destroyed, he's just an old man. He can't hurt us anymore."

Daniel wasn't convinced. Herman would always be dangerous, powers or no. Daniel had learned that the hard way, and it was a lesson he wouldn't forget.

"Take it," said Eric. "Hide it. Keep it safe. Hopefully you'll never have to use it."

There was still one person who hadn't spoken.

"Michael," said Daniel. "Do you agree with these guys?"

Michael looked around the room. He'd changed since getting his powers back. He smiled more, he was friendly and warm, but there was still something slightly haunted in his eyes. He'd been through too much to come out of it unscathed.

"I want it smashed into a thousand pieces and buried in every corner of the earth," said Michael. "I want that thing gone and I don't want to talk about it ever again. Not ever."

"But," he continued, with a look at Mollie, "being Supers means we decide things together, and we trust each other. So I trust my friends, and I trust you, Daniel. After all, you brought us all back. You're the hero, man. Your choice."

Daniel nodded. "My choice."

Then suddenly, and without further discussion, Daniel lifted the sledgehammer with both hands and with a yell brought it down on the ring. The black meteorite exploded in a puff of black dust and green light. A flash, then nothing but bits of broken, harmless rock.

No one said anything until Daniel spoke up.

"You guys put all the faith in the world in me," he said. "But I don't deserve it. Not if I keep this thing around. If I did that, I'd be keeping hope alive in Herman's withered old heart, and he wouldn't stop, not ever, until he became the Shroud again. You're my best friends in the world, and this is how I'll protect you."

His friends just watched him, expressionless. All but one.

"Good call, Daniel," said Theo, smiling. "Good call."

Daniel nodded at the new kid. "No more Shrouds," he said. "Never again."

Chapter Twenty-Nine
The Story of Johnny and Herman

The Mountain View Home wasn't a sanitarium, exactly. There were no straitjackets or padded cells, but it wasn't a day at the spa either. The grounds were lovely, with well-kept lawns trimmed with bright flower beds that gave the place a soothing garden feel. That was, until you wandered past the flowers and bumped into the high-walled perimeter fence with cameras that followed your every move. The security guards all wore neatly pressed suit coats instead of officers' badges, and at least half a dozen rooms actually had a view of the mountain, but these were reserved for only the most special guests. It was one of these rooms that Daniel found himself standing outside—the topmost room actually, with the very best view.

Herman Plunkett, locally famous philanthropist, had been presumed dead right until the moment when he was delivered to the Noble's Green sheriff's station by a group of young Good Samaritans who'd found him roaming the streets the morning after the Blackout Event. Herman Plunkett, who was no longer presumed dead, was now simply presumed insane.

Mountain View was a place for healing, but Daniel would have preferred Herman to be in a place where the walls were just a little bit higher. They really didn't know who they had in there.

The visiting room was just off the main floor, but due to Herman's unique position within the town, he was allowed special privileges. He was allowed to take visitors in his private room, which was at the end of a long, secluded hallway. At one end of the hall was a nurses' station, which was currently unattended. At the other end was Herman's closed door. And seated in one of the chairs just outside was a familiar, well-dressed gentleman with a graying beard.

He was watching Daniel.

The man smiled, but it was all Daniel could do to swallow down the hot pit of anger that had risen in his throat. He suddenly wished he hadn't destroyed the black ring, wished that he had the power to make this man sorry for all the things he *hadn't* done. For all the kids who'd suffered at the hands of the Shroud.

Powerless to actually threaten the man, Daniel had to settle for calling him the first word that came to mind.

"Coward," Daniel said.

The man's smile cracked just for a second, but it didn't break.

"I can understand why you'd think that," he said. "But it's a little more complicated."

"What's complicated about it? The people here have been worshipping you for decades, they've built monuments to you, they even named the town after you, and you left their children alone with *him*!"

What happened next shocked even Daniel. Without thinking about it, without meaning to, he punched the man square in the face. He'd never hit anyone out of anger before, but his face felt like it was on fire, and the more he talked, the hotter he got until he couldn't help himself. He just struck.

It was like punching a cold marble statue. He was pretty sure he broke at least one finger, if not two. He doubled over, clutching his fingers to his belly as the pain in his hand shot up his arm. It hurt so much, the room began to tilt under his feet.

Someone took him by the shoulder and sat him down in one of the chairs. The man was saying something, but Daniel could barely listen. It hurt too much.

Strong hands took his broken fingers in theirs, and there

was a flash of light that left spots in Daniel's eyes like a camera bulb had just gone off. But the blinding pain was gone. He flexed his fingers experimentally and found that they were a bit stiff and sore but definitely no longer broken.

"I wouldn't try that again," said the man. "I'm hard to hurt."

"You . . . healed me? You can do that?"

The man stood up and smoothed his beard where Daniel's fist had connected with his jaw. The tousled hair was the only mark Daniel had left.

"I can heal small things," said the man. "Although it's not really healing—more like *sharing* my own body's healing power with you. I can only do it for a second, but a second is usually all it takes."

Daniel took the opportunity to get a good look at Johnny Noble. He'd only ever gotten glimpses before, and then he hadn't even been sure that this was the fabled superhero. The statues and few surviving photographs were all of Jonathan Noble as a young man, around the time of the St. Alban's fire. Though this Johnny was older, he didn't seem decrepit like Herman. Something had preserved him so that he looked maybe sixty, and a very healthy sixty at that. Remarkable, considering the man standing before him had to be nearly a hundred years old.

But if there was any doubt as to his identity, all you had to do was look into his eyes. He had Herman Plunkett eyes, only less reptilian. The two men shared the same brightness, the clarity. Those eyes had seen much.

That and the fact that his skin was as hard as stone. That was pretty much a dead giveaway.

"So why are you here?" asked Daniel. "Visiting your friend the Shroud?"

Johnny's face darkened slightly at the mention of that name.

"I could ask the same of you," he said.

"But I asked first."

Johnny smiled again. "All right then, far be it from me to argue with a child's logic. I'm not visiting, but I like to check up on him now and then. He never knows I'm here, but I like to make sure he's keeping out of trouble."

Daniel laughed at this. He actually laughed out loud. He couldn't hit Johnny again or else he would have. The situation suddenly became so absurd it was funny.

"Out of trouble? What do you call the Shroud? What do you call what he'd been doing to those kids for all those years?"

"Necessary, I guess," said Johnny. "I called it necessary."

Daniel stopped laughing. "I hate you."

"I know. But I need to explain as best I can. I doubt it'll change your mind about me, but I need you to hear it."

"Fine," said Daniel. "Explain."

Johnny took a deep breath. He looked suddenly uncertain. He shoved his hands into his pockets and looked at his shoes rather than at Daniel directly. He looked a bit . . . childish.

"Herman and I fought, you know," Johnny said as he looked at the door to Herman's room. "When I first caught wind of what he was doing here, I confronted him and we fought. Johnny Noble versus the Shroud, just like in one of his stupid comic books."

"He told me," said Daniel. "He said that you won, but I wasn't sure whether he was telling the truth. It's impossible to tell with him."

Johnny nodded. "Oh, he told the truth all right. It was close, but in the end I was just a little bit stronger and a little bit smarter. And that little bit can make all the difference in the end.

"Beaten, Herman begged for mercy. I couldn't destroy the source of his power, that meteor stone, without risking losing my own powers, but I made him promise to stop using it. More than that, I threatened him."

"You threatened him?" asked Daniel. "That's it? You could've figured out a way to destroy the stone without actually touching it!"

Johnny held up a hand to quiet him. It was an unexpected gesture and had just a tinge of anger behind it. Daniel shut up at once.

"I *threatened* him, Daniel. I threatened his life. Do you understand what that means? Herman was just a young boy when I first met him. When we fought, he was fully grown, but all I saw was that scared little kid. And I threatened to kill him. That was no small thing for me to do.

"And he did as he was told. For a few years, at least, he stopped being the Shroud. But then World War Two broke out and I . . . thought I needed to be elsewhere.

"I saw things in that war, Daniel. I saw men die in horrible ways, while I couldn't even be scratched. I kept my powers secret, used them only when no one else would see. I witnessed what men are truly capable of, and I learned a valuable lesson."

"Which was?" asked Daniel.

"Man has never invented a weapon he didn't use. Nothing so terrible that he couldn't resist trying it out. And this town is just full of weapons unlike anything the world has ever seen. Herman was afraid of what these super-kids would do to the world; I became afraid of what the world would do to these kids. In the end, Herman's way was kinder than what was waiting for them out there. No powers, no memories of powers, but they still had their lives to live. They could grow up, have families, live in peace."

"He terrorized them!" said Daniel.

"Yes," said Johnny. "And as the years went on, he got darker and more frightening. By the time you came along, he was teetering on the edge. That's why I helped you in your final fight with him at the quarry. He'd crossed the line, threatening to kill you all. That was too much."

"You helped us?" asked Daniel. "Rose. Rose said she saw you in the Shroud-Cave."

Johnny nodded. "I shared a little of my power with Eric while he was unconscious. The way I just did with you, to get him back into the fight. I knew you'd need his help to defeat the Shroud. Rose saw me do it, though. That girl's sneaky."

"So what's different now?" asked Daniel. "Why show yourself now?"

"Everything's different now, Daniel," said Johnny. "You've changed the world, and there's no going back."

Johnny walked over to the window and gestured outside.

"You've either saved Noble's Green or doomed us all," said Johnny. "I'm not sure which yet."

"Either way, with no help from you," said Daniel.

Johnny smiled and shook his head. "You're right. I'm sure I'm not the first adult to disappoint you. I wish I could say I'd be the last." He held up his hands. "It might be that none of this really matters. Herman told you about the Witch Fire Comet, yes?"

Daniel nodded.

"It's still up there," said Johnny. "And if it follows the same path it's been following for thousands of years, it'll return this year. Then, who knows?

"Of course, that's assuming that it really is a comet. That it's not something else entirely."

"What do you mean?" asked Daniel.

Johnny laughed. "I don't really know. Isn't that a terrible answer? But I've long suspected that there's more to that comet than any of us know. Guess we'll find out soon enough."

Johnny gazed out the window for a moment, lost in his thoughts. After a minute he glanced over at Herman's closed door.

"So are you going in to say hi? Match wits with him for old times' sake?"

Daniel shook his head. "No. I've changed my mind. I don't think I want to see him at all. In fact, I'm done with both of you. I've got friends, people who aren't afraid of the future. I'll stick with them."

Johnny raised an eyebrow. "So you don't even want to know whose side I'm on now?"

"Don't know," said Daniel. "Don't care. We've done fine without you so far. We'll manage. And if you try to hurt me or any of my friends, we'll beat you just like we beat the Shroud."

With that, Daniel turned and walked away from Johnny Noble. He was shaken by the encounter, a mix of emotions tugging and twisting in his heart, but as he emerged from the Mountain View Home into the sunshine, he glanced up at the sky; and if he squinted, he could just barely make out shapes soaring and sailing above the town. Perhaps it was Mollie or Michael. Perhaps Mr. Madison was up there with them, laughing as he rolled and spun through the air like an out-of-control balloon. Daniel knew the feeling. He'd known it for a heartbreakingly brief few minutes, but he'd never forget it.

No one would take it away from them now. And they were in for a real surprise if they tried.